D1005674

A Howl
of
WOLVES

ALSO BY JUDITH FLANDERS

THE SAM CLAIR MYSTERIES

A Murder of Magpies

A Bed of Scorpions

A Cast of Vultures

NONFICTION

A Circle of Sisters: Alice Kipling, Georgiana Burne-Jones, Agnes Poynter, and Louisa Baldwin

The Victorian House: Domestic Life from Childbirth to Deathbed

Consuming Passions: Leisure and Pleasure in Victorian Britain

The Invention of Murder: How the Victorians Reveled in Death and Detection and Created Modern Crime

The Victorian City: Everyday Life in Dickens' London

The Making of Home: The 500-Year Story of How Our Houses Became Our Homes

Christmas: A Biography

A
Howl
of
WOLVES

A Mystery

JUDITH FLANDERS

Minotaur Books
New York

This is a work of fiction. All of the characters, organizations, and events portrayed in this novel are either products of the author's imagination or are used fictitiously.

A HOWL OF WOLVES. Copyright © 2018 by Judith Flanders. All rights reserved. Printed in the United States of America. For information, address St. Martin's Press, 175 Fifth Avenue, New York, N.Y. 10010.

www.minotaurbooks.com

Designed by Omar Chapa

Library of Congress Cataloging-in-Publication Data

Names: Flanders, Judith, author.
Title: A howl of wolves / Judith Flanders.
Description: First edition. | New York : Minotaur Books, 2018.
Identifiers: LCCN 2017061020 | ISBN 9781250087836 (hardcover) |
    ISBN 9781250087850 (ebook)
Classification: LCC PR6106.L365 H69 2018 | DDC 823/.92—dc23
LC record available at https://lccn.loc.gov/2017061020

Our books may be purchased in bulk for promotional, educational, or business use. Please contact your local bookseller or the Macmillan Corporate and Premium Sales Department at 1-800-221-7945, extension 5442, or by email at MacmillanSpecialMarkets@macmillan.com.

First Edition: May 2018

10 9 8 7 6 5 4 3 2 1

For Lynne Halliday

A Howl of WOLVES

Chapter 1

"There are thirteen dead people here." Jake was accusing.

I didn't think it was my fault. "I know. I told you that," I reminded him.

"I thought you were making it up."

"I don't make up dead people." I replayed the sentence in my head. It sounded worse the second time around. "I mean, I didn't need to make them up. Thomas Kyd already did." It wasn't as if I'd gone out and hired a special offer, baker's dozen hit man.

Jake didn't respond, his head bowed, turning the pages of his programme ferociously, as though, if he could just find the right place, a play that had been written more than four hundred years ago would suddenly have a different ending.

"Why are we doing this?" Jake brought me back to the present.

"We're doing this because we're nice people."

In truth, he's nicer than I am. Don't get me wrong, I'm a nice person. I don't race old ladies to the last seat on the bus, or at least, not too often. I pat the heads of small children, if they happen to stroll past. And—I couldn't think of anything else I did that made me a nice person. I'd like to believe I'm a paragon of virtue, someone who is always late because she stopped so frequently to rescue small furry animals from random perils. In reality, I became an editor in a publishing house for a reason. I spend so much time inside my own head that imperilled animals would have to claw their way up my leg, sit on my shoulder, and bat at my nose before I looked up from my book long enough to notice them.

We were in a theatre, though, so the odds of small furry animals requiring assistance were slim. "It's not just for Kay, it's for Bim," I said firmly.

Kay and Anthony were my upstairs neighbours. They were actors, successful enough that they were regularly cast in big parts in small productions outside London, or in small parts in big productions in London. This was one of the latter, a West End company fronted by one television star and one film star–slash–theatrical legend. Kay was only playing the lead actress's maid, but, as she said cheerfully, she got to die in a pool of blood onstage. Each to her own, of course, but dying bloodily eight times a week had never been my ambition. Especially since Bim, Kay and Anthony's son, also had a part in the play. I hadn't realized that six-year-olds watching their mothers die wreathed in gore was in the good parenting guide. But apparently it was, as Bim had acted it out for me with relish, several times. He knew every nuance, since he played the same leading lady's page, and was onstage when Kay was killed.

He also spent a lot of his time running around my garden, quavering "My deeeeear," in an affected, high-pitched voice. Then he mimed reading a script, daintily licking his ring finger before turning each page with it, peering over an invisible pair of reading glasses in a manner that Kay swore could easily have him mistaken for the director's twin, if twins came in sets where one was half the height, and less than a tenth the age, of the other. Nonetheless, he was having a good time, and attending the first night of a play wasn't exactly a hardship, even without friends in the cast.

Jake wasn't quite as convinced. The play was *The Spanish Tragedy*, and I'd made the mistake of looking it up and attempting to pass on the plot summary when the evening was first planned. After I'd described the first couple of deaths, Jake had begun to mumble about not going to the theatre to watch the same sort of thing he saw at work all day.

I considered asking what the CID estimated the annual rate of death by rapier at, but I'd bitten it back. Then I lost points for that heroic suppression of snark by patting myself on the back. Smug wasn't a pretty look, even mentally.

While Jake read, I watched a couple two rows ahead of us. They were greeting, and being greeted by, half the audience. They didn't look like actors. The man was in his seventies, I guessed, and gave the impression he'd rather be spending his evening in front of the telly with a hot drink. The woman didn't look any more like a performer, but she was exactly where she wanted to be, at the centre of attention. She was probably a decade younger than her partner, although she was dressed as if she hoped everyone would think it was two, or even three: a lot of Polyfilla had gone into both her face and farther down. I didn't feel unkind staring at her chest, since her dress was cut lower than most bikinis: pay and display.

I was pulled away from my supercilious judging of total strangers by a hand on my shoulder. I turned, and there was Anthony, together with a couple he introduced as Kay's parents. We did polite London chitchat—did you come far, isn't traffic terrible this evening—and some parental stuff—did they get a chance to see Kay perform often, wasn't Bim adorable in his page's costume—and then the lights went down. I settled in. There's nothing I like better than an onstage bucket of blood.

Jake appeared not to agree, if his shifting about was any indication. And initially I could see his point. The first act seemed to be entirely made up of people telling each other what had already happened, and the director and designer had only upped the difficulty by setting the production in the twentieth century, in what looked to be a Soviet courtroom. I could see no obvious reason for that decision, while the uniforms made it hard to tell the characters apart.

Then the play captured me. The important things—in the sixteenth century, a Soviet courtroom, or now, in a West End theatre—were still the same: betrayal, love, revenge. By the time the interval came, Jake's arm must have been black and blue where I'd grabbed it every time a weapon came out.

In the second half, he reached for my hand as the lights went down, either in a show of empathy, or to try to ensure he retained some circulation in his arm as the bodies began to pile up onstage. Kay was number four to go, and I discovered that Bim's garden re-enactments had been uncannily accurate, so much so that I was surprised to hear her own deep voice, rather than a high-pitched six-year-old's reciting the lines.

We were, by my count, up to the tenth body when things went astray. According to the story, the tenth body wasn't in reality the tenth at all, but belonged to a character who had been killed before the interval, whose body was now being displayed by his anguished father, who drew back a curtain to reveal it hanging from a rafter, all green and mildewed and nasty, one hand clawing outward in a ferocious death-spasm, fingers splayed and frozen in the air.

Certainly, to modern eyes it was ludicrous, and you would expect the odd nervy giggle in the audience. But it was in fact the cast that started it. They worked hard to cover things up, but the moment the curtain was pulled back, everyone onstage stuttered and stumbled, all of them refusing to look at one another, shoulders silently shaking.

It spread quickly. These were regular first-nighters, theatre people themselves, or the families and friends of theatre people. Whispers and not-so-smothered snickers buzzed through the house.

Jake turned to me. Without taking my eyes from the stage, I shrugged. I had no idea what was happening. Then Anthony leaned forward from the row behind. "The dummy's been made up to look like Campbell Davison," he whispered.

I shook my head. *Who?* the headshake said.

"The director. Someone is playing a practical joke." He paused. "And someone is going to get sacked." He sounded amused and appalled in equal measure.

A hissed "Shhh" had me turning guiltily back to the stage. So the dummy was Bim's *My deeear* man come to life. Or, rather, to death. Kay had implied he wasn't universally loved, and this prank suggested that she wasn't alone in that view.

The cast doggedly continued, but no one was paying any attention anymore. All eyes were glued to the figure swinging at the rear. I had no idea what Campbell Davison looked like, my entire knowledge of the man being based on Bim's imitation, but I could see now that the dummy bore no resemblance to the young actor from the first half. This body was stockier, an old man's shape, and, under the green mould makeup, the face was older too. The hair, which at first sight had appeared blonde, was grey, and longer than the brutal 1930s buzz cuts sported by the men in the cast.

In theory, this was the climax of the play. But even the ghost of revenge, who summed up the moral after the lead committed suicide, promising eternal torment for those who caused misery to their fellow men, could make no impact on the so-carefully-not-laughing actors and the smirking audience.

That is, until the curtain came down. In the few seconds between the blackout and the curtain rising for the cast bows, the performers had sobered, some now looking downright frightened. I imagined that they realized that while physically they were facing a delighted audience, tomorrow's reviews would be very different.

When I turned to Jake, though, he was as sober as the actors, checking his phone hurriedly rather than joining in the applause. A shake of his head, and he put it in his pocket. "Come on," he said, pulling me up. "We need to go."

We did? I would have stayed to the end, if only to say the right things to Kay's parents and Anthony, but getting up the endless stairs before the crowd wasn't a bad idea. I bent and whispered a few *She was marvellous* sentences to them, but Jake had my coat, my umbrella, my bag, and me—he really wanted out.

"Mr. Hustle," I grumbled at his back as he sped up the stairs two at a time, phone out once more.

"There's no signal down there," he replied, as though that were an answer.

I knew that there wasn't any football, or he would have dodged out at the interval to check, so I had no idea what had made this mad dash necessary.

"Do you know where the stage door is?" he asked, before continuing without waiting for a reply. "You'll be all right going home on your own?"

Going home on my own? I was about to repeat that out loud, when he pushed open the street door. Three police cars, lights flashing wetly in the damp night air, were double-parked in front of us. Another two were lined up in an alley beside the theatre.

Jake steered us over to the nearest one, pulling out his warrant card as he went. "Field, CID," he said to the uniformed constable blocking the alley. "I was in the audience. I saw it."

I stumbled to a halt.

"Oh god, he was really dead, wasn't he? That was Campbell Davison. That wasn't a dummy."

Chapter 2

Jake didn't get home all night. I slept sitting up on the sofa. I'm not quite sure why, but going to bed seemed frivolous, a sign that I didn't care about what had happened. And since I didn't *know* what had happened, but I did care, well, I slept sitting up on the sofa.

Jake had handed me over to a constable in the street. "She doesn't know anything," he said, "but you can process her quickly now, and it's one less for you."

There's really nothing I like better than being spoken about as though I weren't present, much less having it announced that I'm entirely ignorant of whatever it was, but in this instance Jake was right, I didn't know anything.

He kissed me absent-mindedly and said, "You'll be all right on the bus home?"

I nodded, too shocked to respond as I normally would have—*No, of course I won't be all right on the bus that I take every day of my life. Everyone knows I need a keeper and three assistant keepers to get me onto public trans-port.*

"Processing" me turned out to be police-speak for taking my name and contact information. Once that was done I was told politely that they wouldn't keep me any longer, which I easily translated back into English: *Now, would you please get out of our hair?*

So I did. I headed to the bus stop, where the first group of theatre-leavers stood waiting, and eavesdropped shamelessly. They, like me, hadn't known anything was wrong until after the performance, when they were stopped at the exit by police taking names and addresses of everyone in the audience. No one would say what had happened, referring to it vaguely as an "incident," and the guesses ranged from blackmail to some sort of theatrical sabotage (which was, I gathered, like industrial sabotage, but with costumes and gossip websites). While they spoke about the dummy as though it were part of the sabotage, oddly, none of them seemed to think that the dummy might not have been a dummy. And once I realized that, I also realized that Jake hadn't replied when I'd asked. He hadn't said it *wasn't* Campbell Davison, and so I had assumed I was right. I had also assumed that the number of police responding to the "incident" meant it was more serious than sabotage or blackmail, no matter how high-profile those involved were. But maybe not. Jake was right: I didn't know anything.

Once I was on the bus, I texted Anthony: *If you need me to look after Bim, or anything else, let me know.* He hadn't replied by the time I got home, so I decided to leave a note on their door. That way Kay's parents would see it if they came back without Anthony. I wrote out my phone numbers, and that I was in the flat below, and added an arrow pointing down, in case they weren't sure where "below" might be.

Then I stood on the landing for a moment. I had no idea why, since I knew perfectly well I wasn't going back downstairs. I looked at my watch. Nearly 11:30. I headed quietly up to the top-floor flat, to see if Mr. Rudiger was awake.

That he was home wasn't in question, since Mr. Rudiger never went out. Not rarely, but never. He was already living in the house when I had moved into my flat twenty years before, and in all that time, as far as I knew, he'd been downstairs perhaps half a dozen times, and he'd only gone past the front door three times—two of those times being when we all had to leave because of a fire. He was probably in his seventies, but he wasn't ill, or frail. He just didn't go out. He had been a famous architect decades earlier, before he retired in his forties and, as far as I knew, had lived in the top-floor flat of my house, peacefully minding his own business ever since.

Well, our business too. The man had hearing like a bat, and always knew who was coming and going in the house. Tonight was a coming and going he'd definitely want to know about.

I could see a light shining under his door, but still I tapped lightly. He might have fallen asleep reading, or, for all I knew, he might leave his hall light on all night. But no. Within seconds of my knock, steps could be heard.

"It's me," I called. "Sam."

He opened the door, no more surprise on his face than if I'd dropped by on a Saturday to see if he wanted me to pick up something at the market. "Coff—" he began, then looked more closely, and modified his offer. "A drink?"

"I think someone was killed. In the play. The one Kay's in. And Bim." I blurted.

"Camomile tea," he decided, as though what one drank after watching a play in which someone had been killed, with one's friends in the cast, had been formally and statutorily laid down in a handy pamphlet, a copy of which he kept by his front door.

Once I had my hands wrapped around the cup, I realized that even if there wasn't a pamphlet, he was right: a hot drink was exactly what I needed. Death was cold, and its ripples spread. Herb tea couldn't ward off death, but it could warm the edges of those it had touched.

I sat in my regular spot in Mr. Rudiger's cosy sitting room, its rich burgundy curtains pulled against the night, a single lamp illuminating the matching burgundy sofa and a fat, welcoming chair as I told him everything, both what I'd seen, and what I thought I'd seen: that I'd made a guess, from Jake's reaction, that Campbell Davison had been killed and somehow had ended up hanging from a meat hook, in a spotlight.

I rubbed my forehead. "It doesn't make much sense. Why would anyone want to highlight his death, rather than hide it if it were . . ." I searched for a neutral world, and settled on "purposeful." I couldn't quite bring myself to say "murder." "Or maybe—maybe someone found him— maybe he'd had a heart attack and . . ." I trailed away. If he'd died of a heart attack and someone painted him in green makeup and strung him up then it might be even worse.

Mr. Rudiger didn't respond. He didn't say much in general, and never chat for the sake of chat. If he didn't know something, he stayed silent.

"I looked up Davison on my phone on the way home." I waved it in his general direction, in a do-you-want-to-look gesture, but went on immediately. "Apart from loads of theatre, he did a few films." It went without saying that Mr. Rudiger didn't go to the theatre, so he wouldn't have seen any of the plays, but he surprised me.

"There was a Shakespeare season he directed for the BBC a few years ago," he said. "The history plays. Very bloody."

I was getting the feeling there was a theme there. "Have you ever seen *The Spanish Tragedy*?"

He shook his head.

Most people haven't, even if they aren't agoraphobic. "After tonight, I know why it's hardly ever done. It has a big cast; it needs lots of different sets; and there's blood. So much blood." I took several sips of tea, trying to calm my stomach.

Then I tried to calm the rest of myself. "I might be completely wrong. I don't know what happened, and the dummy might just have been a stupid prank. It might be something else entirely." Even as I said it, I couldn't think of anything apart from violent death or a bomb that would warrant five police cars and the processing of an entire West End audience. But we hadn't been evacuated from the building, so the bomb idea was out. And whatever it was, Jake had recognized it from his seat in the audience.

Mr. Rudiger couldn't think of anything else either. I knew that from the polite way he pretended to believe me.

By morning, Jake still hadn't let me know where he was, or what he was doing, but the news was everywhere. FA-MOUS DIRECTOR SWINGS was my least favourite headline in the dozens of articles already online, but even the respectable papers were shrilly titillating, with photos everywhere—production photos, or stock shots of Davison, not images from that final scene, thank god.

I shut down my laptop and headed for the tube. At least there was no internet reception there, and I wouldn't be able to read about it on the way to work. But even if I couldn't read about it, there was no way of shutting my brain down.

So once at the office I made coffee and, while I was waiting for it to brew, I picked up my phone and hit "speed dial 1": my mother.

"You heard?" I asked. Helena knows everything, usually before it happens. There was no way she hadn't heard. Really, the only surprise was that I had been at a first night, not her. She went everywhere, saw everything, knew everyone. My idea of a big night, on the other hand, was forgetting to turn off the front-door light while I was tucked up on the sofa indoors. So I modified my question. "Did you know him?"

The shift got me a soft noise of approval before she replied. "No, but then, from what I hear, I was out of his age group."

"His age group? He can't have been more than ten years older than you."

She gave a delicate little huff of breath—Helena never did anything that wasn't delicate, and she was about as fragile as a Sherman tank. "I was too old, not too young. Don't forget he lived with Sylvie Sander when she was nineteen and he was in his thirties."

That wasn't something I could possibly have forgotten, because I had never known it in the first place. I didn't even know who Sylvie Sander was. Luckily, Helena's maternal superpowers picked this up, and she went on without my having to ask. "She's the designer he always works with—she must have done the play you saw last night too. But they only lived together when she was in her twenties; after that, his women stayed the same age while he got older."

"So he was Dorian Gray, except he didn't keep a portrait in his attic."

Sensibly, she didn't try to untangle that. "According to the news this morning, Frances Singer was his latest."

I didn't have to ask who she was. She'd been the lead last night, and Kay had been her maid. But—but— "She

has to be half a century younger than he is. Was. Whatever."

Helena was dry. "Which is why I was out of his age
group."

Ick. Moving on. "Apart from his entirely predictable
penchant for women young enough to be his grand-
daughters—and really, what a surprise that is, 'Famous
man hooks up with much younger woman shock'—did you
hear anything that wasn't in the news?"

Because, really, there hadn't been any news. Davison
was dead, cause unstated, his body hung up on a hook, for
reasons, and by persons, unknown. In effect, what I had
managed to work out last night.

"No," said Helena slowly. "And that's strange, isn't it?"

I didn't want to make her already entirely confident
ego swell so hugely it became unmanageable, so I didn't
reply, but I did silently agree. If Helena hadn't heard anything, either there wasn't anything to hear, or the world
was coming to an end, and we were all going to die in a
screaming fireball of terror. I was hoping for the former.

I couldn't worry about either eventuality right then,
though. Publishing offices don't get moving at the crack
of dawn, but I had a meeting scheduled with an author
that was going to take up my entire morning. Mostly, the
actual editorial part of being an editor was straightforward. An author delivered a manuscript, I'd read it
through a couple of times, making notes as I went, before
emailing all my comments to the author. Some would be

major: *Why does Character A undergo a personality transplant in the second half of the book, behaving in a way s/he would never have done before chapter 7? I know the plot requires it, but don't you think you have to give your readers a reason for the change? And if there isn't a reason, you'll need to invent one, no?* (That faux-naïve "no" and the question mark at the end was a standard editorial ploy to soften the blow of a query that could only lead to heavy rewrites, if not a whole new draft.) Mostly the points would be minor—sentences that were weak, or meandering; inconsistencies in plotting, chronology, narrative (*His eyes were brown on p. 87, they're blue here; She's eaten lunch three times in this chapter, and doesn't seem to be aware of it*).

That, as I say, was the norm. But there were always a few authors who needed a face-to-face meeting. Sometimes this was because the editorial queries were so huge that that kind of bombshell couldn't be dropped in an email: the news had to be broken gently, and in a space where we could discuss how to proceed, rather than a hit-and-run—*Here's the problem, bye now!* Sometimes it wasn't the editorial work, but the author, that made it necessary: all authors hated being edited, but some were stubbornly resistant, and needed to be coaxed into looking at their work with fresh eyes.

Most authors have what publishers dismissively and, it must be said, unkindly refer to as separation anxiety, equating a writer's frequent inability to let go, their constantly wanting to rework a supposedly finished book, with a new mother's disinclination to leave her baby with a stranger. But today separation anxiety wasn't the problem. This morning's meeting was with Carol Dennison. This was her third book with me, and don't get me wrong, it was as smart, funny, well constructed, and well written as her previous ones. It was just that Carol had the opposite of separation anxiety.

Her method was delivery, run, and never look back. Whenever I thought of Carol's attitude to a book she'd finished, I thought of those convents in the Middle Ages, where people left foundling babies on the doorstep to be raised by the nuns. Because Carol never lingered, worrying about her newborn once it was trundled off into the convent. She was the mother who dumped the little darling and promptly legged it down the road, even as passers-by ineffectually called after her, "Miss, miss, you forgot your baby!" So I'd long learnt that the only way to get her to respond to editorial questions was to lead her into a room, close the door firmly behind her, and all but build a barricade in front of it until we'd covered everything that needed to be discussed.

Once she was there, and she knew there was no way out, there was never a problem. It was getting her there that was tricky. Hence the meeting. Hence my preparations. I looked around the meeting room I'd booked. Nobody could claim Timmins & Ross spent too much of their budget on extras like interior décor. The walls were that weird plaster-board wall-divider stuff with the aluminium edging. At some point, no doubt, they'd been white, but that was a long time ago, in a galaxy far far away. Now they were yellowing, which made them tone harmoniously with the orange moulded-plastic chairs around a chipped Formica table. Those chairs might be ugly, the feeling was, but by god, they were uncomfortable too.

I'd done what I could to dissipate the aura of hapless apathy the furnishings transmitted. I had a large pot of coffee ready and waiting beside a plate of biscuits, and I'd left a message for Miranda, my assistant, to order sandwiches from the café over the road, to be brought in at one. I added a second message, reminding her that this was a Carol Meeting, and to make sure that we weren't interrupted unless blood was actually running in the gutters. Then I thought of the previous evening, and deleted the last part of that sentence, retyping it as "Don't let anyone interrupt."

Bernie in reception rang up at nine sharp to say Carol was there. I checked my phone one final time to see if Jake had left a message. Nothing from him, but a text from Anthony: *Thx for the mssge. Any chance you cld collect Bim from school at 3 & keep him till we get home? I'm filming, Kay's parents went home, police interviewing cast, no idea when she'll be done.*

Of course. Txt address of school, I tapped back. Then I turned off my phone, and "Ask her to come up," I told Bernie, putting my editorial hat firmly back on. I needed to think about this book—about what it had to say about families, and inheritance, both financial and emotional inheritance, and how tragedy was passed down the generations. Being a helpful neighbour might get me into heaven, but it wasn't going to pay the bills until I got there.

The plus of a meeting with an author was that I had no time to think of anything else. As I'd known she would, once we sat down, Carol dealt with all my questions quickly and easily, and over lunchtime sandwiches we even had time to discuss the jacket. Our designer had produced a beautiful image, a decaying Gothic mansion, to symbolize the decay of the family in the novel. Carol liked it, but was worried that the picture of a Gothic building suggested the supernatural, and people would expect a book filled with things that go bump in the night. We spent half an hour quite seriously discussing which architectural periods indicated ghosts would be present and which didn't. Gothic, we agreed, was ghosts, Georgian was rational; Elizabethan was ghouls, but Queen Anne was entirely spook-free. No one ever tells you before you go to editor school just how bizarre some days will be, although that's probably because there's no such thing as editor school.

At any rate, while the plus was I was kept fully occupied, by the time we finished, just after two, the negative was physically visible when I got back to my desk: an email inbox bursting with little red flags, and a chair almost hidden under a pile of proofs, jacket roughs, and marketing copy. That was the main reason I rarely had author meetings in my own office. Too many people came by to drop off things that had to be done "right away!" according to the yellow stickies on them, usually followed with a smiley. If an office was empty, however, these urgent items were never taken to be dealt with "right away!" by someone else. Nor, despite my keeping an almost obsessively tidy and nearly empty desk, were they even left on my desk. The desk chair was always the favourite spot, the theory being, if you couldn't sit down, you'd do whatever it was simply so that you could get off your feet.

I was shifting the pile from chair to desk, flicking through it quickly to see how many of the "right aways" could actually wait when Miranda trailed in with a list of people who had wandered by asking for *just a few minutes to discuss* [insert title of book/name of author/promotional campaign—or, most likely, piece of scurrilous gossip currently doing the rounds]. She also had, cherry on the cake, the sales department's preliminary schedule for our upcoming sales conference.

I held out my hand, a little cloud of doom forming over my head and beginning to drip a steady rain down on me. "Gimme."

"It's not that bad." It was always sunny in Mirandaland.

Silly girl. "Sure it is."

She shrugged. "Yes, all right, maybe it is." She was learning. Another year in publishing, and she'd be as bitter and twisted as the rest of us. It's like with dogs, where every year of their life is seven human years: Miranda was still a puppy now, but soon she'd be middle-aged in editing years.

I knew it would be "that bad" without reading it because the simple fact was, the sales department was in charge of organizing the sales conference. Put like that, it sounds not merely obvious, but sensible. The problems arose because the sales department thought that the word "conference" was the important part—that what mattered was how the day ran, its orderly marshalling of events, while the editors cared about sales. Editors are frequently dismissed as having their heads in the clouds, not paying attention to the bottom line, but we desperately want our books to sell. And when our books weren't given enough time, appropriate prominence, or the right presenter to be shown off to potential buyers from bookshops, we felt that they had been handicapped before the race even began.

I'm sure if a group of sales directors were asked, their story would be different, but from the editorial point of view there was a permanent feeling of grievance at sales conference time, mostly because we had no control, and little input.

I scanned the page Miranda was still patiently holding out, petulantly refusing to touch it, as though that would somehow semaphore my disgruntlement down two flights of stairs to the sales department—take that, you grey drones in thrall to Electronic Point of Sale figures!

"Really, it could be worse," said my assistant, still masquerading as a little ray of sunshine.

I didn't want to admit it, I wanted to hang on to my snit, but she was right. Not only could it have been worse, but it frequently had been. At least this year two of my lead titles—those books we thought would sell the most, and to which we therefore allocated the most resources—were in decent slots, even if I had eight minutes in total to present them both. How I was supposed to convey to the massed ranks of sales reps, book-chain account managers, trade journalists, and assorted others why these books were fabulous and ought to be stocked in vast quantities in every bookshop in the land, in 240 seconds each, no one could ever explain.

But that was the deal. Last year, some bright-eyed little genius in sales had even installed a huge, pulsing LDT clock on the wall facing the speaker, the seconds ticking away inexorably as we gabbled faster and ever faster to finish before—a horrifying touch, this—a gong was struck and Bruce, our sales director, pranced up to the podium to introduce the next editor, and the clock started to tick down her 240 seconds.

I wouldn't win any battles on the time I was allocated, but if need be I would fight a rear-view skirmish over which titles were chosen, and in which order. I skimmed the list. "Carol's book needs to be moved into a better slot. And she should be presenting it herself." An author presenting told the buyers that we thought their book was special, worthy of particular notice. But this was not a new battle, nor even a new war. Carol wrote what is generally called "women's fiction," or, as I was constantly pointing out, the type of books that actually sell. But while her sales figures meant that the mostly male sales department was forced to acknowledge her value, they weren't ever interested in her books themselves. And this new book was even more of a headache to pitch than usual. Its theme was the invisibility of women as they aged, and the mere word "menopause" when I had dared say it aloud in the acquisitions meeting had made Bruce look queasy. So I was struggling.

"That's a fight for another day. Is there anything on my chair that can't wait?" One of the great things about working in publishing was that, as long as the work got done, no one much cared when you did it, or where, if you weren't too blatant about it. If I wanted to write my sales conference presentations at home, no one would blink. And given that I needed to collect Bim in—I looked at my watch and stifled a scream—half an hour, not only were the presentations going to be written at home, but so was everything else.

I didn't give Miranda time to reply. "I'm hideously late. Will you email me anything screamingly urgent, and I'll deal with it in about an hour?"

She nodded, unconcerned by my disappearing act. Miranda dressed as if she'd fallen asleep in 1982, and had somehow magically woken up unchanged three decades later, appearing every morning looking like she'd spent the night at a gig at the Batcave: black everything, from her Doc Martens on up to her dyed black hair, currently highlighted by a single nod to colour, a small pink rose-bud hairpin, of the sort more commonly favoured by kindergarteners. But despite the hibernating, she was the sharpest assistant I'd ever had. So much so that she was now my assistant only three days a week, and the other two she was a junior editor.

Today, happily, was not one of those days, and I felt no guilt at all about abandoning her with the backwash of my administrative work. "Email me, otherwise I'll get to everything first thing tomorrow," I called as I fled down the corridor.

"Good luck with that," she said, calmly seating herself behind my bulging in-tray. "Tomorrow is Saturday."

Well, damn.

Chapter 3

I made it to Bim's school about thirty seconds before the children started to spill out. The mothers waiting at the gate gave me looks that were so uniformly disapproving that they must have belonged to a team of synchronized matronly disappointment, where they practised in front of mirrors twice a week at noon. I surreptitiously checked to ensure I had put on both a shirt and a skirt that morning. Miranda would probably have mentioned it if I'd forgotten, but their glares made me uncertain. Whether it was that I'd arrived at the last minute, or just an in-gang vs. out-gang thing, I had no idea. Having no children, I had missed the school-gate experience up until now, and no one was giving me the warm fuzzy-wuzzies to make me regret that decision.

Then Bim appeared. "Sam!" he shrieked. "You came to get me!" That was warm and fuzzy-wuzzy enough for me. Then he continued, still at top volume, "Did you know that Campy got hurt last night? *And I was there!*"

I spoke in a low, soothing tone, as if to an aged relative not expected to survive past the morning, rather than to an overexcited six-year-old almost levitating with happiness at having been part of something unpleasant. "I know he did. Poor Campy," I added meaningfully.

"Mmm," said Bim, unpersuaded, and we set off for home. The rain the previous night had diminished to the odd shower, and it was clear now, but still wet enough that Bim could hopscotch his way across the pavement, aiming for the centre of each puddle as we went. I veered in the opposite direction to avoid the splash-back, and apart from resembling a pair of drunk and slightly incompetent tango dancers, we got home with no problem.

"Snack and then homework." I phrased it as a statement, but Bim took it to be the opening stage of negotiations.

Bim looked at me sorrowfully, a fool too foolish to know she was a fool. "Tomorrow is The Weekend." I could hear the capital letters.

"Yes it is." I was cheerful. "But your mum said to make sure it was done tonight, so you could play tomorrow."

She'd said no such thing, but I wanted to make her life as easy as possible just now. At any rate, Bim had no trouble believing his mother was the homework witch, and simply moved on, a seasoned wheeler-dealer. "Snack, and then playing in the garden, and then supper, and then homework," he countered. "Or maybe snack, then fix something, then playing in the garden." Anthony had long been the house's resident odd-job man—he was very good at leaky taps, or windows that stuck—and Bim had recently taken to the role of his assistant with enthusiasm, most days going nowhere without his mini–tool belt, complete with mini but real tools that Kay had found on eBay.

It was a tempting offer, but, "Hmm." I pondered. "I know, how about snack and then homework."

"Snack and then play *inside* and then supper and then homework?"

I considered. "Or, we could do homework and no snack."

He gave me the sort of death-stare a dowager duchess would reserve for a scullery maid who talked back. Really, in a different century he could probably have run the British Empire with a glare like that. But since right now he was smaller than your average Jack Russell, and with less bite, its effect was dissipated. I stared back, outwardly unmoved, inwardly chewing my cheek so that I didn't laugh.

"Snack, then homework," he agreed morosely, before moving on to the part of the deal he liked. "What's for snack?"

I hadn't been prepared, and supplies were always low by the end of the week. "There's apples," I began. His face told me what he thought about fruit as a snack, so I continued, "Or we could make toffee apples."

"*Make* them?" he breathed. "People can do that?"

I was regaining the ground I had lost with my insane harping on homework. "Yep. And we can be those people."

My kitchen is small, with counters along two sides. I pulled a chair from the tiny corner table so that he could stand at the counter, and wrapped him in a tea towel before we both washed our hands. All of these activities were new to Bim, even before we got to the toffee-making portion of the afternoon. Kay and Anthony worked strange hours, and while Bim was well fed, cooking wasn't something either of them did for fun.

I collected what we'd need: sugar, water, apples. I looked around. My toffee-apple equipment was seriously lacking, and I had no sticks. "We can use forks instead," I decided. "We'll spear them."

Bim lifted up the bag of sugar and began to pour it carefully into a pan. "Or we can use my screwdriver." He put the sugar down again so he could pull it from his belt and wave it in the air, narrowly missing my eye. "Campy was stuck," he added as he returned it to its loop and picked up the sugar again, moving on.

I hadn't had a chance to ask Kay or Anthony what, if anything, Bim knew of the previous night. "Was he?" I asked neutrally.

"That's what Gordon said."

"Who is Gordon?"

"He's the tutor for the children. When I'm not onstage, Gordon looks after me, and we do my homework together."

He kept his head bent, making little patterns in the sugar with his forefinger, but sliding me a glance under his lashes to make sure that the dreaded "h" word hadn't triggered a reflex urge in me to head for his satchel. "I'm only on at the beginning of the last act, and on regular nights I have to go home right away afterwards. Last night was special because it was the first night. And then, because Campy got hurt, I didn't get to take a bow anyway, even though I'd been practising it for ages. *And* Gordon made me do extra sums while I was waiting."

"That's a pity." I decided not to engage with the Campy-got-hurt part of the conversation, instead going back to what he'd said at the start. "Are there more children than you in the play? I thought I only saw you."

"You did only see me. Robbie and me share being the page, because you have to be twelve before you're allowed to work every night." Bim's eye-roll told me what he thought of the child-labour laws. If the government would only see sense, it said, he'd be down the coal mines like a shot. "He's doing both matinees this week, because I got the first night." He didn't quite high-five me, but his triumph was palpable. Then he returned to his main complaint. "I waited and I waited. Campy told Gordon I wasn't allowed to wash the blood off if I was going to take a bow, and it was all sticky and smelly, but I waited. Campy was sticky and smelly too."

I lifted the pan onto a burner and turned it on low, taking the opportunity as I moved Bim's chair to change the subject too. "Now we watch it very carefully, and wait for it to turn brown."

I made a mental note to keep a stockpile of ingredients for biscuits or brownies for future childcare emergencies: beating butter and sugar was far more exciting than watching sugar heat, and the waiting left Bim lots of time to chat. "I was sticky with blood from when Mama got shot," he boasted. "It goes whoosh—everywhere!" He made a fountain gesture with his hands. I thought of the final scene and tried to smile. "Did you like it when Mama got shot?" he asked. "That's my favourite part."

"That was a good part," I agreed weakly. "Look! The sugar is turning into toffee," I said, adding a silent *thank you, lord* to the end of the sentence. Watching the toffee foam up was absorbing enough that talk of dead people was postponed. Rolling the apples in the toffee, spearing them with forks—and a mini-screwdriver, hastily washed—was all novelty enough that the conversation died, helped by a small meltdown when I said the apples had to chill before they could be eaten, so we'd move on to homework, and they'd be ready when spelling had been done. The Four Horsemen of the Kindergarten Apocalypse rode out at that pronouncement: War, Famine, Petulance, and Death.

Anthony and Kay arrived home together just as Bim and I were sitting down to supper. They looked as if they hadn't slept for a month. Anthony took the bowl of pasta out of my hand and put it in front of Bim. I moved over to where Kay stood leaning against the door. "Do you want to join us? There's plenty," I offered. "Or do you want to go home, and we'll come up when we're finished eating?"

Kay rubbed both hands across her face in the most un-Kay-like gesture I'd ever seen. Kay is very tall, and very thin, and very blonde, and very beautiful. She's also goofy beyond measure: she wears dresses that no one over the age of five would be seen dead in, all glitter, and ribbons, and bows; and she can't walk past anything without bumping into it, or knocking it over, or both. But she carries it off because she is so completely self-possessed that she makes everything—the sparkly outfits, the clumsiness—appear to be carefully made choices.

She didn't move from the door: it appeared to be the only thing keeping her upright. "I don't know if I want to shower and then sleep for a week, or if I want to sit with Bim so I can pretend everything is normal."

I looked over to Anthony. He was Kay's opposite. Short, and dark, and square, he didn't look like a magazine idea of an actor at all, he looked like he did something with his hands. But I'd seen his work, and he was good: intense and focused. When he wasn't performing, that focus was on keeping Kay grounded. He did that now, reaching out a hand to tug her into the room. "If Sam says she has enough to feed us, let's eat. I don't know the last time you had a meal."

Kay stared into space for a moment. "I'm not sure. I think I had an energy bar before the performance last night."

That was twenty-four hours ago, so I moved Bim back

and pulled the table away from the wall to make room for all of us. "Come on," I said firmly. "Supper, then shower, then bed." I managed to stop before I asked if she'd done her homework.

We ate. Kay was mostly silent, and I headed off Bim's discussions of blood and death by prattling on about my meeting with Carol. "That reminds me, I have a bunch of new books for you," I said to Kay. Kay was one of my best test-readers, giving me feedback, and also enthusiastically passing on the books she liked to her friends, giving them that crucial but all-too-often elusive word-of-mouth validation that publishers dream of. "There's a bag of them by the door when you leave. And when Carol's book is in proof I'll get you a copy of that, too. You liked her earlier ones, didn't you?"

Kay roused herself marginally. "Can't remember. What does she write about?"

"This one is a family story, covering four generations, all living in this mouldering house, handed down together with emotional baggage—hatred, feuds." I paused. "Does that sound grim?"

She smiled briefly. "It does. But right now I'll take everything you can spare. I'm onstage for what feels like hours in the first two acts, and after my line and a half, I just sit in the background and embroider. I can easily put a book in my embroidery basket and read."

She shot a look at Bim, and Anthony slid in with a conversation change to the squeaky hinges on our shared street door: "Bim and I will take care of it in the morning," he promised.

As far as I knew, the door hinges were just fine, but Bim patted his tool belt with one hand while he gulped his milk with the other, and we managed to stay away from all discussion of the theatre until he was finished.

Anthony took him upstairs, leaving Kay sitting staring, theoretically at my garden, but more likely at nothing at all. I looked at the dishes on the table, then at Kay, and reached into the fridge for some wine. "Now that you've got something in your stomach, I think you need a glass or six."

She slumped in her seat, no longer having to pretend everything was fine. "Only six?"

"Do you want to talk about it, or do you want to not talk about it?" I asked, moving the dirty plates to the sink. "I'm good either way."

That was a flat-out lie. I longed to know what had been happening, but I'd never seen Kay so unravelled. If she needed to pretend that everything was normal, well, that was the way it would be.

"You'll hear it all in the end anyway," she said, and when I looked blank, she added, "You know Jake's still there?"

I didn't, but I had assumed his silence meant he was involved, and I nodded, more an acknowledgement of what she'd said than agreement.

"He didn't talk to me himself because of"—she made a gesture toward the ceiling—"because we're neighbours.

But I think I was the only person he didn't interview. He was there all day."

So she wanted to talk about it. I was relieved I didn't have to pretend indifference.

"They interviewed you this morning?"

"I wish." She stared at the wine bottle, picking at the label. "They interviewed us most of last night. Then we were allowed into one of the dressing rooms one by one, with someone waiting outside while we washed and changed. I'd only been home a few hours this morning when they rang to say they wanted us to come in and speak to them again. I've spent the day telling seventy-three different people the same things over and over." She sounded angry, but her hands shook. She was frightened, and sad.

I couldn't bring myself to become the seventy-fourth, so I took the toffee apples that Bim hadn't eaten out of the fridge, and started to wrap them up. That seemed suitably off-topic and lighthearted. "I'm not the Toffee-Apple Guru or anything, but I think these will probably be OK for the next few days, if Bim wants to take them to school to share with his friends. Although," I added, "I wouldn't mind if you substituted sticks for the forks first—I don't expect returning cutlery is high up on a six-year-old's list of things to remember."

Kay snorted, but when I turned to hand her the parcel, she was crying, not laughing. So much for lighthearted.

"They should take Bim away from me," she wailed. "I'm a terrible mother!"

I stared at the apples, and then at Kay, head down on the table. I wasn't quite sure how we'd gone from apples to Kay being unfit and Bim being taken into care. I should probably have said all the soothing things one says when someone is crying, but "How do you figure that?" was what I found coming out of my mouth.

She sniffed. "I put him forward for the part. It wasn't his idea, or Anthony's. I suggested it. I should have been at home, making him toffee apples. Instead it was my bright idea that made sure he saw a murder." Her voice rose in pitch and volume at the last words.

"Of course you did," I said seriously. "I heard you. 'How do I arrange to send my child into a situation where someone will be killed?' It's the kind of thing you do all the time."

She wiped her nose on her napkin, waving her other hand back and forth. "All right, I know, it's not my fault, and I'm being ridiculous. But he's—" Her nose reddened and her mouth wobbled. "He's so *little*. And he was *there*."

"There?" I asked. "He saw something? You saw something?"

She sat back wearily. "No. No to both those questions. I just mean he was around, waiting backstage when it happened. I didn't see anything, and neither did he. No one did."

I nodded, waiting to see if she wanted to continue.

Apparently yes. "As far as I can tell from what they asked, no one saw anything. We all thought it"—she waved her hands, unable to say "the body"—"it was a practical joke. We'd all received a text the night before, after the dress rehearsal, to say that Campbell's sister had died, and he wouldn't be there for the first night."

"His sister?"

She sniffed, regaining her composure. "From the questions I was asked today, his sister isn't dead, or even ill. They kept returning to it: did I know she had been ill, what had Campbell said about her. But I didn't even know that he had a sister. I met him for the first time when I was cast, so I couldn't tell them anything. Most of the others knew him much better. Bill Rose was an old friend, Ed had worked with him before, and of course Sylvie had known him forever."

Bill Rose I translated to William Anderson Rose, the actor who had revealed the dead body. Sylvie was Sylvie Sander, the designer Helena had talked about. "Who's Ed?"

Kay rolled her eyes. "Ed is Edward Vallance. You know, the Edward Vallance who has been in the mega-successful *Hartshorn* for the past three years, and you watched onstage last night?" I looked blank. "He was the reason all the photographers were outside the theatre."

I'd known that one of the cast had been in a successful TV show. "He was Balthazar?" I hazarded. "The baddie?"

She nodded. "He'd worked with Campbell and Sylvie before. And then of course there's Frankie. She knew him much better." She looked sideways at me, as if to check whether I was keeping up and understood her slight emphasis on "better."

Thanks to Helena I could at least look mildly intelligent. "Is she a day over twenty?" I didn't bother trying not to sound censorious. Apart from anything else, the gossip was keeping Kay occupied and her mind off Bim's involvement.

"Don't be disgusting. Campbell is seventy-six. Having a relationship with a twenty-year-old would be revolting." She looked at me severely. "She's twenty-nine. Campbell is barely half a century older than her." She stuttered: "Was. *Was* barely." The joke had gone sour, and she was close to tears again, but she blinked them away. "If it took them a full day to ask me what time I put on my makeup, and when I made a cup of tea, and I barely knew him, they must still be questioning her. I really couldn't tell them that much. Most of the time when I wasn't onstage I was with Bim and his tutor. Gordon is officially obliged to stick to the boys like glue, but it was an opportunity for me to have some time with him now he's in school all day. Anyway, we did his schoolwork together, or played, and so I didn't spend as much time with the rest of the cast as I would have if Bim hadn't been there."

That reminded me. "What—and when—are you going to tell Bim? He told me Davison had been 'hurt,' and I wasn't quite sure what to say, so I just tried to steer him off the topic."

She slumped again, daunted by the thought. "My parents took him away immediately last night, and I didn't want to tell him this morning and then send him off to school. We'll figure out what to say this weekend. He'll need to know before we go back to work."

"Back to work?" I stared at her. When she'd said that she had lots of time to read onstage I hadn't questioned it because Bim was there, but I'd assumed she didn't really mean it. "You're joking. The show's going to go on?"

She gave me a watery smile. "I bet you've always wanted to say that." Then she shrugged. "We were told that the police will probably be out of the theatre over the weekend, and we can reopen toward the end of next week."

"And you will? That is, they will?"

"Ed and Frankie and Bill will be praised for their team spirit, so they won't drop out. The rest of us—the small parts, and the crew—can't afford to drop out, even if we wanted to: this was a fixed eight-week run. None of us have other jobs we can just fall into." She was being pragmatic now, and I saw her point. If a death at the office meant my salary for the next two months vanished overnight, I'd be concerned about the cause, but not to the extent of refusing to go into the office.

Kay continued. "And it's not like there won't be an audience. Jenny said the bookings went crazy overnight after the news broke. We'll be sold out for weeks, which would never have been the case with this kind of play, even with Ed in it. The producers will be ecstatic."

I didn't say *Even though their director's dead?* but I must have looked it, because she shrugged. I hadn't meant to make her uncomfortable. I cast around for a route out of the gaping silence. "Who's Jenny?"

Kay looked blank.

"You said Jenny said the bookings went crazy."

"She's the stage manager. Nothing happens in a theatre without the stage manager knowing. She's the one who passed on the message that Campbell wouldn't be there last night."

"Did you like him? Davison?" I asked.

She paused, as if that were the one question no one had asked. "I—I—I'm not sure. I respected him. Even though he was physically quite frail—he had arthritis or something, and he couldn't move around much—even so, that didn't stop him doing his job, and he was really, really good at it. Lots of directors aren't. I mean, you don't have to have any training, or skills, or pass an exam, to call yourself a director. But Campbell was one of the best I've ever worked with. He was polite, and pragmatic, and efficient, and he got what he needed. But . . ." She trailed away. She wasn't weepy anymore, she was figuring it out like it was a problem to be solved. She nodded to herself, and began again. "I had a small part, so I wasn't in the inner circle. And from that outsider group, you could see that everything that made him a good director made him an unpleasant human being. A good director sees what a production needs, and he makes sure everyone involved believes what they need to believe to make it happen. In real life, that's called being manipulative and underhanded. So no, I didn't like him, and I didn't for the very reasons that he was good at his job."

I stood up abruptly. "You should try to sleep."

Kay blinked at my abrupt dismissal. I wasn't being unsympathetic, though. I was just aware that Jake had been lurking in the hall for the past few minutes. I had no plans to do his dirty work for him. Kay was my friend, and if he wanted to interview her, he could do it himself.

She stared at me, trying to work out my sudden distance. "It wasn't me. In case you were wondering."

I laughed out loud at that. "I never thought for a moment it was." She looked mildly insulted, as if I'd questioned her abilities. "I'm not saying you'd never kill anyone," I soothed. "If someone was trying to hurt Bim, you'd have no hesitation in pushing them into the path of an oncoming bus. But would you kill someone so that it screwed up your first night?" I shook my head. "Can't see it."

She was mollified, and I walked her to the front door. Once I heard her footsteps on the stairs, I said, "You can come out now." Jake stepped out of the bedroom. "How long were you there?"

My tone indicated I wasn't impressed, and Jake had the grace to look slightly ashamed. "Not long. You were asking if she liked Davison." He held up his hands. "I didn't plan to eavesdrop. I didn't realize she was there, or that you hadn't heard me come in until I was virtually at the kitchen door." He smiled. "And I agree. It's unlikely Kay had anything to do with Davison's death."

I snorted. "What I was too polite to say was that if someone tried to hurt Bim, she'd absolutely push them into the path of a bus. And then she'd trip over the curb, and take out six innocent bystanders with her when she fell."

Chapter 4

Jake was in the shower when I woke the next morning. When he came out, I didn't lift my head, or even open both eyes, but said accusingly, "It's seven o'clock."

"It is," he agreed, transferring the contents of his pockets from the suit he'd been wearing the day before to today's.

"You're wearing a suit," I added, even more accusingly.

"You're two for two."

I summarized. "It's seven o'clock in the morning, you're already dressed, and you're wearing a suit." I got to the point. "On a Saturday you're supposed to be off-rota."

"And the lady wins the purple plush panda." He sat down beside me. "Are you really surprised I'm working today?"

I stopped pretending and sat up. "No, of course not.

It's just that I thought if I ignored it for long enough, it wouldn't be true, you know?"

He knew.

"It's the job. That doesn't mean I'm not going to bitch and moan about it, but I do get it." I thought about our plans. "Where are you going to be? If Kit and I change our meeting place to somewhere near you, do you think you could still have lunch with us?"

Kit was one of my authors, or, rather, he had been my author first, but he had long passed into the small group that had moved from the pleasant work-acquaintance category to the friend group. He was a fashion journalist, and he wrote books on the intersection of fashion, celebrity, and gossip. Not only did I love him dearly, but he and Jake had bonded, even though Jake's idea of fashion was rotating his four Marks and Spencer suits, two for summer, two for winter, while Kit was the man who had put the "camp" into a Boy Scouts' jamboree.

Jake considered. "That might work. I'll probably be at the office all day. Text me the restaurant, and if I can make it, I will." He stood. "Stay where you are and I'll bring you coffee. There's no reason for both of us to be up this early on a weekend."

I knew there was a reason I liked the man. I snuggled back down and pretended I was still asleep.

Finding somewhere to eat near Jake's office was easier said than done. For decades Scotland Yard had been in an ugly office block near Victoria station, and Weird Rule of

English Life Number 938 decreed that no good restaurants were permitted to exist near train stations. Recently, the ugly office block had been sold off, like so much of London, to a Middle Eastern developer, and the CID had been relocated to a building on the Embankment, just near Parliament, hidden in with a mass of other government buildings. Now, I discovered, Weird Rule of English Life Number 938 had a sub-section (b) which decreed that no good restaurants were permitted to exist near Parliament or other governmental buildings. Googling left me with a pizza place, which I didn't bother to mention to Kit, because he would rather eat his left arm than go somewhere so unfashionable, or—or nowhere that I could find. Kit kept texting me places that were miles away, would have four types of cutlery and a bottle of wine that cost more than all my shoes put together. Jake's sole contribution, when I texted him to ask, was that the pub he and his colleagues routinely met at was off-limits. Not that I would have considered it for a moment and, anyway, Kit would have fainted if I'd suggested a pub. We finally settled on an Italian place that I expected would only solidify my adherence to the don't-eat-near-a-station-or-now-Parliament-too rule, but after a dozen texts, I would have eaten pretty well anywhere that didn't have hot and cold running cockroaches, if it ended the discussion.

When I arrived, Kit was already there, busy charming the waitress. He probably didn't even know that's what he was doing, but Kit loves people to love him, and they do—he is lovable. And attractive. He's very tall, and very dark, and always dressed as if he's about to head to a photo shoot entitled "The Well-Dressed English Gent." Today being Saturday, he had substituted a beautiful cashmere pullover for his usual beautiful suit, but the charm was a Monday to Sunday deal, no special schedule for Sats, Suns, or hols.

The waitress probably had nothing better to do with her time than be charmed. The restaurant didn't go in for Italian stereotypes, settling instead on what I could only think of as European airport-lounge chic—a 1960s-ish beige and orange carpet, Danish modern-style wooden tables and chairs, lots of beige on the walls, and those hanging light fixtures that were once very designerly, but were now IKEA basics. And in all that beige, all those tables, Kit, and one other table, with a young couple who were all but sitting in each other's laps, were the only occupants.

I kissed Kit's cheek and sat, saying, "Jake asked me to order him something cold. He'll get here, but when, and for how long, is up for grabs."

Kit tossed his head, as though being a police detective was an eccentricity Jake chose to assume for no other reason than to disrupt his friends' meal plans. But his heart wasn't in it. "Tell me *everything*," he said, his hands braced on the table edge, as though it might get up and dance about from sheer excitement if he didn't hold on tight. Kit never did or said anything without throwing all his energy into it. This time I'd witnessed, if not a murder, the end result of one. His energy was ramped up to stratospheric levels.

So I did. I told him what we'd seen, and what Kay had told me. He made sympathetic noises in all the right places, and for the first time, I allowed the wall I'd built around the evening to come down slightly, and acknowledge the horror of what had happened.

While Kit is dramatic, he's also sensitive, and he saw I was upset, and guided the conversation away from the death itself. "I saw the photographs of the production in the paper yesterday," he said, waving the breadbasket at his new best waitress friend, to indicate our urgent need of breadsticks to bolster us during our conversation. "The costumes were impressive." He nodded grandly: the verdict was in. Kit writes fashion journalism for a living, but he knows more about its history than most.

I waggled my head. "I'm sure you're right about them as costumes, but onstage all those Soviet army uniforms just made it hard to tell who was who."

"East German," he said. "But yes, I agree, uniforms are always a technical challenge."

"East German what?"

Kit waved it away. "The uniforms I saw in the paper were East German, not Soviet. Not that it matters: military uniforms can be theatrically awkward. The purpose of uniforms, after all, is to make everyone look alike. It's strange someone as experienced as Sander would do that, or that Davison would agree."

Apparently everyone except me had heard of Sylvie Sander. "You know her work?" I didn't wait for an answer, replying instead to his unspoken *Duh.* "Well, I didn't."

Kit was diplomatic. "She's been working a long time. You probably have seen something of hers without knowing it. She mostly does the classics. In fact, I don't think I've ever known her to do a new play." He considered that briefly. "No, I don't think she ever has. Anything Davison does that's new, he works with someone else; the classics are always with her. I suppose it's not something that stands out, because a lot of the designs she does, whatever the date of the play, she sets in the postwar period: 1950s, sometimes 1960s. Nothing later. She's famous for that."

I was outraged. "How do you know this stuff?"

"Sam, I've been working in fashion for, what, thirty years. How could I not?"

I hated "everybody knows" answers to things I'd never heard of. I returned to his comment about the period Sander favoured. "I can see why someone might do that. Women's clothes from that decade are very dramatic, and if you go for zoot-suit things, so are the men's."

Kit nodded. "And, from the dramatic point of view, if you set something in the postwar period, you give even trivial matters a sense of importance that they might not otherwise have, just because you know your audience is aware of the historical facts."

"Cynical?" I teased Kit. "You?"

He bowed graciously, accepting it as a tribute.

"Speaking of cynical," I added, glad to have moved

away from the death itself, "you should have seen the cameras out front when we arrived at the theatre. And the audience came dressed for it." I gave him a sequin-by-sequin description of the woman a few rows ahead of us.

Kit knew almost as many people as Helena, although their professional worlds couldn't be further apart. So I was only mildly surprised when he said, "That sounds like it was Liz Henderson. She goes to a lot of fashion events too, and she's at all the parties."

"Who is?" asked Jake, sliding into the seat where the cold stuffed peppers I'd ordered for him were waiting. He began to eat without waiting for a reply, as if food were something he'd once heard of, but hadn't seen in years, and had no expectation of ever coming across again.

"Our Lady of the Displayed Bosoms," I explained.

He didn't stop chewing, just raised his eyebrows, waiting for an explanation.

"At the theatre. A couple of rows ahead of us."

He shook his head.

"Oh, come on, you must have noticed her. She had on a dress that in many southern US states would have seen her arrested for indecent exposure if she'd been wearing it on a beach."

He still looked blank, so I waved it away "Never mind. She was just a woman at the theatre, meeting and greeting."

Kit joined in. "If it was Liz, she likes the parties, the photographers, being somewhere famous people are. A first night would absolutely be her thing. In the fashion world, initially she was asked to events because she donated to charities linked to fashion houses or the art colleges. Now she's invited because she gets her picture in the magazines, which gives them more publicity. Which gives her more publicity, which means she's invited." He raised a hand in dismissal, of the woman, the fashion publicity machine, and possibly the world at large. "She's invited because she's got a profile, she's got a profile because she's invited. But," he concluded simply, "she's no one."

I'd been judgemental as I'd watched her in the theatre, not terribly taken by her over-the-top greetings or her under-the-ribcage décolletage, but, well, ouch.

By mutual consent, we didn't discuss the evening at all after that, and when Jake left after half an hour, giving me a quick kiss and no mention of when he'd be home, I concluded that I probably wouldn't see him for the rest of the day, or even the rest of the weekend. Kit and I walked along the river while there was some weak sunshine left in the day, and then I headed home. I'd done my weekly food-shop at the farmers' market before I'd set out that morning, and my afternoon was scheduled to be filled with even more excitement: I had to put away the groceries, change the sheets and towels, do some laundry, clean the bathroom. My life was, I decided as I sluiced bleach around the loo, so filled with fun and festivity that they ought to make a Broadway musical about it. Only a full chorus line high-kicking past my laundry basket could possibly do it justice.

It was late afternoon by the time I got as far as the pile of clothes waiting to be ironed. I kicked at it gently, deciding. I had two choices. I could do the ironing, or I could ignore it for another week. I nudged the top layers aside. I didn't recognize the clothes from about halfway down. I looked more closely. They were T-shirts, and a sundress: summer clothes. That made life easier. They'd been waiting to be ironed for at least three months, so I obviously didn't need them and I could ignore them for a few more months.

Cheered by that, I filled up a watering can instead, to water the ugly cheese-plant that lived by the front door. It had been left by the people who lived upstairs before Kay and Anthony had moved in. No one liked it, but no one had the heart to let it die by inches slowly in front of us.

As I opened my front door, I heard a thundering on the stairs above, a sound that nature programmes had taught me heralded a panicked herd of rhinoceros stampeding ahead of a ravenous lion. Kay is tall but delicate; Anthony taller and heavy-set. There was no question. "Hey, Kay," I called up.

The stampeding drew nearer, and then stumbled. I mentally slapped myself: *Do not distract Kay while she is in motion.* A few more seconds and we met on the landing between our flats, Kay out of breath and gripping the banister for balance for a moment before she gripped me. "I'm so glad I caught you. I wanted to ask a favour, but face to face, so I could tell if you really didn't want to say yes."

I thought I more or less understood the gist of that. "What is it?"

"Jenny just texted. They've called an all-day rehearsal tomorrow."

"Mmm?" I couldn't see my role in that.

"Anthony is working, so I was hoping"—she gave me puppy eyes—"that you might be able to help out with Bim. I'd try our usual sitter, but Lisa's sister just had a baby, so she's gone to stay with her for a while."

I ran through my schedule for the next day in my head, which was easy, because I didn't have one. Jake had theoretically not been working, but I assumed now he would be, so anything we might have done—a film, meeting friends, a walk on the Heath—would have to be rescheduled anyway. "Sure."

She looked unnerved. "That was way too easy."

"I'm not doing anything. What time do you need to leave? Just drop him off, and we'll go to the park, or whatever you had planned."

"Oh, no, that's the problem. He needs to be at the rehearsal."

I shook my head. "Start at the beginning, and explain. You want me to babysit Bim, but he's working, so . . ."

"They've called a rehearsal to restage the final act. We—that is, no one—" She regrouped, and finished in a rush. "We can't do the last act the way it was, with the body revealed again."

"Of course you can't," I agreed.

"The assistant director will block out a new staging tomorrow. Bim and Robbie, the other page, are on in the first scene, so they have to be there. I'm not allowed officially to be their chaperone, because I'm working too. Gordon went away for the weekend and can't get back in time. So we need to find someone who could come to the rehearsal to supervise the boys." She winced. "I'm embarrassed even to ask, because it's scheduled to last all day. Unofficially, when I'm not needed I'll keep the boys occupied, but . . ." She trailed away. "It's a lot to ask."

It was, but as long as I didn't have to amuse Bim and his friend for six or eight hours on my own, it also wasn't. "It'll be interesting to see. And I'll bring my e-reader, and when the boys are working, or you're with them, I'll read manuscript submissions. It's what I do most Sundays anyway."

Kay, always the performer, threw herself onto her knees and kissed my feet. Either that, or she fell over. With Kay it's never easy to say.

I often dropped round to have coffee with Helena on a Sunday, so I gave her a quick ring before I went to bed. I explained my new role as chaperone-to-the-six-year-old-stars, and after that, filled her in on my lunch with Kit. She hadn't heard anything more than what was in the news about Davison, and although she didn't say it, she was clearly annoyed that Kit had known more about Sander than she had, or that he'd thought he knew who the woman in the audience was. If the Olympics had a Competitive Networking event, the two of them would be a shoe-in for joint golds every four years.

Still, she'd never give me, or him, the satisfaction of acknowledging it.

I didn't imagine Jake would be thrilled to hear I was spending the next day with the very people he was investigating. I could have told Kay to find someone else—Bim's friend Robbie must have friends and family who could help—or I could decide not to share the news. I chose door number two. Jake was home late anyway, and I made sure I went to bed early.

That part was easy. Growing up under Helena's eagle eye had ensured that my avoid-uncomfortable-conversations abilities had been honed to razor-sharp levels. The next morning was less so.

I had hoped that Jake would have left at his usual seven or seven thirty, gone before I had to be up on a weekend, and I could tell him all about it after the event—it's easier to apologize than ask permission. Well, I wasn't quite asking permission. Indeed, as I showered and dressed, I got increasingly annoyed by the idea that I should even contemplate asking permission—who was Jake to tell me what to do, I thought as I stomped down the hall.

By the time I'd walked the few metres to the kitchen, in fact, I was furious with the hypothetical Jake who had hypothetically demanded to approve my hypothetical schedule for the hypothetical day. The fact that he hadn't, and wouldn't, was irrelevant.

When the non-hypothetical Jake handed me my coffee, therefore, and didn't ask anything at all, I was confused, and so I blurted out, "I'm spending the day with Kay and Bim."

"That's nice," he said.

The mental grinding of gears as my careening thought processes were forced to brake sharply in the face of reality could probably be heard in the street.

So derailed was I by reality smacking me in the face that I babbled. "What about you? Where will you be?"

He looked at me for a moment. I never asked his schedule. He dealt daily with death and destruction, and we had a silent pact: home was a death-free zone. He might complain to me about office politics, or his colleagues, but blood and guts had no place in our life together.

Un-asking the question, however, would only bring more attention. I searched for something more normal. "Will you be home in time for supper? Or maybe we can look and see if there's something on locally at the cinema?"

Now Jake knew something was up. I never suggested going out. I didn't quite lie down on the floor in a toddler tantrum when social events were proposed, but it always hovered as a possibility.

A knock at our front door preempted whatever he was going to say. "Mama says you're coming to the rehearsal with us!" shouted a small voice on the other side of the door.

"Does she?" said Jake.

Busted.

I headed to get the door. "She couldn't find a sitter for Bim. I'm going to look after him while she works," I called over my shoulder.

Jake didn't reply. But his silence followed me audibly down the hall.

Chapter 5

On our way to the bus, Kay lowered her voice even though Bim had run ahead. "We told him last night that Campbell was very old and sick, so he died, like Thumper." Thumper had been Bim's bad-tempered, smelly, and decidedly not-lamented rabbit, who had left his hutch to go to the great warren in the sky the year before.

I raised an eyebrow. "Is that going to work? Won't he hear people talking about what happened?"

Kay still looked as though she might cry at any moment. "I don't know. I spoke to Robbie's parents last night, and that's what we agreed we'd tell both boys."

"What about the police? Isn't he going to have to speak to them?"

"They've asked to interview him tomorrow. He knows there are regulations covering how many hours he can work. We told him they check up to make sure, so he has to tell an 'inspector' everything he did that day. The police said they could interview him like that." She was silent for a moment, and then added hopelessly, "It might work."

And it might not: children ended up hearing everything. But it wasn't my business. "How have you explained today's rehearsal to him, then?"

"I said that this sometimes happens. If things don't go well on opening night, they change it afterward." She added with a tired smile, "Which also has the benefit of being the truth."

The rehearsal was in a building not far from the theatre, in what looked as if it had once been a warehouse. Now, at street level, it housed a couple of chichi shops, and upstairs there were, from the names on the door, chichi companies—an advertising agency, a TV production company. These were bypassed by Kay in favour of a side alley.

Bim reached up to punch in a code by an unmarked door. So, "You've been here before." I didn't need to make it a question.

Bim sang a little song to the tune of "Mary Had a Little Lamb": "Thirty-nine-and-seventy-one" as he moved indoors to press the button for a huge freight elevator, which made a groaning noise on its approach. Kay explained, "The company Campbell put together is doing a nine-month season, with four plays. This is their second, and we rehearsed here until we moved into the theatre. The third play is in rehearsal here now, which is why we have to be squeezed in over the weekend."

On the top floor, the lift opened directly into a large white room. From the upright piano pushed into the corner, the long table to one side covered in a paper tablecloth with coffee urns and disposable cups, a dozen or so wooden chairs, and not much else, I concluded that this was the workspace itself.

Kay walked us over to a square-set woman with fine brown hair ending in a fringe cut bluntly over her forehead, partly feathering down to a pair of funky red reading spectacles set firmly on an upturned nose. She was maybe in her late thirties or early forties. The nose might have given her an air of childlike charm, if the mouth under it hadn't been so firmly set, the lips so tightly pressed together. The lines radiating around it said her mouth always was firmly set, and probably had been set for years. I looked at the lines, and then at her hands, which were twisted with arthritis. She was older than she looked.

Kay ignored the bad temper radiating out from her in waves. "Morning, Jenny." So this was the stage manager. Maybe I'd judged too quickly. Wrangling a couple of dozen actors on their day off—which had been her day off too—couldn't be a lot of fun. Kay didn't wait for an answer from Jenny, which was probably smart, since pleasantries didn't look to be her thing. "This is Sam Clair. She'll be the boys' chaperone for the day. Sam, this is Jenny Rogers, the stage manager. Any questions you have about the day's schedule, or anything else, in fact, Jenny will know the answer to."

She might have all the answers, but she didn't look up

when I said hello, she didn't look at Bim when he said hello.
She ticked off a couple of items on her tablet and looked
away, pushing up her spectacles crossly, leaving them to
rest on her forehead as she moved away without speaking at all. They promptly fell down again, a distinct full-
stop to her disdain.

"It's not you, it's just her natural charm and bubbly
good nature shining through," Kay said under her breath
as she guided Bim to a row of coat hooks and began to unwrap him. She nodded toward the table. "They'll feed us
at intervals. Help yourself whenever you're hungry."

The lift behind us opened and another child around
Bim's age appeared. Bim took off, shouting, "Robbie, Robbie, they've got the good kind of juice today!" as Kay
continued even more quietly. "Jenny *really* doesn't like
children. I thought it was just Bim at first, since he's a bit
noisy sometimes, and he runs around backstage when
Gordon isn't paying attention, but Robbie is quiet, and
never gets in anyone's way, and she doesn't like him
either." She shrugged. "So I just keep Bim away from her
as much as I can. She's not unkind, she just doesn't want
to deal."

That seemed fair enough, and I hustled over to the table
to make sure that Bim and Robbie got their juice and then
set them up out of the way of the group of adult performers now congregating around the coffee urns. "Let's find
a space where we can get out the games we brought," I
said, thinking that I'd keep them at the back of the room
until they were needed.

My day was not onerous. Kay had packed books as well as games, and Bim had brought a shoebox from home that he wouldn't be parted from even to put in Kay's bag. He and Robbie sat cross-legged on the floor with it, and with an identical box that Robbie had brought, and we managed to kill at least an hour going through the contents of both "pirate treasure chests": pirate maps that closely resembled train schedules; some pebbles that were classed as "jewels"; a bit of cord that came from the "noose" used to hang the pirates' arch-rival, Black Bart; and "pirate grub," which looked suspiciously like a half-sucked sweet covered in lint, that I decided not to inquire further about in case it inspired one of the boys to finish it.

They were called shortly after to work for an hour or so with the assistant director, a man called Tom, whose last name I never heard. He was thin and pale, in his mid-twenties, and his default mode was deferral. He deferred to everyone around him: to Bill Rose and Ed Vallance, the stars, who were very workmanlike and serious; to Frances Singer, who was very starry and prefaced every refusal—and there were many—with "Campbell said/did/liked," which made everyone else flinch each time; and most of all, Tom deferred to Jenny, who ran the day with only slightly less organization than the D-Day landings had required.

She hadn't been nice to me—she hadn't even been ordinarily civil to me—but I admired the sheer efficiency with which she ensured that the work that needed to be done was done with a minimum of fuss. And I was fascinated with her very quiet grandeur, a way of being starry without Frances's giddy showing off. Jenny sat to one side, watching, timing, noting, very rarely tossing in a comment, but when she did, everyone bobbed their heads in unison—yes, Jenny; no, Jenny; three bags full, Jenny. She even handed her bottle of water to Tom to open. He did it automatically, without her needing to say anything: an *I'm too important for this* that was so routine no one thought twice about it.

Kay was killed early on in the final act, so as soon as they'd blocked that out she came and joined us in our little huddle. The boys were on the floor, having abandoned their pirate chests for a game on Kay's iPad, with Bim, having refused to take off his tool belt, lying humped over the bulge made by the hammer like a baby seal. I was sitting on one chair, and had my feet up on a second one I'd pulled around to face it. Kay arranged two chairs in a mirror image facing me.

She sat and I dropped my e-reader, which I'd been deluding no one that I was working on. "Where's the loo?" I'd been drinking coffee since seven.

She nodded to a hallway behind the catering table. "Through there, to the end of the corridor, then left."

Now she was with the boys, I saw no need to hurry. The rehearsal room had framed costume drawings all along two walls and the model of a set, but the actors were working there, and I'd only seen them from a distance. There were more, however, in the corridor, which I could stop to look at properly. They were mostly for *The Spanish Tragedy*, and so I took some pictures and texted them to Kit, since he'd said he'd liked what he'd seen in the papers.

It was more than an hour later, and I was playing a game with the boys, when Jenny looked at her watch, cut off Tom, who had been giving notes, in mid-sentence, saying, "Let's take a break. Everybody back in an hour, please." Tom didn't argue, or even look surprised, just closed his mouth and his script as everyone immediately stood, most heading for their coats, a few raiding the catering table, where sandwiches and fruit were being laid out.

Kay stood. "I'll take the hooligans for a walk," she said. "There's a playground in Drury Lane where they can run around for half an hour, and still have time to stuff down a sandwich before we're called. Do you want to come, or do you want some time to yourself?"

I looked at my watch. "I've got a few errands it would be good to tick off my list, if you don't need me. I'll be back by two."

I had no errands, nor even a list off which to tick them, but while I was fond of Bim, there were only so many zombies I felt the need to kill, and by quite early in the day I had met my weekend quota, not only of killing, but of discussing them, which I knew from experience automatically followed zombie-related activities. Instead I went and stretched my legs for twenty minutes, then returned to the rehearsal room. Or tried. As I walked down the alley, I cursed myself: I'd forgotten the code for the door.

I rang the bell, hoping that someone was still upstairs. No luck. I was weighing up texting Kay for the number, which would blow my "running errands" cover story, or just retreating to sit in a café until everyone was due back, when a figure blocked out the light at the end of the alley. I looked up, and then up some more. It was Ed Vallance. I hadn't realized how tall he was until he was standing beside me. He reached past and punched in a number—39-71, which I now carefully sang again in my head to Bim's tune as I scuttled into the lift behind him.

"Thanks," I said. "I forgot to get the code. I'm looking after—"

"The boys," he supplied. "I saw." He held out his hand. "Ed."

"Sam. I'm a friend of Kay's." We moved into the rehearsal room. "I mean, I'm not really a chaperone, so I don't know if it's OK, but before you start work again, may I look at the model?"

Ed waved a hand. "Knock yourself out."

He was outwardly pleasant, even as he did that thing that I'd seen in other very successful actors, of never quite making eye contact. I supposed it was a way of fending off hordes of strangers, keeping up a barrier. And certainly, Ed didn't seem to want to chat, immediately dropping his head to his phone, eyes to the screen. That was fine with me. Asking to look at the model wasn't a way of starting up a conversation; I just wanted to look at the model. And anyway, I was all chatted out after my morning with Bim and Robbie, although if Ed had needed any facts about either pirates or zombies, I had several dozen new ones at my disposal.

It didn't appear that he did, however, so I turned to the model, which was for *The Spanish Tragedy*, and had tiny white model figures spread across it to represent the players. They had no faces, and weren't in painted costumes, but they'd been posed as if they were making miniature speeches to their miniature colleagues, making their white, faceless silence eerie. Beside that was another model, for *The Taming of the Shrew*, which Kay had told me was the next play, also with Frances Singer and Ed Vallance. The sketches on the walls were for those plays, and for another, or possibly others, that I couldn't identify. Characters' names were pencilled in below them, but I didn't recognize them. Whatever they were for, they, too, as Kit had said, were in a 1950s style.

I could have asked Ed, but he hadn't looked up, he hadn't looked in my direction at all. Short of holding up a sign that said, *Thank you, I have enough friends, I don't need more,* he couldn't have made his lack of interest more clear. I turned back to the sketches. If I googled the names of the characters, that would probably lead straight to the play. I pulled out my phone.

"Christ! Don't do that!" I spun around. Ed was striding across the room, hand out like a traffic cop.

I jerked my head around to see who had come up in
the lift behind me, and what they were doing that they
shouldn't. There was no one. He was talking to me. I
squeaked, "Me? What am I doing?"

His face was stern. He was probably only in his late
twenties or early thirties, but what were normally heavy
lines between his nose and mouth were now pronounced
and deep. Given that he was nearly two metres tall, and,
as he bore down on me, it felt like he was also two metres
wide, too, I backed away.

"You can't take photos. Sylvie will have a cow." He
was giving me the sort of frown I use on authors who think
dream sequences add gravitas to their novels.

"I'm not. I mean, I didn't." My back hit the wall, so I
held out my phone—*See, guv, it warn't me wot did it.* "I
was googling the names on the sketches to try and figure
out what the play is."

Either my wide-eyed stare, or the sheer nerdiness of
what I was doing, persuaded him. He backed off, raking
his hand through his thick dark hair—a gesture that
seemed both genuinely *aw-shucks*-ish, and carefully practised. I was sure his tween fans loved it. "All right then.
But Sylvie is crazed about photos of her drawings. She's
permanently convinced her work will be stolen. No reproductions are allowed, ever."

I raised my hand. "I really and truly wasn't. Boy
Scout's oath." My mind flashed back to the pictures I'd
taken in the corridor earlier. How fortunate that I'd never
been a Scout. Or a boy.

Before I had too much time to feel guilty, Jenny, Frances Singer, and Tom came through the door, wrangling about something Davison would or would not have wanted. They swept Ed into their argument, and I was left by the table. I slid my phone into my pocket and collected a sandwich before retreating to the children's corner.

I confessed my false step with Ed when Kay got back: since she had hired me, I didn't want her to get in trouble for my actions.

"Don't worry. I think everyone's on edge because of"—she gestured to the missing Davison. "Sylvie was a nightmare to deal with, and Campbell was the only person who could keep her on track. I think it's worrying everyone now, with the other plays coming up."

"What does being a nightmare involve?" I would have said half the behaviour I'd seen that day would qualify as nightmarish in most regular offices, so I was curious.

"As a person, day to day, nothing. She's a perfectly nice, perfectly harmless woman. If you'd never seen her work, you'd think she was a secretary in an old Hollywood film—the loyal, overlooked drone who's secretly madly in love with her boss. Except Sylvie wasn't in love with Campbell. In fact, I think they hated each other."

"Even though they'd been working together for decades?"

"Maybe because of it. Everything has to be Sylvie's way, all the time. She's heard of compromise, but it's something for other people to do; it doesn't apply to her. She and Campbell only take on projects they initiate, and they have it in their contracts that no one can override them on the design, not even the producers."

"Is that unusual?"

Kay rolled her eyes. "That's freakish beyond the realms of science fiction. No one in theatre ever overrides a producer. The producer has the money, so the producer is the difference between people seeing your work, and your work staying in your head."

That I understood. People outside publishing think authors have control over their own books, but you have to be really successful before that is true. If a book-chain doesn't like a book cover the author loves? The author isn't going to get that book cover. If the publisher thinks the title the author has given their book doesn't work? The title will be changed. So, translated into my world, Davison and his designer were J. K. Rowling: so successful that they were therefore powerful enough to tell the money people to take a flying leap.

I was about to share this insight when Kay and the boys were called on to work. Instead I did what I'd been doing all morning: I picked up my e-reader and then ignored it completely and watched the rehearsal instead. Despite his weedy demeanour, Tom knew what he was doing. He had the entire attention of the two boys, who were required to perform a new and elaborately choreographed entrance behind the leads. As they repeated it for the eighth or tenth time, I watched Jenny at the rear time each segment with the lighting designer, who had appeared with the stragglers from lunch.

A voice above me said, "I've been trying to work out what you're doing all day."

I looked up.

"Bill," said the voice, now accompanied by a hand.

I shook it. "Sam," I said.

If Ed Vallance had seemed bigger in life than on screen, Bill Rose was the opposite. He'd filled the stage the other night, his enormous, brown-velvet voice and sheer personality making everyone else respond only to him. He'd done the same when he was rehearsing that morning. But now as he sat in Kay's chair, like her putting his feet up on the seat beside me, I saw he was a small, fine-boned sixtyish-year-old man, someone you wouldn't look at twice on the bus.

In response to his first question, I lifted my e-reader. "In theory I'm reading for work. In practice, I'm watching all of you. Watching other people's work is always far more interesting than doing your own."

"For an actor, agreed. I spend my visits to the dentist memorizing how he lifts his tools, just in case I'm ever asked to play a dentist." He mimed lifting an invisible dental tool with a deliberate, heavy gesture. "And if I go to a concert, I copy how the French horn player shakes the spit out of his instrument." He twirled his hand, each idea mirrored in his body to be read like a sign. Then he deflated. "Of course, I never have been asked to play a dentist, or a French horn player." He seemed to brood on the many great dental and horn roles that had unfairly passed him by.

I looked over at the boys, who were repeating their entrance once more. "I don't think it's the same for non-performers. I'm not thinking about replicating it, but just working out all the different parts that go into making it. Usually I see the end product, but never the timings, the masking tape on the floor, the discussion about lighting. And listening to the director, and then seeing how you all change what you're doing after he says the most anodyne things. He hasn't said anything this morning that didn't seem obvious, or even dull, yet you all made important changes afterwards."

He laughed shortly. "It's not always like that: more often, directors say important things and we don't change anything at all. Tom's good. Very good. Much too good to have been an assistant director for so long, but then, Campbell was special." He looked pained.

Kay had said he knew him well. I made the kind of meaningless noises that we all make after a death to express sympathy, adding, "This must be hard," nodding toward the rehearsal.

Bill shrugged. "The only thing harder than changing things would have been not changing them. And at least Tom gets to flex his muscles a bit. Campbell was brilliant enough to keep someone like Tom to do all the routine work. If it hadn't been for the reason behind it, I'd say it was a blessing for Tom to get out from under Campbell's shadow. But," he went on, "you still haven't said what you've been doing, what your 'work' is."

Before I could explain, Jenny called sharply, "Bill, we

need you." She looked down at her tablet again without waiting to see if he responded, brushing her spectacles once more down from her forehead.

Bill didn't keep her waiting. He was up like one of Pavlov's dogs on hearing the bell, pushing back both chairs, which elicited a shriek from Bim: "No! My treasure!"

He shot forward, diving under my chair to rescue his box, which Bill had unknowingly kicked when he stood, scattering the pirate hoard across the floor.

"Hey, little man, I'm sorry." Bill dropped to his knees to help collect the jewels and maps and other piratical paperwork, but Bim was having none of it, furiously slapping the objects out of his hand.

"They're *mine*," he shouted.

I was slow to respond, forgetting that this was my job, until Jenny's tone cut across Bim's wails and Bill's apologies. "Bim! Really!" She half bent down to pull him away, and then froze, seeming to remember that wrestling with children was beneath her dignity. The only one who behaved sensibly was Kay, who picked a kicking and screaming Bim up by his midriff and marched off down the hall, her "That's enough. We don't shout at people, and we don't hit them, even if they—" getting cut off as the door swung closed behind her.

Robbie and I silently worked to right the box, me collecting the treasures, Robbie laying them out in the order they belonged and checking to make sure they were all accounted for, crouched between a circle of adult legs.

Finally, Tom clapped his hands and said, "Just a few

notes," and they moved away to their workspace, sitting, or draping themselves across the prop cushions on the floor. The lighting designer came forward and stood with Tom, while Jenny directed one of her nameless assistants to pack up the bits of costume that had been in use. I assumed that this meant things were winding down. I couldn't hear Tom, his voice was too low, but the actors were leaning in, listening intently, and I could guess the tone of his remarks from the expressions on their faces. Ed was hearing nothing but good; Bill Rose, not so much. Frances Singer must have not been mentioned: she wasn't even making a pretence of listening as she checked her makeup in a compact.

Kay joined the group quietly, a subdued Bim holding her hand. She tugged on it, prompting him silently, and he walked over to Bill. "I'm sorry I bit you," he said. I hadn't seen that, nor had most of the cast if the quickly hidden smiles were anything to go by. Bill was gracious. "Don't worry, little man. We all want to bite people from time to time."

Kay cleared her throat meaningfully again, and Bim turned to the group, speaking to their toes. "I'm sorry I interrupted the rehearsal." Tom said something in his soft voice, and Bill pulled Bim down to sit beside him, Kay smiling her thanks at them both.

My eyes skipped back to Jenny. Her mouth had thinned when Kay and Bim had returned, and then she'd looked away, ostentatiously ignoring Bim's apologies, and sniffing loudly when they were generously received. Now I paused. She was turned away from the group, so they couldn't see her face. I could. She was staring with an expression of such sick longing that I felt like I'd seen her naked. I tried to follow a mental dotted line to work out the object of her desire, but I couldn't. Tom? The lighting designer? He was a new entry, and it was only since he'd arrived that she'd appeared anything except armour-plated.

She stood, and I dropped my eyes to my e-reader and determinedly didn't look up again. I had made a good start on a new manuscript when a body plopped down across from me. I tried not to scowl. I'd agreed to babysit, so I couldn't be bad-tempered about babysitting. Or, rather, I could, but I was obliged to hide it. When I looked up, though, it wasn't babysitting duties that were calling, unless this twenty-nine-year-old needed help with her juice box.

"Hey," said Frances Singer, smiling and twirling a bit of hair around her forefinger in almost a parody of look-at-how-delightful-I-am.

"Hey," I replied. Not a scintillating response, and she probably was delightful, but hair-twirlers never did it for me. Like Kay, she was tall and thin, but she didn't have Kay's obvious punch-to-the-gut beauty. At first glance, all I saw was nice enough features, and mousey brown hair sticking up all ways in a clip. If it wasn't for her over-the-top posing, in fact, she'd probably get overlooked at first glance. But not, ever, at second. Her skin was whiter than paper, and it looked so thin she was virtually translucent;

it was as if she shone from inside. I wasn't sure if it was beautiful, or slightly creepy.

"Kay says you're a publisher."

My smile became fixed. The woman had either written a book she wanted me to read, or she hadn't bothered to write it, but had thought "one day" of writing one, and wanted to talk to me about it. Because, as all writers and editors know, to write a book you don't need hard work, or skill, or hard work, or talent, or—did I mention hard work? You just had to imagine yourself doing it "one day," and then talk about it. Talk about it a lot.

"I am." Even to my ears, my tone was grudging.

She wasn't put off. "My agent thinks I should do a memoir."

That was better than a novel. Frances Singer was relatively famous. There might be some mileage in that. And the way she'd phrased it was interesting.

"Your agent thinks? What do you think?"

"I think I don't know how to write, and I don't know anything about books. I think when people tell me they want to be an actress, but they have no training, they never go to the theatre, they don't analyse the films or television programmes they watch, and they make no effort to learn anything about technique, or the business, I think it sends me crazy with rage." She smiled sweetly. "I can't see why you wouldn't feel the same way."

If I told her I was in love with her for that speech, it might seem an overreaction. So I just smiled back, honestly this time. "Pretty much. But you don't have to write the book yourself if you're famous for something else. It depends on how interesting your life has been, and if you're ready to tell people about it." I shrugged. "If you want to do a look-at-the-fabulousness-of-me book, I'm not the right publisher. I'm not saying there's not a market for it, just not with me."

Frances grinned like she'd just won the lottery. "Definitely not look-at-the-fabulousness-of-me. But I love the phrase and I plan to steal it."

I waved an it's-yours gesture. "Tell me what you had in mind."

Just then, Jenny called, complete with martyred frown and omnipresent tablet. "Frances! Please! If we can get through this final scene, then we can all go home."

Frances's face slid from open to professionally polite before the sentence was complete. "Absolutely, Jenny, I'm with you now." She stood, muttering as she rose, "Sir, yes, sir, how high shall I jump, sir?" before she raised her voice and said neutrally, "The agent who suggested a book is Miles Markov. If you're interested, will you get in touch with him?" And she resumed her "Campbell says" drama-queen persona like a coat.

I stared after her. She'd been open and friendly and, for want of a better word, normal with me. And she'd been a pouting ingénue starlet all through the rehearsal, one whom it was easy to believe had been having a relationship with a man half a century older than her. Who was this woman?

Chapter 6

The day had gone to hell before it had even begun. I stumbled out to go for a run at six. I sit at a desk all day, and if I didn't move myself first thing in the morning, it was possible that, like mildew, I would become inextricably attached to my chair, and they'd have to peel me off with acid. I certainly never want to go running: I don't like it, I don't like six o'clock in the morning, and I particularly don't like the two together on a cold, dark autumn day. I pulled the door behind me firmly, so that I didn't go back inside with a whimper when I discovered that it was not merely cold, not merely dark, not merely six o'clock, but also raining. I set off at the shuffling trot I referred to in public as "running."

When I got back forty-five minutes later, sweaty, puce-faced, and panting, it was to find that Jake had already left. I narrowed my eyes meaningfully at the empty flat. Jake had not come home until after I was asleep the night before, and when I'd left he'd been asleep. Our lives frequently overlapped, or failed to overlap, in that manner, but at the moment it felt like it meant something, and that something was Jake's unhappiness that I had become involved in a case he was working on. That it wasn't my fault, or that I didn't even think I *was* involved, was what my narrowed eyes were meant to convey. To whom, I had no idea. So I showered and headed off to work.

The rest of the day was worse. We had an editorial meeting first thing. First thing by publishing standards, which meant ten o'clock officially, in reality ten twenty. It should have been routine, but the meeting was run as always by the editor-in-chief and my boss, David, who is so terrified of conflict that he allows discussions that should be ended with a quick decision to spiral out of control, into the very conflict that he hates and fears. Today's meeting ran true to form: we were all cross about the time slots we'd been allocated at the sales conference, and what those timings said about how the sales department would treat our books, and we felt free to share that annoyance by making snide remarks about everyone else's books. There was no outright hostility, just scratchiness and bad temper, but it was noticeable among a group of people who were normally collegiate—indeed, who normally enjoyed one another's company.

When the meeting finally dragged to its weary close, I called out to our sales director, who, for a big man, was scarpering pretty nimbly to the door, "Bruce, have you got a moment?"

The beauty of the passive-aggressive have-you-got-a-moment gambit is that it is ambiguous—how long is a moment?—and yet the unstated unit of time is small enough that, if you say no, you haven't got a moment, politeness demands that you must then say when you will have a moment. So you might just as well say yes, and get it over with.

Bruce understood. "Sure," he said, lying through his teeth.

"Fab." I grinned at him, letting him know that I knew he was lying. We'd worked together for years.

"Or, I should have said, sure, unless you're going to moan at me about the sales conference."

"Me? Moan? At you?" I drew back with a theatrical hand to my breast. "Of course not. It's your joyous personality that draws me into conversations with you like a moth to a flame."

"Christ," he said. "I think I'd rather you moaned."

"In that case . . ." He was still standing, looming above me, as though he might still make a break for the door and freedom. Bruce wasn't that tall, but was big and bulky, with a white shirt buttoned tightly over his middle-aged work-at-a-desk gut that was now riding disconcertingly at my eye level. I kicked out the chair next to me in a silent invitation.

Since he'd known I was going to moan at him, and he knew that I knew that he knew, we'd performed this elaborate preamble merely to amuse ourselves. He gave up all hope of escape, and sat, stretching out his legs in a show of insouciance. "Go for it. Tell me why everything I've planned is crap."

I got down to business. "Not everything. Just Carol. Since *The Alien Corn* is a lead title, since her sales are great, and rising, I'm not sure why you don't have her down to present. You've met her, you know she's funny, she's good at this kind of thing, she's got a personality people engage with. Instead you've given both author slots that morning to literary first novelists. Even if they get reviewed—and we know with first novels, that's a big 'if'—and even if the reviews are great, their sales are unlikely to break four figures, and you've got them presenting to the chain-buyers, who won't stock their books anyway."

He sighed, as if I were being a tiresome puppy still demanding walkies after we'd just come back from walkies. "Look," he said, pretending to be the voice of reason, "I know Carol's book is not for me, and I know that everyone who is in the demographic it is for thinks it's great. But it's a small subject for a select group."

He did not just say that. He did not. I waited a beat, to make sure I had a grip on my temper. "Growing older is a small subject?" I was proud I managed to sound mild, almost uninterested. "There are only two possibilities, surely: growing older, or dying young. Or have you got a third option lined up for yourself?" All right, maybe I didn't sound mild. Maybe I sounded snotty.

Bruce clearly thought I did. "No, of course I don't have a third option. It's a small subject not because it doesn't happen to everyone, but because most people don't want to think about it, much less shell out £14.99 to read about it."

"I agree. Which is why *The Alien Corn* is so brilliant.

It's set in a good old-fashioned story of a family, a suspenseful plot that makes the reader keep going to find out what happens to the characters. The ideas are in the background, there to be taken in without it being soap-boxy. Families, and what happens to them as one generation succeeds the last, what happens to the emotions, and just the sheer *stuff*, how you pass things on, is something that every single person on the planet has to deal with. I can't see why you think it's niche."

He stared at me, sad-eyed, as if I were being wilfully obtuse. "It's not just the subject. It's that . . ."

I waited. I wanted to force him to say the words.

He started and stopped a few times. "Carol isn't that promotable," he said, finally.

"Pro-mot-able." I stretched out the syllables, pretending to mull over the word, even though I'd known it was the one he would use. I furrowed my forehead in a passable I'm-adorably-confused manner. "The willowy blonde twenty-four-year-old Cambridge graduate is promotable, right?"

"Of course." He didn't have to think about that one.

"But Carol isn't." Bruce was getting pissed off, but that was fine, because I was incandescent. I summed up. "You've got two literary novelists with no track record presenting to buyers who don't stock their sort of book, but you've invited them because they're twenty-four, posh, and have shiny pretty hair. Carol, whose father was an electrician, and whose hair isn't pretty or shiny, but who sells books by the shed-load, hasn't been asked to present because she's fifty and writing about women getting older." I tried to moderate my voice, but it kept rising. "About women getting older, to a group of buyers who are themselves mostly women who didn't go to Cambridge, don't have shiny pretty hair, are getting older and who are selling books to women who are also older, and who *as we know* are the one demographic who can reliably be depended on to put their hard-earned cash down and *buy books*." I banged on the table in emphasis as I finished.

Even as I shouted, I knew I'd blown it. I'd let my anger show, and now Bruce could say what men said to women who raised their voices. He did. "Why don't we discuss this later, when you're not so upset." He pushed his chair back and marched out, looking victorious.

Bruce and I were roughly the same age, in our midforties. When he was angry, he shouted, and people were obliged to listen. When I raised my voice, however, it was called "being upset," and people could refuse to listen. In my twenties, if I'd been angry charmingly enough, I might have got away with being called feisty. Now I was just a bitch. I looked at my watch and sighed. Only another forty years and I'd be eligible for the charmingly feisty zone again.

I stopped on my way home and picked up enough Chinese food to feed, if not the entire Red Army, then at least a good few battalions. Indian food is the default ethnic takeaway in Britain, but I'd grown up in North America, and when I was upset, my body required monosodium glutamate and yellow dye no. 5. By the time Jake got home, I had all the silver-foil boxes laid out, and the kitchen resembled a "before" photograph for one of those alternative health programmes, where they show you the terrible diet the family had before they were introduced to the wonders of whatever paleo-low-carb-low-fat-low-sodium-low-taste diet was being promoted.

Jake knew the symptoms. He paused briefly in the doorway, before cautiously heading for the fridge and pulling out a couple of beers. (I'd trained him well—everyone knows beer is the only appropriate drink to accompany Chinese food.) "Bad day?" he asked the bottle.

"It was Sam and the Terrible, Horrible, No Good, Very Bad Day," I elaborated.

I'm not sure Jake recognized the mangled children's book title, but he got that I wasn't happy. "The kind of bad day you want to tell me about, or the kind of bad day you want never to think about again?"

I leaned back in my chair and closed my eyes. "Probably the former, but not now. It will just make me angry again. Tell me about your day instead."

There was a silence, and I opened my eyes. Jake was staring at me speculatively, as though he were having a conversation in his head. Then he turned away and got out plates. He handed me one and started spooning rice out. I stood and put my plate away, replacing it with a bowl and chopsticks. Jake had been raised on Indian takeaway, so he stuck to a knife and fork; I flashed my chopstick technique at every opportunity, and after the morning's debacle I needed to feel I was good at something, even if it was only eating. I sat and speared a piece of lemon chicken.

Jake sat too. "Campbell Davison died of anaphylactic shock," he finally said. "He had an extreme allergy to peanuts."

I thought about that for a moment as I chewed. "It was an accident, and then someone took his body and—" I shook my head. "No." I rejected it firmly. "I can't think of any circumstances in which a person died from an allergic reaction, and a passer-by just happened to see his dead body and thought, *Oh, good, I was looking for one of those,* and hung it up to be revealed in the final act of a play he was directing that, coincidentally, needed one."

Jake choked on a mouthful of beer. When he could speak, "That was our conclusion too," he said mildly, "although no one expressed it quite as colourfully."

I waved my chopsticks at him, in a you-should-diversify-your-hiring-practices motion. "Who knew about Davison's allergy?"

"Everyone."

"I didn't. I'm everyone."

Jake itemized. "He mentioned it frequently in interviews, so it was public knowledge. The crew, the performers, and the rest of the company were all regularly reminded not to bring peanuts or peanut products into the rehearsal rooms, the offices, or the theatre. So were the people who catered the rehearsals, and the company that had the bar concession at the theatre. The backstage staff who were the official first-aiders had EpiPens to inject in case he was exposed accidentally, and had all been sent for refresher training."

That *was* everyone, wasn't it? "But doesn't that make your inquiries endless, if someone just had to sprinkle a bit of residue from the bottom of a pack of peanuts on something he was eating?"

Jake looked tired. "Worse than endless. Davison was apparently sensitive enough that if there was peanut dust in the air, or peanuts had been on a plate that hadn't been washed carefully enough, he would still have had a reaction. But it wasn't an accident. It wasn't bad dishwashing, because otherwise he would just have been found collapsed somewhere."

I thought about that. "The person didn't have to be near Davison at all when it happened, did they? They didn't need any particular knowledge, or strength—" I stopped. "No, that's not right. They needed to be strong enough to get him up on that hook." I tried to visualize the performance. "He was a big man, wasn't he?"

"He was tall enough: over 180. But no strength was needed. There are hoists for the scenery, and the hook was operated by an electric pulley. Which is why no one noticed that the weight on the hook was much greater that night than when it carried the dummy. Anyone can press a button. Someone took the dummy off, and hooked up Davison, but the lifting was done mechanically."

"As long as he died near where the hook was."

"Possibly. There is machinery to move the sets around,

which could have been used to get him near the hook, but access to that is more restricted."

That was taking us into alibi territory. "Why are you telling me this?"

Jake stood to get another beer. He held one up to me in a question, and I shook my head. "I'm telling you because most of it will be in the newspapers tomorrow. Kay will hear more, and she'll tell you. So you might as well get it directly from me." He drank. "If you quote me, I'll deny it, but also because you saw it, and it upset you, and it somehow makes me feel that you're owed honesty about what you saw."

That was nice.

"But I'm not going to discuss the investigation with you."

Sure he would. "When did he die?"

"The day before. Probably the evening of the day before."

"He'd been dead for a day?" I pushed my bowl away.

"Sorry," said Jake. "I should have waited to tell you this after dinner."

Which made me feel ridiculous. Why did knowing when Davison had died make any difference? It did, though. Leaving a dead man lying around, uncared for and unregarded. I imagined a deserted corridor and a lot of dust. It was just—heartless was the only word I could come up with. As though killing weren't heartless too. I pulled my bowl back and lifted a mouthful of virulently orange sweet-and-sour chicken to my mouth. "So he died sometime on"—I counted back—"on Wednesday evening?" Then I remembered. "Kay said they received texts after the dress rehearsal telling them that Davison's sister had died, and he wouldn't be there for the first night."

"Jenny Rogers got a text from Davison informing her of his absence, and she texted the cast, the creative team, and the producer. Meanwhile, Davison's sister is alive and well. They weren't close, and when we contacted her, she said she hadn't spoken to him in perhaps a year. She lives in Edinburgh, is a retired teacher, and the only trip she's made out of the city in the past six months was to the seabird centre in North Berwick, to go bird-watching."

She didn't sound a likely candidate. "Either someone rang him and told him his sister was dead, and he believed it and texted the stage manager, or—can you tell if he sent the text?"

"It was sent at ten, when he might have been alive, or he might have already died: the medical examiner can't pin it down further. The text came from his phone, and only his fingerprints are on it. There are some scuffs and marks overlaying the prints, which might have been someone using the phone while wearing gloves, or might be the phone knocking around in his pocket."

"Did he make arrangements to go to Edinburgh? Did he ring anyone?"

Jake nodded approvingly. I was going to get a gold star in kitchen-detection. "No calls that we can trace, not from his flat, his office, the theatre, nor his mobile. And no online bookings from any of his devices, nor any made in his name from elsewhere."

"Someone told him, he texted the stage manager, and then died before he could do anything else. Or he died, and someone used his phone to text the stage manager before they—what, they just left the body lying around somewhere?"

"We don't know. The dummy was used at the dress rehearsal. Afterwards it was hoisted up into the fly-tower, to be lowered again just before the final act. That hook and hoist weren't used for anything else, so the dummy was left on it. The switch could have been made any time after Davison's death and before the final technical check thirty minutes before the curtain went up, according to the stage manager."

I swallowed hard. "How was it—how was Davison hooked up?" It sounded worse when I said it aloud, and I tried to make a joke out of it. "My intensive reading of crime fiction says that you can tell how long after death bleeding occurred. Is that true?"

"A pathologist can, yes, but the hook was designed to fit into a piece of reinforced leather at the neck of the costume that was put on Davison." Jake stopped sharply, as if he had suddenly noticed that, for a man who wasn't going to discuss the investigation, he was telling me an awful lot. I could see the precise moment when he decided he didn't care. "Davison was left lying on his back for a while after he died. We know that from the lividity—from how the blood pooled after his heart stopped. Putting the costume on a body in full rigor would have been difficult without leaving some evidence of the struggle, and there was none."

I started to ask a question, but Jake was already there. "Rigor lasts from twenty-four to forty-eight hours, although it's hot in the fly-tower, which means if that's where he was, it would have been closer to twenty-four. So the clothing change might have been done right after his death, or just before the final act. The latter seems less likely, unless the person who did it knew how long it took for rigor to pass. They probably wouldn't have risked it, unless they had to."

"But anyone could google 'how long does rigor mortis last' and they'd know."

"True, but it's more complicated to kill Davison, nip off to look rigor up on Wikipedia, and then return to tidy up. And more complicated is always less likely than less complicated. The costume itself wasn't elaborate: a cloak that buttoned all the way down the front. Apart from having to put a pair of boots on him, everything went over Davison's own clothes, so it didn't need a lot of time, or a lot of effort."

I summarized: "Putting him in costume wouldn't be difficult. Anyone could have killed him if they knew about the dummy, the hoist, and how it operated."

"And that there was a hoist, and how the play ran—that the dummy would be revealed in the last act. Someone with access to and knowledge of backstage practices." He sighed. "The crew. The creative team. The actors. Davison's wider theatre company—the people involved with the other productions. His business partners."

"Surely not the last? How would they know about hoists and how a play that hadn't opened was staged?"

"The dress rehearsal. They were all invited, and most of them were there. They saw the staging with the dummy, and quite a few of them were backstage at least some of the time. So far none of the crew has remembered anyone asking about that hoist in particular, but who's to say what was overheard?"

From what I'd seen at the rehearsal, they all also gossiped endlessly—almost as much as publishers. No one would remember a casual comment or question.

Jake broke into my thoughts. "Tell me about the rehearsal."

"Really? You want me to stay out of things, and when I don't, you turn me into a spy?"

He didn't rise to my snark. In fact, it might be that our relationship was based entirely on Jake not rising to my snark. I decided to think about that later as he said calmly, "You can't have it both ways. You are visibly distressed at the idea of Davison being killed, his body abandoned and then mocked, but you don't want to 'betray'"—he didn't make finger-quotes around the word, but his tone of voice made them clear enough—"the person who might have done it, just because you shared a cup of coffee and a chat?"

Put like that, I was ashamed. But I was damned if I'd admit it. I went for grudging, instead. "What do you want to know?"

He made a generalized hand gesture. "Tell me whatever you like. Who was there? What were they like?"

That seemed like less of a—to use Jake's word—betrayal. "I'll preface this by saying most of my day was pirates and zombies. And I'm fairly certain Bim and Robbie are in the clear."

He smiled. "Noted."

So I told him about my limited interactions with the others—Ed's polite standoffishness, Bill's approach, Frankie's array of personas, Jenny's awe-inspiring regimentation and lack of charm. "I didn't speak to most of them, didn't even hear their names—Jenny had a couple of assistants; there was the lighting guy. Tom was so quiet I barely heard a word he said."

"Did anyone else drop in?"

"I don't think so. Not while I was watching, at any rate, although I spent a lot of time reading and playing with the boys and might not have noticed. Who were you thinking of?"

He didn't reply. Instead, "What did you think of Jenny? Is she reliable?"

I'd told him what I thought about Jenny, so I waited until the real question came out. Jake chewed it over for a while first, then, "The woman you saw in the audience."

"The chest lady?" I couldn't remember what Kit had said her name was.

Jake nodded. "And her husband: Elizabeth and Hugh Henderson."

"What about them?"

"They were on the list of the people who were backstage after the dress rehearsal. Other than that, she's exactly what Kit described: a socialite who's interested in being seen and does it by giving money."

I modified, "What about her?"

"She said she spent part of the interval at the dress rehearsal with Jenny Rogers. Jenny Rogers says she didn't see her."

I didn't know anything about Elizabeth Henderson, but I'd spent a day in Jenny's presence. "Jenny probably has spreadsheets listing out everyone she's spent more than five minutes with since she was in nursery school. At night, she goes home and plots them out on a graph, and she can tell you qualitatively as well as quantitatively with whom she's spent the most time, and what in future the optimum time to spend with each would be, all in neatly tabulated columns."

Jake's lips quirked. "Are you saying you'd trust Jenny's memory over Mrs. Henderson's?"

"I didn't see Mrs. Henderson's memory, only her chest. I'm saying Jenny is a fiend for detail. It's her job."

"Mrs. Henderson said she also spent time talking to Frances Singer."

"That wouldn't surprise me. If she wanted to be part of things, the leading lady would be the one to latch on to, no?"

Jake began to reply, and then thought better of it. We were back to his not discussing the investigation with me. I decided to pretend I hadn't noticed.

Chapter 7

When the phone rang, Jake was watching a football high-lights programme, even though he'd already seen the match that this was the highlights of. But then again, he thought rereading a novel was a waste of time. We'd come to accept each other's oddities. Neither of us, however, was expecting a call. I'd chatted to Helena while I washed our supper dishes and Jake put away the leftover Chinese food, catching her up on the past few days, while she in turn caught me up on the thirty-seven museum exhibitions, forty-three films, and sixty-two dinner parties she'd attended in the same few days. I exaggerate, but not by much. When she was finished I was exhausted from just think-ing about dashing about like that. I lay on the sofa with my book facedown on my stomach and thought deep and beautiful thoughts. Or possibly I dozed.

When the phone rang, I looked over to Jake. It wasn't Jake's office calling, because it was the landline, which nobody used anymore. I'd reached the stage of barely thinking of it as a phone, treating it more like one of those ornaments some great-aunt had brought back from her honeymoon—ugly, but with enough sentiment attached to it that you didn't take it to Oxfam, although not enough sentiment that you didn't think of doing just that every time it caught your eye.

My greeting was "Hello?" My tone added, *This better be good.*

"Well." It was Kit. Of course it was. He was the only person I knew who used a phone to chat, not to text, or to email, or to google whether or not the young Carrie Fisher had ever been in a movie with Warren Beatty. (She had. I'd covered that with Helena.) "Well" was his all-purpose, single-word opening when he had a particularly juicy bit of gossip to share.

I was always happy to talk to Kit. "Well, what?"

"Those drawings you sent me were fascinating."

I pulled the receiver away from my ear and stared at it for a moment. This wasn't gossip, and "fascinating" would not have been my word of choice. "Oh. Good," was all I could come up with.

"I've seen them before," he went on, either not noticing or ignoring my bemusement.

"I know. You told me that you'd seen the production photos in the paper."

He made a clicking sound with his tongue—one that had no spelling, but meant not just *That's not what I meant*, but *Do keep up.* "I saw the photos, yes, but now I'm telling you that I've seen these drawings before."

"Oookay." I drew it out. I didn't know why that was worth a late-night phone call, but whatever.

"Not OK. Not OK at all." Kit was peeved with my inability to understand the point he was making. "Sylvie Sander doesn't let her sketches be reproduced. It's a fetish, a *thing* with her. She's famous for it."

I contemplated pulling the receiver away and staring at it again. Really? You could be famous for not doing something? Then I snapped back to what Kit had just said. Ed Vallance had told me more or less the same thing when he thought I was photographing the ones in the rehearsal studio: he'd said she'd have "a cow."

Kit hadn't waited for me to catch up, and I tuned in halfway: "—the problem is I don't know where I saw them."

"Mmm." It didn't seem like a great problem to me.

Kit must have agreed, because he hung up.

I was lying in bed, staring at my clock in the dark. I was hoping if I stared hard enough, the minutes would stop ticking down. Jake was already up, though, which meant my alarm was about to sound. I had just reached out to forestall it when the doorbell rang. Jake poked his head out of the bathroom. "What the—" the rest of his words buried in toothpaste foam.

I double-checked the clock. No, a tear had not been ripped in the space-time continuum: it was still only six forty-five. My eyes met Jake's. "Helena," we chorused. I headed for the shower, leaving him to get the door. I needed to be washed and dressed to face my mother before coffee.

By the time I reached the kitchen, Jake and Helena were sitting at the little table in the corner, seemingly at an impasse. Helena looked up. "We thought we'd wait for you, darling." Translation: *Don't you know meetings begin on time in my office?* It didn't matter that this was my flat, not Helena's office. Nor, for that matter, that no meeting had been scheduled, so it wasn't actually possible to be late for it. I looked at the table. Helena had set out cups and saucers beside the coffeepot—no casual mugs for her. She'd also stopped somewhere and bought croissants, although I would have been willing to bet that there was not a single bakery in London that was open at six thirty in the morning. There probably wasn't, and Helena had simply willed the croissants into being by sheer force of personality.

She sat quietly waiting while I took this in, a pad and a file open in front of her. Jake, I noticed with some amusement, had taken out his notebook. In fact, the only thing that indicated that this wasn't Helena's office, and we weren't in one of her fiercely regimented meetings, was that I was late, and my good cups weren't nearly as nice as her everyday office ones.

I slid into my seat and poured some coffee. "What couldn't wait until—ooh, say seven o'clock?" I asked. Sarcasm never worked with my mother, but I never stopped trying, either.

"I wanted to catch Jake before he left for work," she answered serenely.

Since she was right, if she'd waited even another half hour she would most likely have missed him, I didn't respond. She left a pause, to underscore her point, then carried on. "After our conversation last night I made a few inquiries." Helena was a solicitor. "Inquiries" might mean anything from chatting to a friend to leaning on someone to pull the tax records of the entire population of northwest London. "I thought it would be useful to look into the money side of things, don't you agree?" she asked Jake, before carrying on without pause, taking that agreement for granted.

Although Jake had occasionally used Helena's contacts, he was less than enchanted to discover that my previous evening's idle what-I-did-on-my-holiday chat with my mother had turned into a stepping-stone into his investigation. "I'm not quite clear why—" His voice was firm, although he left the *why you're poking your nose in* unsaid.

Helena wasn't deterred. She never was. "I assume you've spoken to Cal Bancroft at Caliban?" She glanced at me to add an explanatory gloss, "The producer," before returning to Jake. "And I also assume that, as yet, he hasn't given you a list of his investors."

She didn't phrase it as a question, but Jake answered anyway, clearly giving up on keeping Helena away, at least for the moment. "He says there were no individual investors for the production, that all his investors invest in his company, in Caliban, not in any particular production. His position is that since they are not linked to our investigation, he has no obligation to hand over their names. Until we've got further along, we're allowing that to stand."

Helena slid a piece of paper out of her file, past me and to Jake. "The investors," she said. She managed not to look smug, which I felt showed real class.

This was not Jake's first interaction with Helena, but even so, his eyes widened.

I leaned sideways to look at the list over his shoulder. Three company names, one with an asterisk beside it, and beside that, a single name: Elizabeth Henderson.

"The two companies at the top are regular investors in Caliban, going back years. Smithfield, the company I've asterisked, has never had any connection to Caliban before; it is a personal trust vehicle, with no publically listed beneficiaries. But I've talked to a few people, and I can tell you it's a family trust, with a sole beneficiary, a woman named Elizabeth Henderson. She's dabbled in theatre a little in the past two years, but until this production never via Smithfield. That she used the trust directly would suggest a greater financial contribution than the few thousands she's spent over the past twenty-four months."

She slid out another sheet. "I only heard about this last night, so I haven't been able to glean much information." The second sheet was passed along in the same manner, Helena summarizing as she went. "Elizabeth Henderson, fifty-six, known as Liz. Married to Hugh Henderson, a retired stockbroker, aged seventy. One child, a daughter, now married and living in Germany. She has never worked. She sits on the boards of several charities, none having to do with theatre." Helena paused, looking almost apologetic. "I haven't been able to trace any interest in the theatre that dates back more than two years, but I'm working on it." She returned to her file, taking out the final document. "In the last two years, however, she has become a first-night regular."

I peered over Jake's shoulder again. It was a screen-grab, a series of thumbnails of the same blonde woman with an older man, most of which, if the glasses in their hands were anything to go by, had been taken at parties.

"That's her," I said, as though there were any possibility that Helena might be wrong.

Jake cleared his throat and closed his notebook, folding the pages and putting them in his jacket pocket. "Thank you, Helena, that's very helpful," he said, in one of the worst attempts at an official manner I'd ever seen.

Helena ignored that and gave a demure little smile, the cat that got the cream. "I'll let you know when I hear more."

Jake's eyes flicked over to mine. He still wasn't used to her. Me, I'd have been astonished if she'd said "if," not "when."

Helena's meeting might have delayed me by half an hour, but it did have the advantage of bringing croissants, and by the time I hit the publicity department on my way to my office, I was contentedly brushing crumbs off my jacket. Publicity gets all the newspapers, and as it was still early in publishing-land, I planned to snaffle them and take them back to my desk before their assistant combed through them for mentions of our books—after that, there would be only fragments left, as she snipped and cut for the files.

I was still Luddite enough that I got a paper delivered at home, and I'd read the news reports of Davison's death over the weekend, but now they'd had time, the obituaries were appearing too, with fuller retrospectives of his career. I read through them all, then made copies and put them in my bag.

When I got home that evening, I read them again. They still said the same thing they had said that morning, so I rang Helena.

I didn't bother to say "hello," or "how are you." Helena rarely does, and normally I think it's rude, but today I understood her point—you have something to say, you say it; why faff around? "Did you see Davison's obituaries?" I demanded.

She replied as though people frequently rang her at eight in the evening to quiz her on the day's obituaries. "I did."

"It said he worked for nearly a decade with the Berliner Ensemble."

"Yes," she said, her tone adding, *I'm losing patience here.*

"And you said this morning that Liz Henderson's daughter was married and living in Germany."

"Yes," she repeated, her tone no different.

She didn't think that was a coincidence worthy of comment? I had been sure it was significant, but her lack of interest brought me up short. "It's worth looking at, surely?" I'd started the sentence as a statement, but by its end it had turned into a question. Still, I'd set off down this road; I'd walk it a little further. "I know Germany is a big place, and more than one or two people live there, but here is a woman with a daughter in Germany who previously made only small investments in theatre, who now makes her first big investment in a company whose director spent a significant period working in theatre in Germany."

Helena didn't speak. She was thinking. Then, "Let me get my notes."

Helena was a solicitor through and through. Everything of any importance was written down on yellow legal pads, which could be found on almost every flat surface in her house, as well as in her office. If she'd researched Liz Henderson, then she'd made notes on her, and if she'd made notes, they'd have been filed. I had never checked her filing system, so I had no idea where this particular one would be stashed. In a cardboard hanging folder with a printed tab saying, "Directors, Stage, Deceased"? Or maybe, "Investors, Dodgy." Or, possibly, "Directors, Stage, Deceased, Linked to Investors, Dodgy," right in front of the one for "Directors, Stage, Deceased, Linked to Investors, Sound."

I didn't have time to build more elaborate imaginary filing cabinets, because Helena was back. Her tone was approving. "Well done, darling. But it's not the daughter, it's Liz Henderson herself. Her parents were German. And her maiden name was Maurer."

She paused significantly, as if Maurer should mean something to me.

It didn't. "All right," I said, leaving an inaudible *and . . . ?* after it.

"And Richard Maurer was a designer with the Berliner Ensemble when Davison was there. That was in the obituaries: they worked together until Maurer's death."

That was the sort of thing that seemed important, but on examining it, I couldn't see how. So Maurer was Davison's friend and Liz Henderson's—father? Brother? Was that the reason she invested more heavily, at least according to Helena? And so what if she did, and he was?

I wandered into the kitchen to begin on supper. I trussed a chicken, and found myself in front of the oven, holding the pan and staring into space. We had an explanation of why a wealthy woman who courted the famous had chosen to direct her interest towards a particular art form, and particular company, but it didn't seem to get us much further. Still, it filled in a gap. I'd tell Jake when he got home. I closed the oven door, and then the front door as I headed upstairs.

I visited Mr. Rudiger regularly because I enjoyed his company, but sometimes I felt like a St. Bernard. Instead of bringing the traveller stranded in an avalanche a flask of brandy, however, I carried in news from the outside world. Today, though, I was hoping he would have, if not news, then information from the outside world for me. On my visits we often talked about theatre and art. While Mr. Rudiger never went out now, before he retired he had seen, it sometimes felt, everything: he had a formidable range of references, in his head and in what appeared to be the thousands of books on his shelves.

Normally after I knock on his door we run through a routine we have refined to comedy-smooth cadences. I ask him if he'd like to come down for tea, or supper, or just to visit; he says "not today," as though most other days he's champing at the bit to leave the flat that, in reality, he leaves perhaps once or twice a year. Then he invites me in, and I pretend to consider for a nanosecond before I accept, as we both had known would be the case from the moment I knocked.

Today, I treated him like Helena. No "hello," no "how are you," no "would you like to come downstairs and eat roast chicken with us when Jake gets home." Instead I demanded, "Do you know who Richard Maurer was?"

Mr. Rudiger tilted his head quizzically. "Is there a prize?"

I backtracked. "Let me begin again. Hello. How are you? Would you like to come down and have supper with us? We're having roast chicken," I added, in case the menu might add weight to one side of his decision or the other.

"Not tonight, thank you. But unless Jake is home

already—?" He widened the door, beckoning me in. He knew Jake wasn't home. His hearing was exceptional, and he was always aware of who was in the house. Given our noisy old pipes, he probably knew how often we showered, too, and whether my dentist would approve of the length of time I spent brushing my teeth. I began to think of other things that he might overhear, and decided that that way madness lay. I went in, instead.

I moved automatically to the sitting room, but Mr. Rudiger stopped by a bookshelf in the narrow hallway. "So," he said, head tilted to read the book spines. "Richard Maurer."

"You have heard of him?"

He shrugged. "Of course."

I felt my nose. Yes, it was out of joint. Helena had heard of him. Mr. Rudiger had "of course" heard of him. "I've never heard of him," I complained.

"He was before your time, and his fame didn't last." He waved away both the fame and my ignorance. "Also, he worked in Berlin, and I knew about him from the German or Czech papers." Mr. Rudiger had come to England from Prague some time after the Second World War. I didn't know when, but as an adult, certainly—he still had a strong accent. He returned to his shelves, but it didn't take long: he was as organized as Helena. "Here it is." He pulled out a thin paperback, almost a pamphlet. "He died young, so there weren't that many productions, but the company put together a commemorative book."

He handed it to me, but I didn't even have to open it.

I just looked at the drawing on the front cover. "Excuse me a moment," I said, and pulled out my phone. I dialled Kit. He didn't reply, so I left a message. "Try Richard Maurer," I said, and disconnected.

Then I turned back to Mr. Rudiger. "I won't be a moment, but I need to tell Jake."

"You need to tell him that I have a book about Richard Maurer?"

It seemed easier to explain it to them both. "You'll hear." I hit Jake's mobile number, and he answered right away. He and Helena never seemed to have meetings, or be out of contact. It was annoying usually, but I was grateful now. "Have you got a second to talk?"

There was some background noise, and a "just a minute" to someone else, and then the noises were cut off, as if he'd closed a door. "Go ahead," he said.

"A little preamble," I said. "I think what I'm about to say means something. I just don't know what it means."

I could hear the smile when he acknowledged, "Little preamble duly noted."

I gathered my thoughts, in part to fill Mr. Rudiger in. "I told you that on Sunday, when I was at the rehearsal studio with Bim, that I took some photos of Sylvie Sander's costume drawings. When I did it, I didn't know that she refused to let her drawings be reproduced. By the time I found out, I'd already texted them to Kit. And I told you too that Kit thought they looked familiar, but he didn't know why. That's part one. I was set off on the track of part two by Davison's obituaries." I recapped my conversation with Helena, ending, "Helena said that Richard Maurer, a designer at the Berliner Ensemble when Davison was there, was famous, so I came up to ask Mr. Rudiger about him. And here's where it gets to the bit that I think means something. Mr. Rudiger has a book of Richard Maurer's work. Even just looking at the drawing on the cover . . ." I broke off. It sounded far-fetched, but I'd started, so, "Even looking at the drawing on the cover, I would be willing to bet that it was drawn by the same person who drew the costume designs I saw in the rehearsal room and texted to Kit."

Jake was noncommittal. "What are you suggesting? That Maurer didn't do the designs attributed to him? That Sylvie Sander did instead?"

"Honestly? I don't know what I'm suggesting. That Sander did them. Or that Maurer did, and he let her—No, that doesn't work, he's dead. Yes, I suppose I'm suggesting that she did them. Maybe."

Jake was silent for a moment. "Does Mr. Rudiger agree that they're by the same person?"

I didn't feel slighted by his desire for confirmation, or that he trusted Mr. Rudiger's eyes more than mine, because I did too. "He wouldn't be able to say. He hasn't seen—" I remembered I still had the pictures on my phone. "Hang on. I can show them to him."

I took the phone away from my ear and flicked over to my photographs, turning the screen to Mr. Rudiger. "These are the drawings in the rehearsal rooms where Campbell Davison's company was working," I said. "They're the designs for the costumes in *The Spanish Tragedy*, which the programme credited to Sylvie Sander."

Mr. Rudiger took the phone and scrolled through them. He took the book I was still holding out of my hand. He didn't open it either, just glanced at it and handed it back to me, then raised the phone to his ear. "They're by the same person," he said to Jake. "Yes, I'll tell her," he added after a moment, and hung up.

He turned to me, a small smile on his face. "Jake suggests that you might perhaps like to bring supper up here. And he also wondered if your friend Kit might be free to join us."

I smiled back. I'd heard him say "tell": no suggestion had been made; an order had been given. "It should be ready in about half an hour."

Chapter 8

I texted Kit before going down to my office to print out the four photographs I had taken in the rehearsal room on Sunday. Then printouts, chicken, and I all returned, to find Jake and Kit in the hallway, taking off their coats. We played pass-the-parcel: I handed the food to Mr. Rudiger, and the printouts to Jake, while Mr. Rudiger swapped out the Maurer book for a dish of cauliflower. Finally, we were all settled, and we had all looked at the printouts and the drawings in the book on Maurer laid out side by side.

None of us felt it necessary to say we thought they were drawn by the same person. It was that obvious.

"So," said Jake. He didn't continue. It was, apparently, an invitation to any of us. This was a meeting, and he was bringing it to order.

Kit leapt in, of course. He loved to talk. "So," he repeated. "First question. Who produced these costume drawings?" He tapped the four printouts. "Second, why?

Why has one designer been utilising the work of the other, and why did the other permit it?"

I answered before I'd thought it through. "The third question is surely how—how has it been possible for one designer to utilise the work of the second? The 'how' will tell us why." Jake waited, eyebrows raised at a promising student. I didn't feel promising, and continued slowly, trying to see my way. "We know how it was possible. Sylvie Sander didn't permit her work to be reproduced. She was fanatical about it, and it worked. Even Kit, with his background in fashion and costume design, had never seen reproductions."

Kit nodded confirmation, both that he had never seen reproductions, and that he was omniscient. If there had been any, the nod said, he would have seen them.

I continued. "That's the 'how.' The 'why' must follow logically: she didn't let her work be reproduced because the drawings that go under the name of Maurer are immediately recognizable as being by the same person, even to me, who unlike Kit and Mr. Rudiger, has no training in the visual arts." I was thinking it out as I spoke, so I went step by step. "One of them, Maurer or Sander, has been passing off the work of the other. It has to be Maurer's work that is not his. He's been dead for . . ." I paused.

Jake had his tablet open in front of him. "According to my extensive and in-depth research on Wikipedia, he's been dead for more than forty years. Since 1971." He flicked the screen, scrolling down, and his interest was caught on an entry. "He died in 1971, just before a production of *Medea* that he designed for the Berliner Ensemble, directed by Campbell Davison."

No one said anything. Then Kit drummed on the table with his fingertips. "All right. Maurer died in 1971, which means he can't have designed a production that opened last week. Which means that the designs in a book on Richard Maurer were in reality drawn by Sylvie Sander." He turned to Jake. "Look her up. Is she old enough to have designed anything in 1971, much less to have had a career before that? How many years had Maurer been designing before his death?"

Jake did, and we waited for the page to load. "She was nineteen in 1971," he reported. "Old enough, perhaps, to have designed that *Medea*, but"—he clicked back—"but not old enough to have designed Maurer's earlier productions. You're right"—he nodded to Kit without looking up—"he was only thirty-two when he died, but there's a decade's-worth of productions listed here before that. Sylvie Sander would have been nine when the first one was staged."

I couldn't make sense of the dates that were flying around. I turned over one of the printouts and began to jot down a timeline: birthdates, ages at various points along the way, after a moment also snaffling Jake's tablet and checking further dates. The brief text in the book on Maurer was in German, but it had a list of his productions, so I added those in. The men's conversation gradually faded, until they watched me in silence.

"All right, this is what we have," I said after a minute.

"Davison and Maurer were almost the same age. According to the obituaries, Davison began his career in England, moving to Berlin in his late twenties. He and Maurer worked on"—I counted—"on five productions together before Maurer died at the age of thirty-two. Davison stayed in Berlin, and from then on worked almost exclusively with Sylvie Sander, who, says Wikipedia, was both Davison's lover and Maurer's assist—" I stopped and stared at my notes, before looking up. "Well, that's it, isn't it?"

Kit threw up his hands. If I ever published a book that required an illustration of exasperation, I'd ask him to pose. "What's it? What is 'it'?"

"'It' is your how. Your how and your why. Sander was Maurer's assistant when he died. She was also Davison's lover. Immediately after Maurer's death, Sander began to design for Davison's productions, and only for Davison's productions, even though Kay said they really disliked each other." Kit nodded confirmation of the solidity of this gossip: he had heard it too. I ticked the items off on my fingers: "Sylvie Sander doesn't work, ever, on new plays, only revivals of classics. She doesn't set anything later than the 1960s, the last decade when Maurer was working. And Kay also said that she and Davison originate their own projects, they never take on ones suggested by other people." I doodled around the dates on my timeline while I thought. "Kit says the uniforms in *The Spanish Tragedy* were East German. There's no reason not to design East German army uniforms, but it's not the immediately obvious choice for an Anglo designer, while Maurer would have grown up surrounded by them, and seen them at the checkpoints after the Berlin Wall went up."

Jake summarized. "You are suggesting that Sylvie Sander somehow acquired Richard Maurer's designs, and has been trading off them ever since?"

It appeared that I was. "I can't see any other answer that makes sense, if we start from the premise that these costumes were all designed by the same person." I lifted the book Mr. Rudiger had got off the shelf, it felt like months before. "Some of these designs date back to the early 1960s. Sylvie Sander would have been in primary school then."

Kit was not convinced. "I don't see how that's possible. How could no one have seen it over forty years, when every single one of us here saw it at a glance? And, even if it's true, how do you explain the logistics of someone walking off with a design-studio full of material, and no one noticing that everything of value had vanished?"

Mr. Rudiger hadn't said anything since we'd sat down, and we all jumped as his deep voice broke in. "I can't answer the first question, but for the second question, I can perhaps help." He got up and went to another shelf, lifting down a huge hardback. The title was in German, but I recognized enough of the words to work out it was a history of the Berliner Ensemble. He paged through it quickly, finding what he wanted and turning it to face us. "Yes," he said, "Nineteen seventy-one was probably the only date that that could have happened with no one noticing. The Berliner Ensemble was formed by Bertolt Brecht,

and after his death was run by his widow. She died"—
he put his finger on what I assumed was the relevant
sentence—"in 1971, and it was a while before a successor
took over." He reached over and turned my notes to face
him. "Maurer died within ten days of Helene Weigel,
Brecht's widow. I can well believe that for a while no one
paid much attention to the contents of the studio of a promising, but young, designer, especially if his assistant and
the current production's director were supervising the
staging of his final work without any problem." He gestured to the book on Maurer. "I didn't follow Maurer's
career, but I thought him interesting enough to buy a book
about him when it appeared. I would have bought others
too, but as far as I know, there has never been another one."

This was my territory. I looked at the copyright page.
"This was published by the Berliner Ensemble itself, not
a regular publisher. It's really just a glorified souvenir, and
they probably printed only a few hundred copies, and it
may not have had any bookshop sales at all."

Mr. Rudiger pointed at the price tag on the back,
which had words on it that consisted mostly of consonants.
"I bought it in Prague."

I backtracked. "All right, it had *some* bookshop sales."
I turned to Jake's tablet, which I felt was rapidly becoming
my tablet, and checked a website. "As to how no one has
noticed the similarity of drawing styles, there are no copies of this book in the British Library or the Library of
Congress in Washington. There's one at the Humboldt
University of Berlin, and one in the German National

Library. Otherwise, the only copy I can find in the UK or North America is at a liberal arts college in Massachusetts. Sander's Wikipedia page shows that she works exclusively in Britain and the US, and she's done nothing in Germany since she was Maurer's assistant. That's all it took. The Maurer book had barely any circulation, and, as everyone says, she refuses to let her drawings be seen by anyone. What sounds impossible, has, in reality, proved to be entirely possible."

Jake nabbed his tablet back, and tucked it into his bag, possibly aware that I was eyeing it covetously. It was much nicer than my e-reader. "This is fascinating," he said, "and as Sam said earlier, it sounds as if it must mean something. But I'm investigating an unexplained death. Is the suggestion that Davison didn't know?"

We stared at one another. Finally Kit spoke. "Surely that's not possible. Davison of all people had to have known. He'd worked with Maurer for a decade. He is the single person who could absolutely be counted on to recognize the drawings."

I added, "And if he didn't, that would mean that Sander was the one who decides what their new projects would be. What did she do? Every now and again announce to Davison: *I've got some great ideas for sets for* Mother Courage, *or costumes for* Waiting for Godot, *so hey, kid, let's put on a show in the barn!*"

Jake nodded. "I agree. They worked together for decades. He had to have been part of the deception. But it still doesn't link obviously to Davison's death. Was he going to reveal her secret? Why would he? Everyone would assume, just as we have, that he knew the designs were stolen, and it would reflect as badly on him as on Sander."

"Maybe it was the timing," offered Kit. "Davison was doing more new plays these days, which meant he was working with other designers. Sander had never worked with anyone else, and she's got a reputation for being a difficult colleague. She'd be hard-pressed to find work."

Mr. Rudiger shook his head. "She wouldn't find work with anyone except Davison, and so she murdered him?"

He was right, that made no sense. Unless, "What was her financial situation? Would she have been able to afford to retire on his death?"

Jake stood. "That just moved up to the top of my list." He pulled out his phone and walked out of the room.

I looked at the others, still sitting. "Don't touch that dial," I said.

After dinner at Mr. Rudiger's, Jake moved out of collegiate mode, and went back to reminding me that I didn't work for the CID, and his work was work, not a jigsaw puzzle for random passers-by to stop and play with, squealing, *Look, there's a bit of the zebra!* I didn't argue. One, because he was right, and two, because the mood would wear off, and he'd fill me in. From the few details he'd let slip when letting me know his schedule, his office was concentrating on Sylvie Sander, but that was all.

Meanwhile, back in my real life, Bruce and I were engaged in a silent battle over Carol Dennison's book, a battle no less ferocious for being not only entirely unspoken, but entirely unacknowledged. On the surface, I let it be understood that I had accepted that the sales department had the final say over the content and speakers at their conference; equally on the surface, Bruce had accepted my acceptance. Underneath, however, it was going to be a fight to the death, and we were using the pause to search out strategic ground for the next skirmish.

Meanwhile, Miranda was sulking because she'd missed out on seeing me shout at Bruce. "If you're going to have a showdown at the O.K. Corral," she huffed, "you could at least do it in the open-plan area, so we could all enjoy it."

"I'll be sure to let you know well in advance next time," I promised untruthfully.

"The day before would be best: we need time to buy the popcorn."

I snarled, but, being Miranda, she ignored it, concentrating on essentials: "Maybe we could set up a pool, have a sweepstake about who you're going to blast next."

There was only so much a person could take. "For goodness sake," I snapped. "*Whom*. Whom you're going to blast next." And I dumped a batch of figures that needed reconciling with the profit-and-loss sheets for last season's titles on her desk. Who says passive-aggression is counterproductive?

But when I went to plot with Sandra, I relented. Miranda had a vindictive streak; it would be a pity not to use the tools we had. And anyway, this was part of her publishing training. She needed to move on to the specialist seminar for advanced students: Conniving and Underhanded Dealing 101. "Leave those for the moment," I said as I headed down the hall. "Just bring your mug."

Sandra Stanworth was my closest work friend, and as publicity director, also an important ally. She looked up as we marched into her office. "Operation Justice for Carol begins," I announced as Miranda shut the door.

Sandra's office was minute, with just space for her desk and two chairs, so Miranda trailed in an extra one, kept by her door for the purpose. In the office hierarchy, Sandra was more important that I was, but our chopped-up building meant she could either have a big office one floor away from her staff, or a stuffy mouse hole of a cubicle beside them. A good boss, she'd chosen the mouse hole.

We sat. I didn't need to brief Sandra on the details— almost everyone in a ten-mile radius had heard me shouting at Bruce, and the ones who had missed it had been gleefully filled in within minutes. "What did you have in mind?" she said, pulling out a pen and scratch paper.

"That's what we need to plan. Bruce said that Carol wasn't 'promotable.'" I tried not to look as if I smelled rotten eggs, but I'm sure I failed. "So, let's promote her. Let's get enough traction for the book, enough preliminary noise, that sales will be forced to acknowledge that the interest is there."

One of my least favourite things was when people outside publishing dismissed the success of any particular book by saying it had only succeeded because of the attendant publicity, that it was "just marketing." As though publishers could, through clever promotional campaigns, ensure wild success for all our titles, but for some insane reason that was never stated, we could only rarely be bothered to do so. In reality, marketing, and publicity, could only take a book so far. For Carol, however, we had her proven track record, and there was no question in my mind that the new book would generate interest. Normally we'd start to get trade people—literary editors, festival planners, bookshop buyers—on board once we had bound proofs, so they could read the book.

Given the Great Bruce Blow-Up, however, it seemed wise to hasten the timeline, focusing the trade's attention before the sales conference, forcing Bruce to acknowledge that the book was going to be a talking point. At least, that was my theory.

I laid it out. "Bruce thinks talking about dying is icky, and talking about women getting older is even ickier, and so he has decided people will be turned off by her subject, and won't buy the book. He was smart enough to say out loud that it was the book's subject that was the problem, but it was clear: he thinks that older women don't get press attention, so it's not worth promoting them until and unless there is already a groundswell. In which case," I added between clenched teeth, "he'll tell us he knew it all along." I waved my hand. "OK, I've finished raging. We need to plot. How do we get publicity for this older woman's book about older women?"

"We go to the older women, of course." Sandra was always upbeat. If I didn't like her so much, it would be a definite character flaw. "They run half of London, and almost all of the arts world. We just have to let them know this book is for them. So let's figure out how."

Easy-peasy. Sure. I handed them the draft blurb I'd written. A blurb is the preliminary tool, that enticing précis that goes on the jacket flap of the book, to lure the bookshop browsers into buying. Except that this was possibly the least enticing thing I'd ever written. Or read.

Miranda was never shy. She sucked in her breath audibly as she read.

I nodded sadly. "How do we make it sound like this book isn't going to make you want to slash your wrists? It doesn't, but a bare description of the plot . . ."

Sandra continued, her face horrified as her eyes continued to scan the page, ". . . makes a history of the Black Death sound like *Little Women*."

I winced.

Miranda turned the blurb over and sat, pencil poised. "Let's start again. What is the book about? Not, *Tell me the story*, but what are the ideas?" She'd read the book too, we all had. She wasn't asking, she was thinking aloud, and she answered herself. "It's about inheritance, how we hand on not only money, or property, but emotions. It's about how love is handed on."

That sounded much better than "In a decaying house in the suburbs, an old man lies dying," which was where I'd begun. "It's about transformation," I added to Miranda's theme. "It's about how we are loved, or hated, and then our own experiences transform those emotions into something else. Just as you can inherit money, and invest it wisely, and increase it, or spend wildly, and dissipate it, you inherit love and turn it into—"

Sandra interrupted, scribbling as she spoke, "That's it. That's where we start. Emotions are genes. In good environments, they flourish, in bad they are damaged; you get happiness, or despair."

"Yes, exactly." I paused. "Does it sound selling, though?" We could have the best book since the Bible, and with snappier dialogue, but if the public didn't hear about it because the press thought it sounded dreary, or the bookshops didn't display it prominently, no one would buy it.

Sandra was confident. "Yes, it's selling, dammit. It's the story of why we are who we are, and how we came to be that way. So it's about every family."

Miranda wrote that down. I looked at them both. "It sounds better when you two say it."

Sandra was placid. "It's going to sound even better when Carol says it."

She was like Helena, saying "when," not "if."

She didn't add anything, just turned away and tapped at her computer. Miranda and I waited in silence, since she seemed to have a plan. After a few minutes, she turned back to us: "There," she said, "we've baited the hook. Let's see who bites."

"Who did you email?"

She tried to look modest, although mostly she just

looked pleased with herself. "*Woman's Hour.*" Which had four million listeners, every morning of the working week. "The *Today* programme." Seven million, ditto. "A handful of others. Who knows what we'll get with them, but I'm telling you now, *Woman's Hour* isn't going to be a problem." She was jotting down a list when her phone rang. She looked at the caller ID and winked at us as she answered.

Her side of the conversation was limited, but had Miranda and me leaning forward. "Well," she interjected, "Bruce said . . ." and then sat back and listened some more. She ended, "Of course. I can't promise an exclusive but . . ." and then did the listening thing again, snapping her hand open and closed to indicate to us that the person on the other end had a lot to say. She finally got a word in. "Absolutely," she added. "And Book of the Week?" That was a serial adaptation, every morning and evening, and was guaranteed to pile on sales. I held my breath until Sandra hung up.

Now she was smiling, and it was positively evil. Someone was going to hurt. I just hoped it was the right people. "Done and dusted," she gloated. "Carol's got *Woman's Hour* for sure, with almost certainly a Book of the Week serial to follow. The rest might take a little longer."

There was being good at your job, and then there was being a miracle worker. "All right, confess," I said. "How did you do that?" Getting a prime spot like that took weeks of negotiation, and there wasn't a producer on the planet who replied to an email within two days, much less two minutes.

Sandra looked modestly down at her nails. "Don't piss

off middle-aged women," she said. "You won't like the consequences."

Wouldn't it be nice to think so. "Bruce pissed me off just fine, with no consequences at all."

"Oh, there were consequences," she said. "They were just slow-motion. My email was to the *Woman's Hour*'s producer, telling her our sales director thought that middle-aged women were downers."

"And . . . ?" I pressed.

"And the *Woman's Hour* producer happens to be a middle-aged woman, who, by an unfortunate coincidence, at least for him, also happens to be married to Bruce."

"Since when?" I demanded.

"When were they married?" She dropped the act at my impatient gesture. "She's been at the BBC forever, but only at *Woman's Hour* for the past year. I knew telling her Bruce thought women our age weren't worthy of air space would push the right buttons."

"And yet you only use your powers for good," I marvelled. It really wasn't that marvellous, though, or even that unusual. The London media world was small, and sociable. Consequently we met and ate and drank together. When people meet and eat and drink together, other things follow. And when other things follow, sometimes marriage does too. Sandra's own husband worked in newspaper and media PR; my boss David's wife taught journalism at university; Miranda's ex-boyfriend (or possibly he was current—it wasn't always easy to know with Miranda) was a magazine designer.

Miranda didn't find it extraordinary, at any rate. She chimed in. "Can I be you when I grow up?"

Sandra basked in our admiration for a brief moment, before she got down to practicalities. "Are you going to tell Bruce, or am I?"

Two could be evil. I smiled meanly. "Oh, I think we should leave that until he gets home tonight, wouldn't you say?"

I almost felt sorry for Bruce. Really? Who was I kidding? I was hugging myself at the thought of his evening. "I was reading a submission yesterday, for a biography of Edgar Allan Poe. Poe wrote about self-important men, 'fellows,' he called them, 'who should not, and could not, be entrusted with the management of their own moustaches.'"

Sandra laughed. "If Bruce had a moustache, I don't think he would be entrusted to manage it at home for a long time to come."

Miranda had been tapping at her phone for the last few minutes of our discussion. Now she announced, "Done," in the triumphant tone I imagined obstetricians used after they had successfully delivered quintuplets.

"What's done?" I leaned over to look.

She slanted the screen equally between me and Sandra. "I was going to order the entire editorial departments T-shirts that said, 'Don't piss off a middle-aged woman,' but then I thought, they're going to be worn by middle-aged women. So the front says, 'Don't piss off a middle-aged woman,' and the back says, 'If you wouldn't mind.' We can wear them to the sales conference."

Chapter 9

I returned to my office to find a text from Helena: *Block off the evening of the 5th*. I texted back a snippy *?*, but her immediate reply, *Drinks party*, didn't get me any further forward. I contemplated replying *Yes, and . . . ?*, but I had visions of the endless bland replies from her that that would elicit, leaving me grinding my teeth. So, speed dial 1.

"What party?" Why didn't things work for me like they did for Sandra, with people miraculously responding to my emails with the very news I wanted to hear? Middle-aged women had no trouble pissing me off. From such a glorious beginning, bad temper was now spreading across my day like a glass of red wine spilt across a white linen tablecloth, slowly staining everything in its path.

"Sam." Helena didn't speak sharply. She never did. Still, I felt like I was back in school uniform again.

I tried to sound pleasant, although I suspected that I

ended up sounding both prissy and aggressive—Attila the Nun. "Tell me about this wondrous party, and why I am going to it," I said, my teeth clenched tight.

"It's a drinks party. At Gray's Inn Gardens. Seven o'clock."

I rolled my eyes to the ceiling. No help there. "For the hard-of-thinking, would you back up a little and tell me what you've arranged?"

I heard a small phone-smile for knowing she was up to something. "Connie's office holds an annual party with two barristers' chambers, for their clients and colleagues, to mark the start of the legal term, and I thought you'd very much want to go."

Connie was a friend of Helena's, another solicitor. I was sure she was a perfectly nice woman, but I barely knew her—not well enough, certainly, to "very much" want to go to what was, after all, a disguised office party. And despite Helena having been my mother, and a practising solicitor, my entire life, I had no idea when the legal terms began and ended—indeed, I had only the vaguest notion as to what it meant. But Helena did little without ulterior motive. "All right, I'll bite. What have you got up your sleeve?"

"I just thought you—and Jake, of course—might perhaps like to meet Liz Henderson in a less formal setting."

I joined the dots. "Liz Henderson is Connie's client."

"Connie's senior partner's client, who briefed her barrister, who is head of the chambers that is joint host, and who will be at the party."

I probably missed a few links in that chain, but I got the drift. I dutifully entered the date in my diary. And I texted the information to Jake, so he could do the same. *We're invited to a party at Gray's Inn. Liz Henderson will be there. H's friend is her solicitor.* He texted back almost immediately: *Of course she is.* Then I banged my head on the desk for a while before I went back to work.

I'd emailed Miles Markov the day after my babysitting duties at Kay's rehearsal. I knew him in passing, but had never bought a book from him. Just as many people dismissed the sort of book I edited as "women's reads," so I dismissed the sort of book Miles agented as "celebrity bollocks." I did it silently, though, because you never knew when you were going to have to pretend you weren't prejudiced. Still, Frances Singer had suggested she might have a book for me to look at, and sending an email took no time at all.

Given our lack of work history, or indeed any personal rapport, I wasn't sure if Miles would take my approach seriously, and I wasn't quite sure what I intended by it anyway, so when I got back to my office after what was hereafter to be known as Dennison's Revenge, I was surprised, if also pleased, to discover a message on my voicemail. "Darling, so *thrilled* to hear you've been in touch with Miles. Would love love *love* to talk more. Give me a bell." I grabbed a pen when the voice rattled off a number, and added, as an afterthought, "It's Frankie, of course."

Of course. I had no idea if Frances Singer had a book in her, although I was fairly sure that, if she did, I was the wrong person to publish it. But even so, I could meet her, and then pass her on to one of my colleagues who had a list more suited to whatever it was she wanted to do. As a side note, I thought bringing a celebrity book on board would make Bruce happy. If, of course, he survived his homecoming.

I dialled. The "Darling!" that greeted my name was vehement enough to suggest we were twins who had been separated at birth, and had only found each other now, across continents, after a decades'-long search so extensive that it had had to be funded by a grant from the Bill Gates Foundation.

People called each other "darling" in publishing often enough, but not with that throb of heartfelt emotion. Nor the "So *good* to hear from you," that followed.

I hesitated, not quite sure how to respond to that much enthusiasm. I reminded myself that, when she wasn't acting, onstage or off, I had liked her.

She didn't wait for a response. "I wanted to catch you this week, before we go back onstage, while I've got gaps in my schedule. Any chance we can meet for a drink this evening?"

"Um, sure," I said, not used to being such a social draw.

She laughed again, but a real laugh this time, not a drama-school one, and spoke like a normal person. "Six o'clock? Where do you work and live? Where would suit us both?"

We did the London geography thing—I'm here, you're there, this tube line is less use than a wet Kleenex, that street has been closed for resurfacing for the past decade, what about there—until we found a mutually convenient halfway point.

"Six o'clock, Jimmy's," I said, attempting to hurry things along, as Bruce hovered in the doorway. "See you then."

I hung up and turned casually, as if I didn't know an invisible sword hung over his head. "That might be a fun one for sales, if it comes off," I said. "Frances Singer, the actress."

He thought for a moment. "Sunday evening television. The Dickens adaptation. Bosoms and bonnets." He made a cupping gesture with both hands in front of his chest, which did not make me feel any more warmly toward him.

"Also that cult sci-fi thing, so she hits a few markets. But I don't know if it's anything yet," I warned. "Just a preliminary meeting."

"Sounds promising, all the same. She's very . . ." He paused, and I stared at him. I knew he was doomed tonight, but I didn't feel sorry enough for him to get away with that. He waved it away. "I wanted to have a quick conversation about some of your jackets we presented to the chains last week." He sat, and we went through the jacket designs for the coming season, going over which ones the big bookshops had said they liked, and which they didn't. While booksellers' suggested design "improvements" generally ranged from the unfeasible to the ridiculous, their negative views had to be taken into account, and at least modified, or they would lower the quantities they ordered. Bruce and I had always worked amiably in the past, and it seemed like a good idea to let him go home tonight remembering that.

When five thirty rolled around, I headed out. I had no idea why Frankie had chosen Jimmy's, which was, to put it politely, a dive. For most of the twentieth century, England had clung to the drinking laws that had been passed during World War I, designed to keep factory workers sober and on the job: no drink available before six; no drink available after eleven; no drink most of the time, in fact. So private clubs sprang up, which weren't bound to keep to those minimal hours, and whose members could, therefore, spend the day getting as sloshed as they wanted. Some of the clubs were glamorous, most were not. And some, like Jimmy's were even worse.

Now that alcohol was legally available around the clock, you'd think that the absolute dives would fold up and slink away, but Jimmy's grimly hung on. Once upon a time, it probably had a louche charm, but that time had been, I estimated, when Benjamin Franklin had been the American consul in Britain. Jimmy's pretended to be exclusive: it was behind an unmarked door in Soho, next to an old-fashioned coffee shop. You rang the bell and gave your name, although you could probably say you were the Shah of Persia, or Cary Grant, or Al Capone, and even knowing they were all dead, they'd still buzz you in. Then it was down a steep and barely lit staircase. If you didn't break your neck, you'd find yourself in a basement room decorated last in the 1970s, all pretend-wood veneer, garish upholstery, and smelling of old beer. I'd been in bus station waiting rooms with more atmosphere.

Frankie, as I was now calling her in my head, was already there, and she leapt up from the long wooden picnic table she was sitting at. "You're here!" she cried.

"I am." Her larger-than-life routine made me perversely even more reserved than normal, but we both silently seemed to find the opposition of our personality types amusing.

At any rate, suddenly, just as she'd done at the rehearsal, she switched off. "Thank you for agreeing to meet so quickly," she said at normal volume. "I ordered a bottle of red, or would you rather have something else?"

"Red's fine, thanks," I said, and nudged back the bench that was all the seating Jimmy's provided, surreptitiously checking for leftover food spillage, or drink residue.

Not surreptitiously enough. Frankie laughed, a sound of genuine amusement, not the party-girl-look-at-me laugh she'd used at the rehearsal. "Isn't this place *awful*?" she asked, as she pushed a glass across to me.

"It is," I agreed. Then, with perhaps too much honesty, "Why did you choose it, then?"

Not too much. She was equally blunt. "It winnows

people out. The ones who are disappointed I didn't say Soho House, so they could be seen; or the ones who pretend to love it because it's 'authentic,' although apart from authentically dirty, I can't see what kind of authenticity it has."

"And the ones who hate it are by default all right?"

"Soul mates," she assured me.

Since I was a soul mate, and honesty had worked so far, I figured I'd continue. "Am I really here to talk about a book?" I asked.

She considered. "A bit. And a bit because you know what's going on, but you don't work in my field, so I don't have to watch what I say." We both drank. "Let's talk about the book first, then if it's not for you, or you think it's not anything at all, we can move on."

I wished more of my authors were that insouciant about their books, but then, it was probably easier not to care much when it wasn't your profession. I shared that thought with Frankie, who agreed that, if we had been talking about a part for her onstage, or in a film, she'd be focused and to the point. "And I'd have arranged to meet you at Soho House," she added.

I looked at the drink rings that dated the table as precisely as if they'd been on a redwood tree. "Good to know where I stand."

Frankie wasn't diverted. "The book. My agent thinks I should do something while the TV adaptation is fresh in people's minds. While I'm—" To my surprise, she made the same cupping gesture with her hands in front of her chest as Bruce had.

I wasn't sure what my reply should be—*Always good for women to sell their assets before gravity hits*?

Luckily Frankie didn't seem to think it needed a response. "That would be a look-at-the-fabulousness-of-me book," she went on. "Which you said you don't do."

"I don't." I went through the kind of books I did that she might want to produce, but felt it only fair to add, "A look-at-the-fabulousness-of-me book will probably make you more money. And while the TV adaptation won't be fresh—publishing is a slow business—there will, I assume, be other projects, and you're—"

She filled in before I could finish: "Promotable," she supplied. She was brisk, professional. "I can get any book we do shed-loads of publicity: magazine profiles, or newspaper interviews, and probably whatever talk shows you like, whatever the material. But I'd rather do something that interests me."

I smiled at her. "I'd rather you did something that interests you too, although my sales director would kill me if he heard me say it, because he can sell the hell out of a fabulousness book."

She waved dismissively. "Leave him to me when the time comes."

"With pleasure," I said, with more feeling than was entirely discreet.

She was trained to read emphasis, and looked at me encouragingly.

I'd had a couple of glasses of wine by now, and she wasn't my author yet, maybe never would be. So I shared my Carol Dennison story, and the planned denouement that Bruce was going home to.

She applauded Sandra heartily, and I took a bow by proxy. Then, abruptly, she asked, "Do you know why I was with Campbell?"

However indiscreet I'd been, *Lunacy?* seemed an undiplomatic response, so I just shook my head.

Frankie didn't continue, however, instead staring accusingly at her glass. It was empty. "Do we want more wine?" she asked.

What an absurd question. "Yes, but not here." I was sure of that.

She agreed and reached for her bag. I waved her off with an "Expenses: you're a potential author," and paid, and we headed out, where we found that it had started to rain, a torrential downpour that looked like it was set to continue until May.

"Where to?"

"The Red Fort?" suggested Frankie. That was an Indian restaurant that had been around forever. It was also across the street. Even if it hadn't been good, it would have been good. We splashed across the road.

"Louis," she said, gripping my elbow, "I think this is the beginning of a beautiful friendship."

Actress or no actress, it was the worst Bogart imitation I'd ever heard.

Once seated in the atmospheric gloom that was statutorily required by law in Indian restaurants, I eyed the curries. Frankie opted for a salad, hold the dressing. "If anyone tells you that they're lucky because they have a wonderful metabolism that lets them eat whatever they want and never gain weight, you can call them big fat liars to their big fat liar faces," she told me loudly, waving her fork in my direction.

"I'll be sure to do that," I said.

"Good. Big fat liars," she repeated under her breath, stabbing at her lettuce.

Metabolisms of the rich and thin weren't that interesting. "Had you worked with Sylvie Sander before?"

Frankie blinked at the change of topic, but moved along willingly. "When Campbell was awarded that Perfect Pitch prize, he used some of the dosh to do our four-play season. *The Spanish Tragedy* was the second, and I was in the first one too, an adaptation of a Viennese farce." She wrinkled her nose. "Sylvie was a bitch about it. The costumes she designed for me would have been terrific if I'd been short and waif-like." She gestured at herself. "Even if I mainline lettuce-no-dressing, I'll never be waif-like. I have no idea what she was thinking, but she refused to budge."

If what we thought about her and Richard Maurer was true, she wasn't thinking at all, just using the designs she had. "Did she make a habit of that? Designing against type?"

Frankie stared. "Of course not. If she had, even though they'd got history, Campbell wouldn't have worked with her anymore. Nothing got in the way of the play for him, not even a forty-year working relationship. Why are you asking about her?"

"Just curious," I equivocated. "I liked your costumes in *The Spanish Tragedy*," I added, as though that were an answer. To head her off, I focused on what she'd said before. "What Perfect Pitch prize? What is that? And do you want coffee?"

"God, no," she said, horrified. "It would ruin the buzz. And the Perfect Pitch was what Campbell thought he deserved."

Frankie's fork slid over to my plate, not for the first time. But I'd had several glasses more by now, and she was going for the apricots I'd carefully moved out of the sauce, and saved for last because I liked them best. I poked at her fork with mine, and it retreated. "It's a lifetime achievement award set up by some Silicon Valley mogul with a passion for theatre," she said, returning to her lettuce and pretending the foray had never been made. "The judges are who-knows-who, and as far as I know, it's only been going a couple of years, so it's got no track record. But the winner gets a million dollars."

Wow. "And Campbell won?"

Frankie nodded. "Not that he cared. He liked the cash, don't mistake me, but only because he could use some of it to do the plays he wanted. Cal Bancroft was willing to fund the farce, and *The Taming of the Shrew*, but he'd baulked at *The Spanish Tragedy*: too obscure, too big a cast, and, even with Ed, too little star power. So Cal backed the season, but Campbell funded this play on his own."

"Nice work if you can get it." I yawned.

"You bet. But Campbell was always good at getting his own way and letting everyone think that they were getting theirs. That ghastly Henderson woman was a prime example. She wandered about telling anyone who would listen about her infinite contribution to Theatre and Art—you could hear the capital letters when she said them—poking her nose in to all the departments and getting in the way. But Campbell got to her. He'd stroke her ego for two minutes, and she'd be rushing for her chequebook." Frankie glowered at her glass, which was empty again. "You never said why you thought I was with Campbell," she reminded me.

My glass had mysteriously emptied too, so this time I said it out loud. "Lunacy?"

"Nope," she enunciated precisely, smacking the "p" with a pop. "The opposite. Common sense." She twisted round to face me. "Last year, a West End producer offered me Gertrude." She paused, waiting for a response.

I wasn't sure what it should be, since apparently we'd moved from her sex life to discuss some unknown woman. "Gertrude who?"

She looked impatient. "She doesn't have a last name. She's the Queen of Denmark. Gertrude. Hamlet's mother."

Oh, Hamlet's mother. Sure. Gertrude. Wait. "Why are we talking about Hamlet's mother?" Sometimes I feel like one of those friendly but dim Labradors, sitting up on my haunches and barking at a tree where I saw a squirrel the week before last.

"Because the Hamlet they cast was *eighteen years older than me!*"

I set down my glass carefully. "We were talking about your sex life," I reminded her with all the seriousness that only five glasses of wine can bring.

"Sex life," she snorted. "I should be so lucky. Or maybe not." She shuddered.

I considered that for a while. "You know I have no idea what you're talking about, right?" I finally said. "I mean, I could ask the waiter for a pencil and a piece of paper and see if I could work it out." I paused. "Maybe a flowchart. Or a Venn diagram?" I tried to think if I had ever drawn a Venn diagram. How did you decide how big the over-lappy bits were?

Frankie wasn't interested in my graphing dilemmas. "We're talking about why I was with Campbell. And I'm telling you, last year, a forty-year-old producer—a forty-year-old *male* producer—was happy to assume I was suitable to play the mother of an actor who was, in reality, old enough to be *my* father." She threw out the hand not clutching the glass, as though everything was now crystal clear. "Campbell has always had much younger women. He's known for it, people talk about it. The stress is on 'young.' He cast me for his season, and was looking for new arm candy to remind people he was still in the game, even if the arm I was the candy for was more than a bit wobbly. He was heading toward eighty, and could barely walk. He uses—used—relationships as promotional material. I needed to remind people that at twenty-nine I wasn't old enough to be a forty-six-year-old's mother. We served each other's purpose."

"So you weren't . . ." I scrunched up my nose.

She scrunched hers back. "Don't be disgusting. It was business."

Was dating a man old enough to be your grandfather worse or better than working in a profession where dating a man old enough to be your grandfather was "business"? I got a little lost in the maze of that thought, but my conclusion didn't. "Sometimes the world sucks," I announced.

Frankie's eyes were unfocused. "The world *always* sucks, babe. The world sucks arse. Big fat hairy arse. Especially if you're a woman."

I considered that for a while. "But there are pluses too," I finally protested.

Frankie was talking to a spot ever so slightly off-centre from my eyes. "Pluses to what?"

I tried to find the spot she was speaking to, and crossed my eyes accidentally. I uncrossed them again, and with some difficulty remembered what we were talking about. "To being a woman in a man's world. It's like the part you're playing in *The Spanish Tragedy*. Your character is the moving force, she sets out to get vengeance like the others, but she succeeds where they fail because no one is paying any attention to her, because she's a woman, and so beneath their notice. So she gets to do what she wants."

"Great. So we can do what we want if we don't mind half the world ignoring us."

Put like that, maybe it wasn't such a great option. Maybe the world did suck big fat hairy arse. The conversation moved along from there, but I have no memory of it. I do remember when the fresh air hit, when we left the restaurant. It was still raining. Frankie didn't hesitate. "Taxi!" she bellowed as a yellow light flashed by. Thank god for stage training. She could probably have been heard in Wales. Certainly the taxi driver stood on his brakes as if he'd been shot, entirely ignoring the dozen people on the street, all there before us, all desperately waving and calling too. We didn't wait for their protests, just leapt in.

I was lying on the sofa with my eyes shut when Jake came home, pretending the world wasn't spinning.

I opened them when he started to switch off the lights, watching him move around the room. "Are there really three of you?" I asked, interested.

He laughed quietly. "No, just the one."

"That's good." I lifted my hand to make a point, couldn't remember what it was, and let it drop. Then I remembered. "If there were three of you, it would play hell with your pension when you retired."

Chapter 10

I heard Jake moving around, but I was afraid to open my eyes. A world of pain lurked out there. I felt him sit on the side of the bed and then the pillow was lifted off my face, where I'd pulled it to ward off the morning. "I've put out Nurofen and water. I'll get you coffee if you're ready for it, but I need to leave soon, so speak now, or you'll have to fend for yourself."

I moaned.

He took that to mean I could speak. "How are you?"

I didn't open my eyes, but, "On a scale of one to ten, where one is bunnies and duckies and sunshine and skipping ropes, and ten is the day after the death-star apocalypse, I'm at eleven thousand, three hundred, and ninety-seven." I paused, but I'd been well brought up, so I added, "Thank you for asking. How are you?"

He kissed my forehead. "I'm fine, which is annoying, so I won't tell you."

"I knew I loved you for a reason." He was right, it was annoying. And I had no one to blame but myself. Or Frankie. I could blame Frankie. "If Frankie hadn't been an actress, I'd be fine too."

I could hear him smile. "You would?"

It was too dangerous to nod my head. "If she ate more than lettuce leaves, we could have had pasta for dinner, and that would have soaked up the alcohol."

He stood. "Having seen you last night, I'd be willing to bet there isn't enough pasta in the world to soak up that much alcohol."

I didn't have an answer to that, so I risked opening one eye. Unfortunately, while it was open I saw the clock. "Yes to the coffee, if it's still on offer."

Jake was scheduled to work both days over the weekend. Yesterday I'd dangled the notion that, theoretically, he should have the weekend off, since he'd been called in the weekend before, and people shouldn't have to work two weekends in a row, but he reminded me that, theoretically people shouldn't be murdered, either. It annoyed me that I couldn't think of a snappy comeback.

After he left, I sat in the kitchen with my coffee and stared through the window. I loved rainy autumn days: they meant I didn't have to water the garden. Another theoretically, theoretically I should have been out there cleaning up the fallen leaves at this time of year, but as Jake had pointed out, theory had little to do with real life, so I gazed sightlessly outside instead, running over the day's to-do list in my head: laundry, groceries, cleaning, ironing if hell happened to choose that afternoon to freeze over.

I decided thinking about it could be a substitute for doing it, and refilled my cup and opened my laptop. Jake had unbent enough to say that they had done a preliminary search through Sylvie Sander's flat, but there was nothing to say that the work was not hers. "I'm not sure," he added, "what, after forty years we could hope to find. There were lots of drawings, lots of sketchbooks. Some had no covers, or had pages torn out. That might be because they had Maurer's name on them; or it might be that Sander tore out pages of work she didn't like." He shrugged. "We can find out where the paper was manufactured, and possibly when, but even if it was Berlin in the 1960s, she could say that she liked that type of sketchbook, and had stocked up. And it might be true."

He spoke as if this were a dead end. But if experts could identify a "new" Leonardo after half a millennium, then someone ought to be able to identify the work of a designer after a mere four decades. I believed that absolutely. Because if I didn't, then I'd have to do the laundry.

Being an editor gives you many skills, most of them totally useless, some of them barely sane. I can, for example, spend an entire afternoon discussing how many goats there are in goat's cheese, or cows in cow's milk. This matters, of course, because of the apostrophe placement. Goat's cheese? Goats' cheese? The open-plan area where the editorial assistants sit can, and has been known to, host a huddle of people chewing over this important question for hours, although when they move on to how many babies there are in breath, I tend to excuse myself.

Other editorial skills are more easily transferred to the real world. One of these is research. Many, if not most, editors never get involved with source material. Authors think up ideas for books on history, or a biography, or a political event. They go to an agent, the agent likes the idea, brings it to an editor, the editor likes it, buys the book, and everybody lives happily ever after. But there's another way of working, and that's when I read something, or see a film, or hear somebody talking about a subject, and think, "There's a book in that." So I mess around online, checking out archives and libraries, looking to see if there's any original material, where it is deposited, who owns it, what access the public has to it. And then, if there is a lot of material, but no one has written about whatever it is, I'll ring up an author who works in that field and say, "Have you ever thought about . . ."

In short, I'm good at libraries. And so I sat in the kitchen and began at the beginning. The Berliner Ensemble had been founded by Bertolt Brecht. His fame would have ensured that not only his own correspondence and manuscripts would have been preserved, but so would the records of the theatre itself. It didn't even need basic common sense to find that out: the theatre's website had several pages devoted to its history, in German and English, with a link to the library where all the material was held. Thirty seconds later I was staring at its catalogue. There was no online access to the papers, but it was a list of everything in the collection. I scrolled through it, searching for Maurer's name, and found it cropped up regularly in the decade before his death.

Using Google, I translated enough to see that this was in contracts, office memos, and correspondence, none of which sounded like it would be useful without zipping to Germany to have a look, and with the additional proviso that I somehow managed to learn German on the trip over. Although, I reflected, a trip to Germany, much less time out to learn the language, would mean I definitely had an excuse not to iron or rake leaves.

I pushed that tantalizing fantasy aside, and continued to scroll. There were records of posters and programmes in the collection for productions Maurer had designed, but with no images, so that was no help. I clicked on what I guessed was German for "Contact Us," and wrote a polite note in, I hoped, the right box, saying I was a London publisher, interested in Richard Maurer's work, and was there anyone at the archives who could help me. I doubted it would lead to anything, but it was worth a shot.

Then I googled "archives richard maurer," and got back all the bizarre and seemingly random hits Google throws up: people named Richard Maurer, or almost Richard Maurer; a town called Maurer in Saskatchewan, which, I presumed (I didn't check), had more than one resident named Richard, and an archive; the picture of a grave of William Richard Maurer (1807–1849); and, inexplicably, a video with instructions on how to stuff pasta shells. I also found a Richard Maurer on Twitter, but since he lived in Scottsdale, Arizona, I didn't rush to send him a message.

Instead I headed where I should have begun, the UK National Register of Archives, a compilation of all the archives in the country. And with just one click, my potential trip to Germany, or even Arizona or Saskatchewan, was on hold. I could stay in London and just visit the Theatre Museum, an offshoot of the V&A Museum, because it held an archive donated by the widow of one Manfred Stieglitz, an actor at the Berliner Ensemble, consisting of letters, scripts, photographs and—be still my fast-beating heart—"design material," uncategorized. According to the museum's catalogue entry, he had died the year before Maurer, and I guessed that his widow, who rejoiced in the gloriously Edwardian English name of Winifred Wood, had moved back to Britain, bringing her late husband's possessions with her.

I was feeling entirely smug and superior as I looked up the Theatre Museum to find its location and opening hours. Then the smug slipped a few notches. The museum wasn't a museum at all: that had closed down a decade before. (Being a Londoner, it was one of those places I'd always meant to visit, but had never quite got around to.) Now it was a study centre, which from the photograph on the website meant it was a room with a row of tables and chairs in it, in a building somewhere in west London. It was only open to the public by appointment, and even then, you had to complete two online forms, provide two pieces of identification, and probably sing "Daddy Wouldn't Buy

Me a Bow-Wow" while hopping on one leg. If you couldn't remember how the chorus went, you didn't get admitted. *Bollocks, bollocks, bollocks*, I mumbled.

I pressed my fingers into my aching forehead. Think like Helena, I told myself. It's not what you know, it's who you know. Who did I know who might get me into an archive in the middle of a business park in Hammersmith on a Saturday? I snorted. Come to that, was there anyone else on the planet who not only *wanted* to spend their Saturday in a business park in Hammersmith, but was thinking up cunning wiles to enable her to do so?

I ditched the "anyone else on the planet," and narrowed it down. I did want to go there, so who did I know? I ran through a mental address book. I liked going to the theatre, but I never did any books about it. Theatre Books Don't Sell is one of those publishing axioms that is handed down on tablets of stone to every bright young editor. The only thing more certain than Theatre Books Don't Sell is Dance Books *Really* Don't Sell. Did any of my authors have theatrical backgrounds or contacts? I couldn't think of any. I knew Kay and Anthony, of course, and now Frankie too, but they were theatre-theatre people, not archive-theatre people. It was unlikely they'd have museum contacts.

Then I thunked myself on the head. It couldn't hurt worse than my head already did. Of course I knew somebody. I reached for my phone and dialled with no hope of anything except voicemail. Instead, the phone was picked up on the first ring. The planets must have been aligned in my favour. I crossed my fingers too, in case.

"Kit, dear Kit, who do you know who could get me into the Theatre Museum archive on short notice?"

"Today?"

Wonderful man. "Yep. Today."

"Why are we going there?"

We?

I was standing on a corner waiting for Kit. On a corner of a five-way intersection. In the rain. As buses thundered past. Buses that ploughed through puddles and ensured that the dirty water regularly sheeted across my suede jacket. It was lucky I loved Kit. And even luckier that he didn't just know somebody at the V&A, but knew somebody who was a big donor to the V&A. It's amazing how quickly, and how high, people will jump when money is involved.

I'd set off from home long before our—it was definitely now "ours"—admission had been confirmed. West London is only about five miles as the crow flies from my house, but there weren't any crows I knew of heading in that direction. By tube it was going to take well over an hour to get there on a Saturday. Weekends occur at regular intervals throughout the year, but nevertheless, when each one rolls around, it always seems to take the public transport system by surprise.

The walk from the station was mostly through a residential neighbourhood, until I reached the business park, filled with ugly, cracker-box identikit buildings—the kind of place where, even if you were sober when you came back from lunch, you'd be hard pressed to work out which office you'd left an hour before. Then I turned a corner and came face-to-face with—I took a step back, not sure what I was facing.

The directions on the website had said the archive was in Blythe House, which I'd assumed was simply a swanky name for an identikit building. But this wasn't identikit. It wasn't even office-like. It was red-brick, and vast, surrounded by a wall, and it looked like it should have a moat around it, or a coat of arms, or a flag flying. It was designed to say *I matter*. Which probably meant it didn't matter at all. The English specialize in making important buildings—the prime minister's office, for example—look like nothing special, while lowly tax-record clerks get housed in one of the grandest buildings in the city.

The geek in me, never far from the surface, came out to play, and I lost interest in tapping my foot and counting the seconds until I could be cross with Kit for being late. Instead, I juggled my umbrella to pull out my phone. Yes, I was right. I punched the air, but discreetly, so no one nearby thought I was totally crazy. The monolith that stretched away for what felt like miles was late Victorian, and had been built to house the Post Office Savings Bank, complete, said the website, with a separate wing to segregate the female post office employees, to ensure they didn't get up to nasty stuff in the stock cupboard with the male post office employees. Well, I made that last bit up—Google didn't say anything about hanky-panky in stock cupboards.

But even imagining it meant that, when Kit arrived, I was happy to see him, rather than cross about standing around in the rain.

"We're to go to the south wing entrance," he said as soon as he was in calling distance. "A woman named Alice will be waiting for us." And she was. Helena was—again—right: it's who you know.

Alice was, possibly, twenty, blonde and festooned in scarves and drapey bits of fabric and silver jewellery, sweet and flustered, a just-rolled-out-of-bed-on-a-weekend-because-her-boss-rang-her-and-told-her-to-get-over-there type of flustered, until Kit's grand manner, flamboyant gestures, and his use of her boss's boss's boss's first name sent her straight from flustered into a full-scale tizzy. She dropped the papers she was clutching. She dropped the keys to the study centre. She probably would have dropped more, except that that was all she was carrying.

So I fell into the Good Cop role, her pal, who didn't know anyone important's first name, to set against Kit's Bad Cop, and between us we got the door unlocked, and located the light switches. The study centre was, as the photographs had promised, an only moderately large room with a few tables, feebly decorated with badly framed posters and other theatrical memorabilia hung wonkily on the walls. It looked like a primary school where the teacher had somewhat advanced tastes.

Alice stuttered, "The director's assistant is coming,

she's supposed to be here, to get you what you need. I don't know where anything—"

I cut her off. The poor thing was going to burst a vein before she hit twenty-one. "Not to worry. I'll boot up the computer and find the references for the files we need. By the time I've done that, I'm sure your colleague will have arrived." I spoke in a low, soothing tone, the way I imagined I'd want to be spoken to when I was 103 and in a home for the terminally confused. Kit didn't say anything at all, just leaned against a table, legs crossed at the ankles, his pose shrieking, *I'm here to supervise while you peons get on with the hard work.*

So I did. I switched on one of the terminals, and located the entries for the Manfred Stieglitz archive, jotting down the file numbers. Then I called over to Alice, "I don't suppose you speak German?"

She looked guilty, as though her entire CV had been built around her being a fluent German-speaker, and now she'd been found out. "You don't have to," I said. "It isn't a requirement, just a question."

"N-n-no," she said. "Or, only a bit."

I brightened. "A bit is good. A bit is a lot more than me. Or Kit," I added. I didn't see why he should get away with that know-it-all pose.

Her shoulders straightened slightly, and she was about to speak when the door opened. An older, very chic, very cross-looking woman appeared. I didn't blame her for being cross, although I admired her immaculate suit and coordinated shoes and handbag, all at an hour's notice on a weekend when Kit's friend had rousted her out on her day off. So I smiled, held out my hand, and introduced myself and Kit, thanking her profusely for her time. Not that it helped. She shook hands, and was polite, but it was a severe effort, and she wasn't going to give us an inch more than she had to—not even her name. I pretended I hadn't noticed the omission, and handed her the piece of paper on which I'd written the file numbers. She snatched at it and flounced off, with nothing more than a "This will take a while."

We waited, Kit and I chatting idly, Alice pretending she was invisible. I tried to draw her into our conversation, but the minute Kit spoke, she froze, so it seemed kinder to leave her alone. "A while" turned out to mean ten minutes, and then Sour Face was back, pushing a trolley loaded with folders and boxes. She moved everything onto one of the tables and stood, hands on hips. "I hope this isn't going to take long," she said, before stamping over to a corner as far away from us as possible without waiting for an answer, choosing a chair with its back to us to drive her point home.

I hoped it wasn't going to take long too, but I was daunted by the size of the piles.

"What are we looking for?" Kit asked blankly. Maybe he should have come up with that question before he decided that "we" needed to make this expedition.

I considered. "Obviously, the best things would be sketches or drawings that are signed by Maurer. Or sketches and drawings that are unsigned, but with his handwriting, or in the same notebooks that Sylvie Sander uses. Anything typed, play scripts, or contracts, or office correspondence, is unlikely to be helpful." I looked at Alice. "Since you're the only one with any German, could you winnow those out?"

She nodded, relieved to have something to do.

Kit was a fashion historian, and his ability to read drawings was better than mine. "If we could find drawings or sketches that were from identifiable plays, we could perhaps try and cross-reference them later to costumes and sets from plays Sander worked on." I pulled out Mr. Rudiger's book, which I'd borrowed again that morning. "There's a list of Maurer's productions at the end."

Alice and Kit each took a pile of folders, leafing through the contents. And me? I was standing there like a traffic cone, serving no purpose at all. So I grabbed a pile too. It was painfully obvious after only a few minutes that Sour Face was going to have most of her day free: whatever the catalogue had said, folder after folder revealed no sketches, no drawings, no designs. Nothing.

Then I had an idea. Kit wasn't just personable and charming. He was the ultimate in personable and charming. He could have been put in charge of selling crude oil to the Saudis, and within ten minutes he would have had them lining up, begging for a chance to buy more, at a higher price. I pulled my chair closer to his and opened a folder at random, leaning in and speaking in a mutter. "Do you think you could sweet-talk the old sour puss over there?"

"I don't see why not. What do we want?"

More "we." "Is it possible to find the names of previous researchers who have asked to see these files? Given the hoops they make you jump through to get an appointment, I assume they keep records of everyone who has ever been in."

"There's nothing useful here. Why do we care who looked at it?"

I shrugged ungraciously. "Because I'm desperate. If there's nothing, we've wasted a trip, and we've also hauled all these nice people out on a weekend for no reason. This way we can tell ourselves that they sacrificed for the cause."

Kit was unfazed. "Desperate is as good a reason as any. And it's important to keep those sweet-talking techniques at optimum levels."

As he walked away, Alice kept her head bent over the folder she was still mechanically ploughing through, but whispered, "She's never very nice, but she's furious today."

"Watch the master," I whispered back.

And we did. I wish I'd timed it, because those particle physicists at CERN, the ones who think they've detected neutrinos travelling faster than light, would have been green with envy as Kit jockeyed Sour Face from Sour, to Mildly Tangy, to Heap of Sugar at a speed that would have made their neutrinos feel so inadequate they decided to look for another line of work. After bare minutes, voice raised, Sweet Face exclaimed, "Mr. Lovell, I tell you, that's not something I'm permitted to give you access to."

Alice lifted an eyebrow at me. *See?* it said, but I responded by holding up a finger: *Wait*. My faith was justified, as Kit's new best friend continued, "Yes, of course it's something I can look up. The password"—she threw out her arm theatrically to a binder on the desk—"is available to all supervisors, but I repeat, the Data Protection Act requires that that information be kept confidential." She stood. "And now that I have made myself clear on that point, if you'll excuse me, I'm going to get some coffee. There is probably no milk in the kitchen on the weekend, so I'll have to go to the café down the road. I hope you won't need me for the next twenty minutes or so." And she winked at him before she sashayed out of the room, closing the door firmly behind her.

I just shook my head at Kit, but Alice actually stood and applauded, before she remembered she was shy, and sat down again in a little monsoon of scarves and bangles. Kit's job was sweet-talking, mine was research, so I went over to open the binder. "Let's just hope we find something."

I started up the computer on the supervisor's desk, and fed in the password. It took me a while to figure it out, but eventually with Alice's help I managed to locate the screen that showed the names of researchers by files accessed. Alice read the Stiegliz file numbers out, and I typed them in one by one.

Then I punched the air again, more vigorously than I had on the street earlier.

"Well?" demanded Kit.

"Only six people have asked for these files in the past decade," I reported. "And"—I didn't quite sing out *Ta-da!*, but I certainly thought it—"the last one of them, a month ago, was one S. Sander." I scribbled down the address she'd provided, and then, for good measure, I added the other five names too. Four gave as their addresses academic institutions: they must be university professors or their students, doing research on the Berliner Ensemble. The one before Sander didn't give a full address, just "N. James," from Smithfield. Smithfield was only a few minutes' walk from the Barbican arts centre, so it was likely that someone from the theatre was working on a Brecht production.

That didn't matter. Sylvie Sander's interest did.

I didn't have time to gloat over my find, though. It had taken me long enough to access the register, and even with Sweet Face giving us some leeway, I'd probably reached the limit. I signed out and closed down the terminal, sliding into a seat beside Alice only seconds before heels came clicking smartly down the hall outside, tapping out a Morse code warning to any computer malefactors that might happen to be in earshot. Not that there were any in that study room. No siree. By the time the door opened, three heads were bent quietly over their files, reading peacefully.

Chapter 11

In all the crime fiction I read, I would now whizz round to Sylvie Sander's house, confront her, and have her in a confessional heap of mush, in time for the doltish police to arrive and wrap everything up. There were a few problems with that scenario. I didn't know what I would confront her with, since as far as I knew, visiting a theatre museum archive wasn't yet a crime, and if it were one, I was guilty too. Then, I wasn't sure what I expected her to confess—even if she had lifted the work of a dead designer, I had no idea how that connected to Davison's murder. And last, but by no means least, I couldn't roll up and confront her, for the simple reason that the address she'd listed for the Theatre Museum was that of the rented Covent Garden rehearsal studio, so I didn't know where she lived.

After Kit and I parted on the pavement outside the Theatre Museum, I faced this problem square on. It had finally stopped raining, and I stood there, brooding, as I realized how little further forward I was. I'd perhaps chipped away a little at the puzzle of Maurer and Sylvie Sander, but nothing more. The euphoria of my apparent breakthrough drained away, and I faced a day of household chores with no obvious reason to postpone them any longer.

Feeling as though someone had somehow slipped a fast one past me, I headed off to do my weekly shopping, staggering home with loaded bags in time for lunch, which I planned would be a quick sandwich and then I'd get on with everything I'd happily postponed that morning. As I walked to the kitchen, however, I could hear that my plans would change.

Kay and Anthony had a key to my flat, in part in case of emergencies, or if I locked myself out, but mostly so that Bim could play in my garden. And unless there were other pirate captains who had dropped by unannounced, the shouts of "Watch out for Black Jack, my hearties!" suggested he was out there now.

Even pirates, however, take a break when there's news to share, and I had barely put my bags down when Bim came racing in. He flung his arms about my thighs, leaning back at a ninety-degree angle to look up at my face. "Did you hear about Campy?" he shrieked.

"I did," I said, detaching him to walk to the fridge to stash my weekly haul away. "Poor Campy," I added, even though that hadn't worked last time.

It didn't this time either. Bim didn't say "Phooey," but

that was only because he didn't know the word. "Mama said he died, bang, like that!" He clapped his hands.

"Like that?" I repeated. At a loss, I pulled out one of the juice boxes Kay kept there for pirate incursions into my garden, and handed it over.

He nodded vigorously. "She said it didn't hurt, but he was hurted before. He was sticky, like when we had to have the blood on us." He held up his hands, presumably covered in invisible blood, before he took the juice box and stabbed the straw in with a passing sound effect— *pssssh*—before getting back on topic. "We're going to rehearsal this afternoon again because there is more deads."

I froze. "There is? I mean, there are? What do you mean, more?"

"Mama was telling Billy's mother on the phone. It's why I can't go for a sleepover tonight."

I looked around. "Where *is* your mama?" Bim didn't ever come down alone.

He sucked at the straw for a while, then, "Upstairs. She's getting my treasure box and other things." He patted his tool belt. "Then we'll be ready."

I couldn't pump a small child for information. Food was a reliable distraction. "What do you do when you go to rehearsal from school," I asked, "have snacks before, or wait until you get there?"

Bim's face was a model of indecision. The answer was, very obviously, that he waited until he got to rehearsal, where, no doubt, he was given a piece of fruit, whereas if he told me he ate on the way, it was likely I'd give him biscuits or chocolate. He was weighing his options: chocolate now versus a discussion about fibbing later. I decided to help him out, if it kept him off the subject of "more deads." "We can put some raisins in a bag for you to eat on the way, and then you can have your real snack later."

This was acceptable, and by the time we'd measured it out, we'd moved on to a conversation about the many ways in which it was wrong to finger-paint directly onto the kitchen floor instead of on the paper that had been laid down for the purpose. I already knew Kay's views on the subject, because I'd heard them through my ceiling the day before. Our house was solidly built, but at that decibel level no one in the building could claim to be ignorant of the many ways in which floor painting was wrong. Bim's equally clear views on his need for artistic expression had been inaudible then, but he shared them freely with me now.

He was building up a head of steam on the subject when Kay appeared. She clapped her hands together: "Quick. Collect all your things from the garden so we can go. Pirate hat, cutlass, they all need to be brought in, in case it rains again." She was speaking brightly, but her voice was clipped, and she was holding herself as if she were made of spun glass. One tiny poke was all that it would take to make her shatter in a thousand pieces. After Davison's death, she had been tired, and sad. Now she was afraid.

Finger-painting aside, Bim was a very good child, and

he immediately headed out to retrieve his plank-walking impedimenta.

I was scared to ask, and desperate to ask, both at the same time, so I did what I usually do, nothing. I unpacked my shopping.

Kay said quietly. "Did he tell you?"

I kept moving around the kitchen. "Only that there was someone else dead. I didn't want to ask him."

She sat down heavily. "Sylvie."

"What?" I stopped dead, cabbage forgotten in my hand. "When? How?" And, more urgently. "Why? For god's sake, *why*?"

She raised her hands helplessly and dropped them again. "Friday night, I think. I don't really know much. The how or the—" She broke off as Bim raced back inside. "Darling, take everything upstairs and put it in your toy box. Then come down, and we'll go." She waited until she heard the front door open and his feet hit the stairs.

I didn't wait for her to go on. "What happened? When? How?"

She raised her hands against my onslaught. "I don't know. They didn't tell us any more than that she had died."

I bit my teeth against the questions that wanted to continue tumbling out. They were all variants on "how" and "why," and Kay would have told me if she knew anything.

She shook her head, not a negative, but a rejection of everything that was happening. "It's not a rehearsal at all, of course," she said. "They've called us back for interviews."

I was scandalized. "Bim too?"

She nodded. "Two detectives came round this morning, wanting to know about my relationship with Sylvie, which was easy, since I didn't have one apart from 'Can this dress be cut a little higher so that when I die I don't flash my boobs at the audience?' They wanted to know where we were Friday night. Again, easy for me: Anthony and I were both home with Bim, and I could even tell them what time Frankie dropped you home, which I suspect is more than either of you could do." She gave a half-hearted smile.

"Oops," I said unrepentantly, aware even as I grasped at the humour that it was a shield against this new unknown. "Were we that noisy?"

"You mean apart from Frankie singing 'Hello, Dolly' and you backing her up in the chorus?"

My eyes popped wide. "We didn't!"

She giggled. "No, you didn't. But you *were* noisy. Frankie was reciting. I'm not sure what play it was, but the entire street had a front-row seat."

I vaguely remembered that. "Something about not leaving her children's bodies with me?"

"She was grimly determined that you wouldn't be allowed to have them, and she even asked the taxi driver to watch her kill them, to make sure. Then she must have forgiven you, because she shouted 'good night' about seventeen times. You shouted back, each time slamming the front door behind you until she shouted again, and you popped out like a cuckoo clock. Then you went out again to remind her to take her babies with her." She stopped smiling and returned to the main point. "The police seemed to lose interest when I told them that that was after eleven, so I think she's covered too."

Bim could be heard galloping down the stairs. Kay stood. "I don't know why they need us again, but if they keep me, Anthony will collect Bim as soon as he's done." She took a deep breath. "I can't say I feel like seeing the others, and I'm sure they feel the same way. I have no idea how we're going to work together."

I kept forgetting that the play was going to reopen. It didn't seem real, and I said so. "The whole thing"—I made a vague gesture, encompassing the deaths, and the rehearsals, and the people who couldn't want even to be in the same room with one another—"seems more like a play than a play. And not a fun one."

Kay was sombre. "No one gets up after death—there is no applause—there is only silence and some secondhand clothes, and that's death," she said unexpectedly.

I blinked, and she brushed it away. "That's from a play I was in last year. It seemed flowery and ridiculous then. Now it just sounds like a description."

Jake didn't get home until nearly midnight, but I was determined to find out what was going on. If I left it until morning, I'd get an abbreviated, I-have-to-go, here-are-the-bullet-points brush-off.

I heard him locking up, then he quietly opened the bedroom door. "I'm awake," I said unnecessarily, since few people sleep sitting up, with the light on, reading.

"And clearly waiting to interview me."

I didn't bother to deny it. "I saw Kay before she went to be interviewed this afternoon, so I understand I've alibied Frankie."

He smiled slightly. "If she was in anything like the condition you were in, the only harm she could have done was to herself." He thought about it. "Or if she fell on someone, I suppose." He started to undress without elaborating further.

"Will you tell me what happened? Please?" My voice was small. "I know it's nothing to do with me, but it is, somehow, all the same. Please," I repeated.

He sat down on the edge of the bed beside me. "I agree, it has, somehow, involved you, between Kay and Frankie." I hadn't told him about the archive yet, but that could wait. "I don't want you talking to either of them about this. Or anyone else."

"I won't. I promise."

"All right then. Sylvie Sander was found dead at her flat this morning. The preliminary reports suggest she died on Friday evening, before about ten. The lock on her door wasn't damaged, there were no signs of forced entry. The building is like this one, a converted house, and no neighbours saw or heard any visitors, but she was on the ground floor, so there was no reason for them to. If this death were in isolation, it would almost certainly be classed as suicide. She'd ingested some pills—there was a half-empty bottle of Valium, the prescription made out in her name—and then"—he looked away—"and then suffocated."

I didn't say anything, and he continued, if reluctantly. "A plastic bag over her head, tied at the neck."

I closed my eyes for a moment against the image. It didn't work, I could still see it, so I opened them again.

"We won't know for a few days how many tablets she took, whether it was enough to incapacitate her, which means that it is unlikely she killed herself, or whether she purposefully took just enough to take the edge of fear off so that she could do it. The tie on the bag was at an angle she could have done herself, but it's possible she took the Valium, was asleep, or drowsy, and someone else put the bag over her head."

I said, "She knew someone was asking questions about Maurer." It wasn't a statement, and Jake waited. "I went to the Theatre Museum today." I didn't look at him as I told him what Kit and I had found, but I didn't need to know he wasn't happy. Then again, I wasn't happy either. And Sylvie Sander really wasn't. I swallowed hard. I ended, "There was nothing there, in the files, and I thought it was a waste of a trip. Then, when we found she'd been there too, I thought she must have been double-checking, to make sure that there were no drawings there. But now . . ." I hesitated, thinking it out. "Now I'm wondering if there were drawings there and she removed them."

Jake made a go-on motion with his hand.

"The catalogue says there were drawings and sketches. Unless we missed something, there weren't any. But she went there a month ago. It was long before you were asking about his work." I thought about the study room. "We were there on a Saturday, so it was different, but if there were only one or two people supervising, and they were bringing files, and returning them, and doing admin, I don't think it would have been difficult to slide some pages out unobserved."

Jake looked reflective. "We were looking into her finances. If what we suspected about her appropriation of Maurer's work was true, she had reason to fear, but given what you say, it wasn't our investigation that precipitated it." He made a note of the date I'd given him.

I was confused. "I'd been assuming that her death proved that she had appropriated Maurer's work."

"It fits, but that doesn't mean that that's the only possibility."

"What I don't understand is how this is related to Davison." I ran through the possibilities. "He's threatening to work with other designers, she'll lose her career, so— so she kills him? That makes no sense."

"Agreed. But if he was going to work with others and she would lose her income, she might decide it would be better if he were dead, because Davison's solicitor tells us she's mentioned in his will."

I sat up. "Was it enough to kill him for?"

Jake smiled sadly. "The first thing you learn in this job is that there is no sum small enough that someone doesn't think it's worth killing for."

That was a lesson I didn't want to learn. "Wait. Wait a moment." I remembered something Frankie had said. "Did he leave her an amount, or was it a percentage of whatever he had?" I didn't wait for an answer. "It possibly matters." I told him about the million-dollar prize Davison had been awarded. "If his will said *I leave £10,000 to my good friend Sylvie Sander*, that's one thing; if it was ten percent of an estate valued at £100,000 when he wrote the will, but now the estate had gone up tenfold in value . . ."

Jake made another note.

"His death might have given her financial assistance. What about possibility? Could she have physically killed Davison?" I figured I'd better get all my questions out while Jake was in a mood to share.

"Almost anyone could have killed him," he said wearily. "The pathologist's report says he died in a two-hour window after the dress rehearsal ended. People were coming and going for most of that time, with only a few definitively ruled out. Gordon Cartwright was with either Bim or Robbie during the last act without a break, and he handed the boys over to Robbie's parents and Bim's grandparents at the stage door at the end of the rehearsal before they all walked together as far as the tube. Cartwright joined friends for dinner half an hour later. He didn't have time to double back. Most of the crew are also clear: there was a birthday party for one of the electricians, and they were all there. Only two techs left it for any length of time, and since the party was in a pub not far from the theatre, they could have gone back to the theatre, so they're not covered. Bill Rose's wife met him backstage as soon as the rehearsal ended, and they went out with another couple; he's clear too. Apart from that, most of the cast, the stage manager, her assistant, the producers and their guests were in and out of the backstage area. None of them has a complete alibi for the entire two hours."

"What about Sylvie Sander? Was she one of the ones without an alibi?"

"She was backstage, and people saw her intermittently, but she's like the rest, in and out. She could probably have got Davison on the hook, but she was sixty-three, she had arthritis, she wasn't particularly strong."

"Like Davison," I said, without thinking, and when Jake cocked his head in inquiry, I backtracked. "Maybe he didn't have arthritis. When we saw the dummy—saw Davison—in the last act, I thought how dramatically they had posed the dummy's hands to make them claw at the air."

"Cadaveric spasm," he said. "It looks theatrical if you've never seen it."

I decided I didn't want to know any more about it, and returned to Sander. "She kills Davison, the police follow the breadcrumbs and ferret out her deep dark secret, and she kills herself. Or, someone else kills Davison, the police follow the wrong breadcrumbs and ferret out her deep dark secret, and she kills herself."

Jake looked away. I hadn't meant it to sound like an accusation, but anything I said now would only emphasize it. Instead I reached for the manuscript I'd put down when he came in. "I'm so glad I do fiction," I said. "When it doesn't make sense, you just ask the author to rewrite."

Jake headed for the bathroom. His words floated back over the sound of running water. "That would set me up for promotion, all right: 'I'm sorry, sir, but I'll have to ask the suspects to go back and recommit the crime: as it stands, the motives need to be more clearly defined to hit our demographic.'"

He had the publishing jargon down pat.

Chapter 12

"Why are we doing this?"

It was déjà vu all over again. We were heading for the same seats, in the same theatre, preparing for the curtain to rise on *The Spanish Tragedy*. The only difference was that this time Jake knew how many people died in the play, and wouldn't have to read his programme. I was also no longer looking forward to the evening.

"We're doing this because we're nice people," I reminded him. And we were. "We're doing this because Kay and Anthony are our friends, and it's a horrible evening for them, and so we're being supportive."

That was true, but it wasn't the only reason. Curiosity wasn't the reason either. I'd seen the restaged ending, too many times, during my day at the rehearsal studio. The press, and paparazzi, and cameras outside the entrance were a reason to stay away if anything was. In fact, the press presence brought back the image of the final act, of the audience laughing, of Davison hanging, and it made me feel physically sick.

I had wondered if the death of their designer would once more close down the production, but Kay had shrugged off my question. "By the first night, the designer's job is done. We rarely see them after that, unless something horrible happens."

My silence reminded her that something horrible *had* happened.

"Not that kind of horrible. Ordinary horrible. Problems with a set, or a scene change, or a costume that gets in the way. And those type of things tend only to happen with novice designers. Sylvie was a bitch to work with, and she wouldn't give an inch, but she was an experienced bitch, and she rarely had a reason to."

The police were giving little away publically, while the question of Maurer was entirely unknown. It was only with effort that I remembered this, and managed not to carelessly drop something about Sylvie Sander's expertise. At the moment, it was generally accepted that she had been devastated by Davison's death, her working partner her entire life, and, the tabloids now reminded their readers, for a few years her partner in private life too. Unsurprisingly, the story emerged as a decades'-long, unrequited passion come to a tragic end. That she hadn't lived a tragic life, that she had had a contented private life with happy long-term relationships, as well as an extraordinarily successful career, was not going to prevent the narrative of an ageing woman left adrift at the loss of her man. The sheer moronic rote default of it infuriated me: I wanted to bite someone.

Jake knew that I wanted to be there, and that I didn't know why I wanted to be there, and that I dreaded being there, all at the same time, and he was being endlessly patient with my vacillations. If I was going to bite someone, it shouldn't be him.

Maybe I should bite Helena. She was being bite-worthy at the moment. She'd rung that morning to say that she was going to be at the reopening too, and would we like to go together. Once she'd suckered me into saying yes to that, she suggested I collect her in Lincoln's Inn Fields, where she had a meeting: "Only five minutes from the theatre, darling!"

Why, after more than four decades of being her daughter, I continued to fall for this sort of thing, I will never know. Because while Lincoln's Inn Fields has many things going for it—it is, indeed, only five minutes from the theatre (darling); it was designed by Inigo Jones, and has lovely buildings; it has a great museum almost no one knows about in it—as I say, while it has many things going for it, one other thing it has is that it's prime territory for barristers' chambers. And Helena never does just one thing when she can kill two stones with one bird.

Had it been a nice day, in summer, I would probably have sat outside in the square in the sunshine to wait. But it was November, and raining, and the sun had set more than two hours ago. I went to the address she'd given me. A small, dark, carefully groomed woman who, without makeup, would probably prove to be nineteen, but made-up as she was, appeared to be a terrifyingly sophisticated thirty, manned the reception desk, talking to a small, dour, square-looking older man who somehow looked like his suit didn't fit, and his life didn't fit, and he was gloomily aware of both. He was leaning over her shoulder, both of them staring down at a ledger. Seeing her immaculate polish had me patting pointlessly at my damp and frizzy hair.

As I closed my umbrella and propped it by the door they looked up and waited in silence as I approached. I patted my hair again under their stares. "I'm Sam Clair. I'm here to meet Helena Clair, who is in a meeting with . . ." I'd forgotten the name she'd told me. "In a meeting. I'm a bit early."

The receptionist gestured to the seating area, and offered me tea or coffee in a manner that virtually demanded I say *No, thank you*. So, "No, thank you," I replied, and sat, pulling out a manuscript.

But while my eyes read, my ears were busy. The hangdog man was named Nigel, and he was not happy. Something had caused a loss to "his" barristers' billable hours—the "his" was repeated several times. He was driving the receptionist to return to the ledger and see where the loss had occurred. Frosty to me, she was repeating with much less starch that she had already been over the books twice.

And then, as if a cloth had been wiped over his face, Nigel straightened up and moved with lightning speed out from behind the desk. "Good evening, sir," he said, leaning unctuously toward the silver-lion-maned older man wearing a suit that had probably cost as much as the gross domestic product of many mid-sized nations as he entered.

"Sir" nodded regally in his general direction. While he more or less disregarded Nigel, he stared over at me as if I were a squatter who had appeared in his sitting room.

Nigel waved a hand in my direction. "Susan Clair," he said. "Helena Clair's daughter. Mrs. Clair is here about the Bridgewater matter."

I didn't mind being introduced as Helena's daughter; among lawyers, it was my reason for being. I did, however, mind being Susan. "Sam," I said firmly.

Silver-mane looked down his nose. "Of course I'm not," he said sternly. "I'm Cyril. Cyril Bosworth."

Had I seen the name Cyril Bosworth as the credits rolled in a film, I would have assumed the man had been born Frank Smith, but this man was obviously the child of parents who had looked at their tiny, mewling newborn and said to each other, *How about Cyril? Later in life, that will give him the foundation to patronize everyone he meets.* And now here he was, living up to their every dream for him.

I kept smiling, although it was an effort. "No, not you, me. I'm Sam."

Cyril and Nigel both stared, Nigel with a return to his basset-hound demeanour, Cyril as though I were something nasty he'd stepped in. "Not Susan. Sam," I repeated firmly. "Samantha. And since Helena chose it, I've never argued."

No one argued with Helena, not even this lion. He nodded regally, grudgingly accepting Helena's right to name her own child, just as the inner door opened and Helena herself emerged. She joined us and squeezed Nigel's shoulder. "Dear Nigel," she said. "Just the man I was hoping to see." I swear he grew three inches. Only then did she turn to Cyril. "How lovely," she said, in a tone that was cordial, respectful, and made clear that if she never saw him again it would be a banner day in her diary. If I could work out how to distil and bottle precisely how she'd done it, I could retire a rich woman, and never have to go to another sales conference.

Cyril was the only person not to notice. He smiled benignly, and then said, as one handing out bad news, "Unfortunately, I can't stop. I have an engagement." We all bore up well under this disappointment, and as he left, Nigel said to the receptionist, "It's late, Felicity. You can go now." She gathered her things, and unless I was very much mistaken, followed Cyril out with some purpose. Helena must have thought the same. "Splendid," she said. "They can keep each other occupied."

To my astonishment, Nigel, who just moments before had looked as if he'd last smiled at the coronation, threw back his head and laughed. "What do you want, Helena?" he asked, as an uncle would to a recalcitrant niece.

"You," she replied simply.

Nigel turned to me. "Sorry about the 'Susan'" he said, "but Squirrel is always happier if he can patronize two people at once."

I wasn't sure which bit of this meeting to deal with. Finally, "Squirrel?" It wasn't the most urgent question, but it was the one that came out.

"He's head of chambers, and has an excellent success rate in court, but if you had to work with him could you resist the nickname?"

I waved my hand—obviously not, it said.

Helena had no time for our little meet-and-greet. "We wanted to discuss Liz Henderson with you," she announced, much to my surprise. I had no idea I was there for any purpose at all, much less Liz Henderson, whom I'd more or less forgotten.

Nigel cocked his head, waiting to hear more before he spoke. I took a moment to berate myself for judging by appearances. This was a shrewd, intelligent man.

"I'm assuming you've read about the death of Campbell Davison," she began, "and you know about Ms. Henderson's connection to him."

Nigel nodded, but still said nothing.

"Your chambers acted for her over her mother's estate a few years ago."

Nigel didn't nod now, and continued to wait in silence. "I don't want information on the case," Helena assured him. "It's her family I'm interested in."

Thus reassured, Nigel was prepared to open up. "There was barely any family." He looked sorry not to be able to help. "Ms. Henderson had a brother, deceased, no issue, and a sister, married and living in Potsdam, two children. The case was minor. It wouldn't even have gone to court if it hadn't had the complication of a reassessment of inheritance and division of assets before German re-unification."

I saw why Helena had wanted to speak to Nigel: a small case, several years ago, and he had the details in his head.

She pressed on. "It's the brother I'm interested in. We've been assuming he was Richard Maurer, the theatre designer." Her glance included me in the "we."

"The surviving sister was Helga—or was it Hedwig?—Dichter." Nigel shook his head, annoyed with himself at being unable to dislodge the relevant detail, before he continued. "The brother's name was Richard Maurer, definitely, but he died long before their mother, so there was no need to concern ourselves with him. I don't remember anything about him." He was apologetic, as though not remembering everything about the deceased brother of a client in a minor case years before was akin to forgetting that the Thames was the name of the river that ran through London. "The case revolved around their mother's East Berlin property and possessions, and who had the right to dispose of the assets in the Eastern Bloc. Interesting under international law, but not of great financial importance. Ms. Henderson claimed that she was driven by the principle of the matter, not the financial outcome, but"—his eyes quickly scanned the empty waiting room—"it was plain that it was dislike of her sister that drove her."

"Did the sister inherit?"

"She disposed of the property on their mother's death,

and after reunification established contact with Ms. Henderson to divide the remaining cash. There was a small amount of personalia"—he turned to me and courteously translated—"personal possessions. Ms. Henderson maintained that there should have been more, and her sister must have sold the goods off and pocketed the proceeds." He flicked his fingers in dismissal. "It was a nonstarter. Even if her sister had done so, more than two decades had passed since their mother's death, and it had occurred outside EU jurisdiction at the time. Frau Dichter, indeed, was to be commended for sharing anything at all, and so the judgement was rendered."

Helena was sharp. "There was no mention of the brother's estate?"

Nigel was curious, but he merely repeated, "My memory says that he had died some years before even their mother."

Helena nodded. "Nineteen seventy-one."

"Then no. I would have remembered if our client had wanted to activate a four-decade-old claim." He paused, considering. "Of course, if his estate had been inherited by their mother, then his possessions might well have been the personalia they were arguing over."

Helena looked knowing. "That was what I was thinking too." She patted Nigel's forearm. "What are the chances that you might look up the old case notes, out of interest, and that we might have a drink soon, too? I have a client who wants to instruct a new barrister in a property-liability case, and I think Squirrel might do very well for him."

Nigel drew himself away, offended. "Are you trying to bribe me to pass on confidential details of an old case in exchange for a new client?"

Helena was equally offended. "Of course I'm not trying to bribe you. I *am* bribing you."

Nigel laughed once more. "I'll have the chance to look for the files next week. Send me your client's brief at your convenience."

They smiled at each other: an understanding had been reached. Helena turned to me, tucking her arm into mine, and said, "Come on, we need to move, or we'll be late." As though all this lingering in barristers' chambers was something I was prone to doing, and she had to keep hounding me to break the habit.

As I said, if I wanted to bite someone, Helena was a sensible target.

The street in front of the theatre was bedlam, with photographers and journalists and even television camera–operators jostling one another, waiting for anyone halfway famous to arrive, at which point they shouted out thoughtful, measured comments like *How does it feel to be watching a play where someone died,* and *Hopefully, what do you think will happen tonight?* I didn't see how we were going to find Jake in the chaos, but suddenly he was there, gripping my arm tightly, assuming, correctly, that my permanent urge to instruct total strangers on how to behave in a civil society was about to go into overdrive. "There are at least fifty journalists here," he said firmly.

"There isn't time before the curtain for you to teach them manners one by one."

He was right, but "How about I explain the rule for dangling modifiers, or the correct way to use 'hopefully'?" I offered.

"Good idea," he said, but he kept hold of my arm and didn't break stride.

Sitting in the theatre before the curtain went up was grim. Watching a serenely unconcerned Liz Henderson re-enact her earlier meet-and-greet in the aisle was more than grim. There were minor differences: her dress was silver, not red; her fellow greet-ees were not as unconcerned as she, and anxious to settle in their seats, rather than chat; her husband was, this time, not bored, but looked actively unhappy. But much was the same: the silver dress displayed as much flesh as the red one had, she posed for pictures as if this were just another opening, another show.

Then I nudged Helena, who had, through who knew what witchcraft, organized to be sitting next to us. But she had already spotted him: sitting next to Hugh Henderson, looking supremely comfortable, and taking in his surroundings as though the entire theatre, the entire audience, had been laid on for his private enjoyment, was Cyril Bosworth.

"Was he there last time?" asked Helena.

"I don't know." I'd been gripped by the display Liz Henderson had put on, but I hadn't known who she was, so wouldn't have noticed who she was with, either.

I quickly filled Jake in. The police had "processed" the audience at the first night. If Bosworth had been there, his name would be on file. He nodded, but didn't say anything.

"He's Busy Lizzie's barrister," I reasoned. "There's no reason for him not to socialize with her and her husband." I turned to Helena. "You go out with clients."

"I do. But he'd have to be a good friend to go to the same play twice in ten days. And he's not Hugh Henderson's friend. Look at them."

She was right. Not only were Hugh Henderson and Squirrel not friends, they were carefully looking in opposite directions, and leaning as far away from each other as they could without actually climbing over the arms of their seats.

"Is she sleeping with him?" asked Jake.

"What am I, the extramarital expert of the theatre district?" I looked down at myself for evidence of expertise. Then I realized he was speaking to Helena. Who undoubtedly was the extramarital expert of legal London. She, however, merely shrugged.

I considered them now. "If I had to say yes or no, I'd say no. She looks at Squirrel as if he were lunch, but not as if he were *her* lunch, not a restaurant she ate at regularly." I shook my head and abandoned the simile. "Look at her. In between chatting to people she's doing a cartoon, *Ooh, you big sexy man* at him, but it's the same one she's doing to every man she's saying hello to. It's a reflex response to male chromosomes." Then I remembered I had no idea what I was talking about, and added, "Maybe."

The lights went down, sending those still standing scurrying for their seats. Instead of watching, I spent most of the first act trying to work out where Liz Henderson fit in, if she did. She had invested in the production company behind Davison's four-play season, and had probably put up more money than she ever had before. She had brought a suit against her sister, claiming that their mother's estate had not been shared equitably, according to her will. Her brother was Richard Maurer, and his estate, including all his artwork, might have been inherited by his mother, although it also might not have been. For all we knew, Maurer might have had a wife and a handful of children who inherited his estate, or he'd left everything to a home for retired seeing-eye dogs.

Setting that aside, if Maurer's possessions, including the contents of his design studio, had been inherited by his mother, that might connect to Sylvie Sander. Had Liz Henderson seen some of Maurer's drawings when her sister shared the estate, and later seen Sander's work onstage and recognized it? That was a stretch, though. It wasn't the costumes that were obviously Maurer's, it was the drawings, and Sander's were never published. So that made no sense. And even if Liz Henderson had, somehow, worked out the connection, and spoken of it to Sylvie Sander, that might drive Sander to kill herself, but how did Davison's death fit in? Davison had condoned the fraud, benefitted from it. If it were going to be made public, he might well want to kill himself too, but he hadn't. Or, at any rate, he hadn't stuck himself up on a meat hook, in costume, to be laughed at by his own actors and an audience. And if Liz Henderson had been a threat to him, if she had been planning to use Cyril Bosworth to bring a suit—but I kept coming up against the same problem. Davison might fear discovery, but that didn't explain his death.

By the time I'd reached that conclusion, the play was winding up to its climax, the great pile of bodies on the stage. I had managed to spare a few brain cells when Kay or Bim were onstage, and Frankie's part—a woman who discovers the treachery and drives the planned revenge, but who is ignored by virtue of being a woman in the sixteenth century—resonated even more than it had before. I was impressed that the performers had managed not only to commit themselves to the story they were telling, but to engage the audience too, most of whom had arrived thinking not of sixteenth-century deaths, but of twenty-first-century ones.

Frankie killed, and was killed; Bill Rose gestured to the wings where, he announced, the body of his dead son lay—the dead son that Campbell's body had so gruesomely substituted for the previous week—and before the audience could begin to think of that, he killed his rival, and then himself, and the front-drop came down and the ghost of Revenge prowled out in front to promise an endless cycle of retaliation to come in the underworld.

I breathed deeply, and tried not to believe that message was for us.

Chapter 13

Kay's parents had not returned to London for this repeated first night, so I had offered to pick Bim up at the
stage door and take him home with us, giving Kay a
chance to finish up in her own time with her colleagues.
It was a rough night emotionally, and she welcomed a plan
that allowed Anthony to stay with her as moral support.

Bim had performed in the first first night, and therefore, he had informed me morosely over the weekend,
Robbie was going to be given this second one, while Bim
was permitted to be backstage with the rest of the cast.
He was supposed to be waiting at the stage door with Gordon, but when we arrived, the man at the desk there
sucked at the gap in his teeth and said, "Chance would be
a fine thing with that man."

"May we go and collect him, then?"

"Names?" he asked, bored, and pulling out a clipboard
with a list.

Unsurprisingly, our names weren't on it. And equally unsurprisingly, the sight of Jake's warrant card made that omission a matter of no importance. I wanted a warrant card, although I would use mine to get into sold-out film showings, or overbooked restaurants. "Down the hall, first set of stairs on the right, third door on your left." I shook off my warrant-card lust and followed Jake.

We could hear Bim even before we left the stairs, and as we reached the landing, there he was, getting full value out of watching Robbie being hosed down, figuratively speaking: a man was using an enormous towel to wipe away the stage blood that covered his hands and face, an even more enormous jar of cold cream sitting on the counter beside them. Bim danced around, calling, "There's another bit! Behind his ears!" as Robbie made faces and whined that Gordon was rubbing too hard.

When Bim spotted us, he shot off like a bullet, grabbing both our hands to ferry us toward Robbie, letting go only to throw out his own two in a gesture that implied Robbie had been painted in stage gore entirely for our benefit. "Look!" he cried. "Doesn't the blood make a *mess*?" It did, and I suspected you had to be six before having that wiped off you four times a week was the peak of pleasure. "Everyone's sticky!" he gloated.

Sure enough, Kay leaned out a door further down the corridor, wiping her face with a similar-sized towel—the blood was a constant for all the cast. "I won't be a moment," she mumbled behind it. "Gordon needs to sign them out before Bim can leave. Between having to be on a list to be collected at school, and logging him in and out of the theatre, he's had more signatures than a FedEx package."

Bim had already lost interest in the now almost-pristine Robbie, and had taken charge of Jake, showing him around backstage. Both were happily occupied, so I leaned in the doorway of Kay's dressing room, where she and three others chatted as they took off their makeup and wigs, half watching them, half keeping an eye on Bim and Jake.

Bim steamed along the corridor like a small, self-powered train, ticking off the occupants of each dressing room as he passed. "And this was the room where Campy liked to sit. He was sticky and smelly." The room was directly across from Kay's room, and I could see a couple of armchairs and a lamp, with a few prints on the wall above. Bim perched on one of the chairs and flung out a hand affectedly, dropping into the imitation I'd seen dozens of times over the past few months. "My *deeeear,*" he quavered, leaping up again and mincing down the hall, peering at an invisible script through invisible spectacles, licking his finger daintily before elaborately turning an invisible page. Kay, now in street clothes, swatted the invisible script away.

"Stop that," she said firmly. "I've told you it upsets people."

Bim wasn't an unkind child, and he dropped it right away. "I forgot," he said.

She squeezed his shoulder. "I know. Let's get you ready to go home. Coat," she instructed. "Hat. Shoes." She called down the hall, "Jenny, do you know where Gordon is? He needs to sign the boys out."

Jenny replied just inches behind me, making me jump. "He's with Helen again. *Gordon,*" she added firmly. She didn't shout, but no one could mistake that one word for anything other than *Here. Now. No fooling around.* And Gordon didn't fool around. He was there, front and centre, almost before she'd finished saying his name. She stared levelly at him in a way that would have shrivelled me into a tiny ball, although I also decided I needed to practise it, to see if I could replicate it at work. Gordon must have been on the receiving end of The Stare before, or maybe it was a side effect of wrangling six-year-olds for a living. He was unmoved, just taking a clipboard off a peg beside Kay's door, signing it and saying to Kay, and to an adult standing behind Robbie, "They're good to go."

Jenny turned to the boys, speaking as though they were seasoned professionals of several decades' standing. "Bim, you're on tomorrow, half hour, please, at seven. Robbie, the same for you on Wednesday, and the Thursday matinee, the half hour at one thirty." She ticked off an item on her tablet, and nodded once each to Kay and a woman I assumed was Robbie's mother. "Kay, stage call for Tom's notes in fifteen minutes." And she turned, speaking into the wireless headset about blue gels and scrims: we were dismissed, and she was on her multitasking way.

I was at work early the next morning—early even for me. Since I normally arrive around eight, and it was Novem-

ber, that meant it was still dark as I walked from the tube.
After seven, the front door was always left on the latch
by the cleaners, but the lights weren't on yet. I didn't bother
to search for them downstairs. Our office had once been
three eighteenth-century terraced houses, and I'm convinced that when the buildings were knocked together,
the architect on the job was tasked with ensuring that
they created as many dead ends, odd turnings, and random steps up and down as possible. And then, to make
sure everyone fell down or bumped into as many of those
architectural anomalies as possible, all the light-switches
were installed in inaccessible or unlikely spots—behind
doors, or on the walls opposite the entrances, with as much
furniture strewn in between as could be fit in. If they had
thought of it, I'm sure half the switches would have been
inside cupboards.

I was used to this, and regularly made my way upstairs in the gloom cast by the streetlights through the
windows. I was halfway across the front hall when a passing car's lights threw my elongated, contorted shadow
across the floor. Displayed with my hand lifted toward
the banister, I had a flashback to Davison in the last act of
the play, his hands reaching out, clawing at the air as if
he were trying to claw out a future he hadn't lived to see.
I don't think that I'm fanciful as a rule, but the sudden
image made me shriek. Then, even alone in the hall, I
blushed bright red. There's jumpy, and then there's literally jumping at shadows.

By the time I reached my desk, I was steadier. I knew

where all the switches were upstairs, and I quickly had the place looking like Oxford Street at Christmas, turning on the lights in every room as I passed. And once I had some coffee, I felt entirely calm: light, caffeine, and a computer. What more could a person need?

First I trundled round to the publicity department, raiding their shelves for reading material for Kay. I was halfway back to my office with my only slightly ill-gotten booty when I paused, then reversed. I dug up a copy of Carol's previous book, and added it to the pile. Frankie might like something to pass the time backstage too.

Back at my desk, I went to work. I'd had enough of dead stage designers, or directors, or mysterious lawsuits in East Germany. That was not my world. Books were, and with a sales conference coming up, I needed to focus on that. So I did. I pulled out all the Advance Information sheets for my books that were going to be presented, and all the jackets and cover copy. I went over the material and checked the promotional plans. And then I went over my presentations for my two lead titles, both Carol's book and a first novel by a woman who had worked for a fashion magazine.

I'd like to imagine that I'm able to do these conferences with insouciance, making up my presentations as I go along, blessed with the perfect metaphor on the fly to suit that audience's response on the day. But then, I'd also like to imagine that I'm faster than a speeding bullet, and more powerful than a locomotive. In reality, I'm slower than old-age pensioners with hip replacements, and I've known earthworms that have more upper-body strength than I do. So I also prepare what I'm going to say carefully ahead of time.

The fashion book was easy: half love letter, half blowing-the-author's-chances-for-future-employment-sky-high. The only trouble with that presentation was deciding what to leave out, there were so many behind-the-scenes stories of the famous and the famously weird, all of them perfect for a four-minute presentation. Carol's book took me longer. Even after input from Miranda and Sandra, whatever I wrote made the book sound like *The Grapes of Wrath*, but with fewer jokes.

Still, eventually it was done, just in time—I looked at my watch and sighed—just in time for our scheduling meeting, a weekly two-hour funfest that usually contained ten minutes of real importance. Unfortunately, when the ten minutes would occur was unpredictable, so everyone was forced to sit there, dozing gently, or playing on our phones or tablets, surreptitiously answering email or reading manuscripts under the table, texting jokes to the person opposite until that crucial moment arose.

I was distracted enough that I missed that moment, and David, my boss, got snarky, but my "I'm tracking an auction for a book I want," got me a pass. And it was true, I *was* tracking an auction, and it *was* for a book I had wanted to acquire, although I had dropped out of the auction three days previously: the bids for a book I'd loved, but wasn't sure how well it would sell, were now nearly half a million more than my upper limit. I was famously cautious with advances, and I was watching the bids mount with the appalled fascination one tracks a natural disaster.

When the meeting drew to a close, I was making a break for it when I heard, "Sam, have you got a moment?" I turned, and saw Bruce still seated at the conference table. It was a replay of our previous meeting, only this time I was the one who couldn't exactly say that a "moment" was too long.

I smiled an entirely false smile and moved back into the room. "Sure, what's up?"

He didn't look at me, keeping his eyes on his phone as he thumbed through some pages. "We've had a chance to reconsider, now Carol Dennison's book has the Book of the Week slot."

"It's been confirmed?" I asked. "That's great." I noticed he didn't mention *Woman's Hour*, and I couldn't say I blamed him.

He nodded, still not looking up. "So if Carol is available for the sales conference . . ."

Leaping up and down and shouting *Yee-ha!* might be misconstrued. I replaced it instead with a carefully neutral, "I'm sure she will be when I tell her how important it is. But I'll confirm as soon as I've had the chance to speak to her." Normally, I would share my happiness at the news, but in this case it would sound like gloating. And, while it totally was gloating, I had to work with Bruce in the future. So I carried on as though it were a minor detail, not a major concession. "Thanks, Bruce, that's great," I said, before changing the subject. "By the way, did you hear that *The Maypole* was shortlisted for the *LA Times* fiction prize yesterday? I'll email everyone when the official confirmation arrives, but it might help you here, since it's her first UK publication." *Really, Carol is just one author out of many, nothing to see here, move along now,* was the idea I was pushing.

Bruce finally looked up and smiled. It wasn't a great smile, but he made a valiant attempt. It said that he knew I'd won and he'd lost, and he appreciated that I wasn't going to make a big deal out of it. We were OK again, so I smiled too, and headed back to my desk, making a mental note to warn Miranda not to wear her Middle-Aged Woman T-shirt where the sales department might see her.

By the time I got home that night, I felt, for the first time in ages, that I'd actually done a full day's work. There had been a launch party that evening for a novel published by my colleague Ben. The author was a fairly successful literary novelist, if "successful literary novelist" wasn't a contradiction in terms, which it was. She made a living writing adaptations for television, so could afford to take the tiny advances we paid for her books. As long as they were well reviewed, they sold enough to wash their faces, as the publishing expression went, and we lived in hope that one day one of them would itself be adapted for television. Then we might do more than just break even on them.

In the meantime, because of the television adaptations, she attracted enough press that it made it worth having a launch party. I went so I could talk up my own authors to the journalists and literary editors there; and to listen to agents, who might have authors they wanted to talk up to me. Publishing parties sound very glamorous, and I'm not saying many people didn't enjoy them. I just wasn't one of them. For me, they were work, and I attended, I spoke to the people I needed to speak to, chatted to a few others who might conceivably one day write a book that I might conceivably one day want to publish. Then I left.

I'd managed to eat my body weight in crisps at the party, so when I got home, I stood at the open fridge door and stared at the weekend's leftovers for a while, as a substitute for actually cooking and eating something healthy. Jake was working late. I closed the fridge door and went upstairs. Officially, I was returning Mr. Rudiger's book on Maurer; unofficially, I was looking for company. I was tired, I was nervy—I hadn't had a repeat of my morning-jumping-at-shadows routine, but I'd felt all day as if I might. I'd also had a glass of wine at the launch: not enough to make me mellow; too much to make settling down to read manuscripts or edit seem enticing. So instead of pretending, when he opened his door, I just said, "I hate this."

Mr. Rudiger pulled the door wider and I went in on his unspoken invitation. "Have you eaten?" he asked.

I shook my head. "If there's a world crisp shortage tomorrow, the International Court at the Hague will have no difficulty in bringing in a guilty verdict against me."

"I'll get us something to drink," he decided, and before I could say I didn't want a drink, he was gone, to return with two glass mugs. "Tea with fruit preserve," he said. "It makes everything seem better."

I took a sip, the same dubious look on my face Mr. Rudiger wears when I make him drink iced coffee in the summer. It was surprisingly good, but "Hmm," I said, not prepared to let go of all my prejudices at once.

He gave a small smile, and sat. "What do you hate?"

I put my mug down and drew up my mental list. "I hate that I watched someone dead onstage. And that I laughed. I hate that Bim saw it, even if he doesn't know what he saw, and that he knows Sylvie Sander died too. I hate that we don't know why. I hate that Frankie works in a world where she had to pretend to live with a man old enough to be her grandfather to seem young." I shrugged ungraciously. "That's all I can think of at the moment, but if you hang on, I'm sure I can come up with more."

Mr. Rudiger, who often looked amused, but rarely smiled, was grinning broadly. "That's enough to begin with."

"I'm just bad-tempered. I don't know why I'm taking it out on you." I felt sheepish. "That wasn't actually why I came up." I put the book I'd brought down on his coffee table. "I meant to return this earlier, but it's so small I keep forgetting I have it in my bag."

"Was it any use?"

I hadn't had the opportunity to fill him in on my abortive trip to the Theatre Museum. "Not really," I admitted, "unless no news is good news." I told him what we'd found, or, rather, what we'd failed to find.

"Who were the people who had accessed the files previously?" I loved Mr. Rudiger for assuming I'd followed that up. Which I had.

"Three of the people were British academics, and I located their profiles on university websites: two were specialists in Brecht, one in German theatre history, so no surprise there. There was one I couldn't find. 'N. James, Smithfield' could be 'John Smith, London' for all the clues it gives. I assumed it was someone from the theatre at the Barbican, so I looked for any Jameses working there, but couldn't see any. Otherwise, it's a needle in a haystack: Smithfield has hundreds of offices. The fifth person was German. I found him online too. He teaches in Berlin, and he published a paper after he visited at the museum. I ran it through Google Translate, but you know how useless that can be for more than a phrase or two. I can see he was writing about Brecht, and he mentioned Maurer, but I don't know more than that." I looked up. "You speak German, don't you?"

Mr. Rudiger lifted his laptop off the side table next to him and passed it to me before sketching a small salute. "Present and reporting for duty, ma'am."

I found the paper online again, and Mr. Rudiger put on his reading glasses and stared down at the screen. I sat quietly while he read, drinking my jammy tea—which was becoming more comforting with each sip—and thinking about nothing at all. When he sat back and took off his spectacles, I jumped: I'd been miles away.

"It's an article on the continuing influence of Brecht at the Berliner Ensemble," he said. "He uses three productions of *Medea*—one under Brecht himself, the one that Maurer designed just before his death, and one that was staged ten years ago—to develop his argument."

"Nothing about Sylvie Sander then, or her work with Maurer?" I hadn't seen her name, but when Mr. Rudiger shook his head, I was disappointed all the same.

"Nothing. It's about how Brecht's vision of theatre was continued when his wife was the director. The *Medea* that Maurer did was just after her death, so very little had been altered, he thinks—for example, that production used very obvious plastic dolls instead of real children, so when Medea killed them it produced laughter, not horror, to create Brecht's alienation effect."

Just as we'd laughed at Davison's body. But that hadn't been a theatrical device. I shut down that thought, and rubbed my eyes. "I'm sure it's fascinating."

"It is. But, I admit, not very helpful. No footnote saying, 'Richard Maurer's sketchbooks show . . .'"

I heard the front door to the house open and close downstairs, and looked at my watch. It was later than I'd thought. "Jake's home," I said, as though without my profound knowledge of front-door noises, Mr. Rudiger would be confused as to what we'd just heard.

He was polite enough not to respond.

"I should go," I said, but didn't move.

Neither did he, so I went on sitting. After a few minutes, the front door to our flat closed, and we heard footsteps on the stairs. "Jake," I said, again translating for Mr. Rudiger. When Jake knocked, I managed to hold back from telling him that that's what it was, and instead I simply held up my mug when Jake appeared. "Tea with fruit preserve," I explained. "It makes everything seem better."

Chapter 14

I had felt virtuous when I got home: I'd got in to work by eight, and accomplished a lot all day. But I should have known, there's always someone to one-up you. When I plugged my phone into the charger before going to bed, I saw a text from Helena: *Meeting Nigel for breakfast. 7, at St. Paul's café.*

There were so many questions raised by those nine words that I wasn't sure where to begin. Was this the announcement of pending news, or an invitation? Or was Helena telling me *I* was meeting Nigel for breakfast? And if I was, where? The only St. Paul's I knew of was St. Paul's Cathedral. Could that be where Helena meant? If it was somewhere less known, wouldn't she have said? And, while it shouldn't have taken precedence, the question that was uppermost in my mind was, when did people start putting cafés in cathedrals? And, more importantly, why would anyone do that? I shook my head. Only the Church of England would think a nice cup of tea was the appropriate accompaniment to cleansing one's soul of sin.

The next morning, thoughts of tea and religious doctrine were swept aside when the alarm went off at five. Now my question was, when did breakfast meetings become a thing? And, again, more urgently, why would anyone do that? In New York, sure—we all loved to picture go-getting Noo Yawkahs, commuting to Grand Central from Lawn Guy-Land before dawn, their fourth shot of caffeine in hand, having already run a half-marathon, read the papers, and bought a bagel. But in genteel London, where a sign of seniority in many companies was not showing your face in the office before ten? Seven? Really?

I staggered to the bathroom as Jake turned over, mumbling something only semi-coherent about "your mother" and needing to be committed. Probably not untrue, and not news, either, but also not helpful. I set myself onto autopilot, refusing to think or feel until I got to the tube.

The joys of travelling before the rush hour, however, were enormous, and couldn't help but make me feel, if not better, at least a little awake. The tube wasn't empty— there were plenty of stony-eyed people heading back from night jobs, and more stony-eyed people heading off to jobs in the City, where they'd put in twelve-hour days so that they could turn around and do it all over again the next day. But the quiet of the walk to the tube, the half-light of the cars sliding by, the damp streets glinting in their headlights, put a softer context onto the day, made it seem safe, cocooned.

Soon, however, my thoughts by necessity moved on to wondering where cathedrals located their cafés. By the baptismal font? In the nave? Did they pass the espresso along the pews? At six fifty, however, the great front doors to the church were firmly shut. I walked around the side of the building. And there, to the rear, in a pedestrian alley, was a small sign: CRYPT RESTAURANT. But that door was firmly shut too, a sign beside it saying the place didn't open until ten thirty. The combination of croissants and crosses still flummoxed me, but at least their opening hours met my preconceptions. Still, that didn't help me locate Helena. I was getting my phone out to text when I heard the tappety-tap of heels along the alley. I didn't even have to look up to feel the mothership approach. Helena is small but fierce, moving down the alley like one of Santa's elves on a tear because a toy invoice had been misfiled. That tappety-tap was known to have produced frissons of fear even in the hearts of Supreme Court judges who had otherwise never surfaced from decades'-long immersion in ponds of warm self-satisfaction.

"I thought you might be here," she said, as if I weren't exactly where she'd told me to be.

She didn't pause, continuing her tappety-tapping past me, and I realized I wasn't, in fact, where I was supposed to be, because at the end of the alley was a small, dingy, old-school café—the kind that in Britain used to be pronounced "caff"—with "St. Paul's" lettered on its window. Or, actually, "St. aul's," since the painted "P" had worn away, probably around the time St. Paul himself had been wandering through the desert telling people that women should be silent. Helena would not have been a big fan of St. aul.

Or his café, I decided on entering. There were four minute Formica-topped tables to the right. On the left, a heavy-set, gloomy man out of central casting stood behind an old-fashioned stainless-steel counter, next to a hissing coffee urn—no newfangled espresso machines here. To be totally authentic, he ought to have had a half-smoked rollup behind one ear, but times change. He stared at us, but didn't speak, didn't even blink as we both asked for coffee. I looked at the buns, but as they appeared to have been baked in the days of St. aul too, it was easy to pass. After our cups were pushed across the counter, both achieving small lagoons spilled in the saucers as though that were a house speciality, we joined the caff's sole customer, who had been sitting, back to the door, with a cup of tea in front of him. Its contents were also out of central casting: mahogany coloured, and therefore, as the saying went, brewed strong enough for a mouse to trot across. Behind the cup, Nigel did that half-crouch thing polite men do—*I'm standing because you're female, but I'm not getting all the way up, because then I'd look like an extra in a David Niven film.*

"Helena," he said. "You find the most interesting places to meet."

She gave him her small cat smile.

"And Sam," he continued. "Helena said you might join us."

I didn't bother to tell him I hadn't been offered the option, just made polite noises for the half-second it took Helena to take off her coat. Then she called us to order. "Nigel has been looking into Liz Henderson's old case," she explained to me, followed by a gesture to give him the floor.

He pulled out a folder. "Helena has told me of your interest in Ms. Henderson," he said, "and as the case is long closed, and this is part of the public record, I can't see any reason not to fill you in." He opened the file and stared at the top page for a moment, as though he were reminding himself of the essential points. I wasn't going to be fooled by his act a second time: he had everything neatly arranged in his head. "Ms. Henderson's mother died, as I said, over twenty-five years ago, before German reunification, in the then Eastern Bloc. Her will left everything to her two surviving children, one of whom, Helga Dichter, lived in Potsdam. The other, Ms. Henderson, was at that stage unable to claim—indeed, she was not aware of her mother's death for some time."

Nigel paused courteously, in case I wanted to comment. When I didn't, he nodded once, sharply, as if I'd done something intelligent. Maybe I should try the silence thing more often.

He continued: "Ms. Henderson's claim was that her sister, in overseeing and disposing of the assets that made up her mother's estate, had failed to make an equitable division. There was, therefore, a deposition itemizing the estate, and I have that document here." He laid down a thick sheaf of papers held together with a bulldog clip, but while he pushed it in my direction, he kept his hand flat on top of it. "This information is, of course, confidential, and not to be seen by parties unconnected with the suit. I'm sure you understand."

I slid my eyes to Helena, who was quietly drinking her truly execrable coffee and reading email on her phone. She neither looked up nor spoke, although I knew she was taking in every word. I looked back to Nigel. "Of course," I replied politely.

He nodded once, briskly, as though to say to an invisible watcher, *I've made my point.* Then he made a great show of pulling out his phone. "Drat," he said, in the tone a toddler might have used to say "Lo, a star!" in an infant-school nativity play. "I must answer this. It will probably take five minutes or so, and when I return I'll explain some more about why I can't tell you anything further."

He didn't wait for me to speak—or, for that matter, for his phone to ring, which it hadn't—but headed outside, where he stood in the doorway and casually joined Helena in the reading-email school of activities. I pulled the papers toward me.

Helena dropped her own email pretence and inched her chair near mine, so we could read the papers together. As I knew she would, she took over. "You'll want the appendix," she said. "That's where any itemized lists will be." She flicked through the papers at lightning speed. "Here. This is the original, provided by the German lawyers; there'll be a translation behind, but photograph both." I was just following orders at this stage. I pulled out my phone and photographed the German list, and then the pages of translation.

Nigel was still outside, unmoving, so I pulled the clamp off the pages. I pushed the main pile over to Helena. "You'll know what's important here," I said.

She started reading and I returned to the lists and the back, and copied her, running through them as swiftly as I could.

Five minutes later, Nigel returned, stopping at the counter to order another mouse-trot tea, giving us time to reorder the papers and put them back in front of his empty place. Then, after a two-minute back-and-forth with Helena about one of her clients his chambers was acting for, he looked at his watch, and with an equally dramatically inept "Is that the time?" he left.

"Lucky he's not a barrister, with those acting abilities," I said.

"He's too clever to be a barrister," Helena replied.

"Barristers aren't clever?" That was news.

"Good barristers are shrewd, and very good barristers are excellent at engaging with large quantities of information for a brief period of time, during which they roll it out in digestible chunks on demand. But clever? No." She was quite sure of that. But then, she was a solicitor.

I decided that this thrilling insight into the rivalries

of the legal world was not my business. I picked up my phone and pulled up the photos of the file. "Did you see anything in the papers that was helpful?"

She shook her head. "As Nigel said, a very silly case, one that only a silly woman would have brought."

I hadn't heard Nigel say anything like that, but then, I didn't speak legalese.

I pinched at my screen, zooming in on the translated lists. They didn't say any more that they had when I'd skim-read them five minutes earlier. A house and its contents made up the bulk of the estate, with various other assets, from a car to jewellery. There were a few pieces of art too, but all were of named artists, none were by Maurer, nor was there any mention of sketchbooks, or drawings, or designs.

"I don't understand," I said, almost to myself. "She was there. People saw her in the audience. Then afterwards, backstage, she lied about where she was, saying she was with Jenny for most of that time, a lie easily disproved by Jenny. She brought her barrister from this case to the theatre, presumably to further some legal end, since it was plain her husband doesn't like him, so they weren't just out for a fun evening."

I pushed my chair back. "Lots of questions, no answers. But this"—I waved my phone—"this seems like a dead end."

Helena nodded. "It does. Good to have that ticked off our list." Sometimes Helena's relentless can-do-ery could grate. Then I mentally rolled my eyes. Sometimes? Always.

"What next?"

Helena thought for a moment before she responded. "Did Jake confirm whether Cyril was at both opening nights?"

"No. Or, if he did, he didn't tell me."

Now she was brisk. "Find out. And find out if he's been on to the German probate court to inquire about Maurer's will. If he hasn't, he should."

Apparently it was my job to direct the CID's next moves. I stared up at the café's yellowed ceiling. "God," I begged quietly, "dear, kind god, is it too late to put me in a time machine, and send me back so that I can be stolen out of my playpen to be raised in the forest by wolves? Is it too late for that, god?"

Helena was unruffled. "That wouldn't help, darling. Wolves have pack leaders too."

By mid-afternoon, sitting at the back of the office's biggest meeting room, I was thinking longingly of St. aul's and its horrible coffee, and even more longingly of a life spent living in a wolf pack. Days in the forest would involve nothing more than hunting and scratching for fleas. Both sounded much better than my afternoon. Bruce had taken it into his head that, not only did we need to spend two full days at his wretched sales conference, but before that, we would spend an afternoon rehearsing. Lord alone knew why. The editors who were good at presenting presented well at the rehearsal. The editors who were crap at presenting presented badly, and however much coaching Bruce and his merry men gave them, they were going to continue to present badly, because they were editors, not presenters, and it wasn't in their skill set. I liked to think I was somewhere in the middle, neither crap, nor good, and anyway, now I was only presenting my fashion-gossip book, the afternoon was a total waste of time and energy.

The sales department people present were all channelling enthusiasm as though the government had announced National Good Cheer Day, with a lowered tax band for those who exhibited the most bonhomie. The editorial and marketing department attendees, however, had missed that memo, because to a man and woman, we were exhibiting Boring Meeting Behaviour, with no attempt at hiding it: we were on our phones and tablets, heads down, hands moving vigorously in our laps. In truth, it looked as if we were all playing with ourselves.

Bruce broke into our attempts to get on with our own work. "Right," he said. He clapped his hands like a geography teacher about to explain what made igneous rock different from sedimentary or metamorphic. "Let's talk venue."

A few of us looked up, with carefully blank faces. I, certainly, had no idea what facial expression was best worn when "talking venue."

"As you know, we'll be at Spritz! in Camden."

We did know, because he'd told us about seventeen times. Each time with the exclamation mark carefully mentioned. Bruce seemed to feel that holding a sales conference in a club where Madonna had played twenty years before gave us some sort of glamour by association.

After a pause, we realized that he was expecting more than silence, and the odd nod of acknowledgement. Sandra did her best. "It'll be like the year the conference was at Madame JoJo's," she offered. Then she paused, doubt on her face. "Or was that a hen night?"

I snickered, which drew Bruce's attention from Sandra's inability to differentiate his sales conferences from drunken evenings watching drag queens. "Something we need to know about, Sam?"

He *was* a geography teacher. Any second now he was going to demand I name the major rivers of Europe for the rest of the class. "Not a thing," I assured him with truly radiant insincerity.

Chapter 15

The sales conference was a two-day extravaganza, divided up by type of book, so that the appropriate buyers could be shuffled in and out to hear about the books that concerned them and, equally, the appropriate editors only had to appear when needed. Commercial nonfiction—sports, cookery, and film and television tie-ins—was scheduled for the afternoon; my area, commercial fiction, was set for the morning. Spritz! (with exclamation mark) was not far from where I lived, but in the nightclubby, trendy end of Camden.

The streets were somewhat less trendy by day. The bars and clubs were shuttered, giving prominence instead to the mobile-phone shops and kebab takeaways between them. And, once past the front doors, Spritz! was not only not trendy in the daylight, it wasn't even attractive. When the smoking ban in commercial premises was first enforced in England, it quickly became revoltingly obvious that the smell of cigarettes had masked all sorts of other nasty smells—spilled beer, stale cooking oil from the kitchens, bleach and chemical cleansers from the loos. In a similar fashion, at Spritz! funky lighting at night masked a multitude of nasty sights—stained carpets; smeared, dirty furniture and fittings. There was probably worse, but I worked hard at not looking.

Whatever hip-ness Bruce had been aiming for with his venue choice would have, in any case, have been eliminated right away by the rickety wooden table in the foyer, the one without which no conference is complete, where two interns sat ticking off names and handing out little plastic badges. It is impossible to be hip while wearing a plastic badge. Really. There are scientific studies.

Nonetheless, like a good employee I pinned on my badge. Carol wasn't due to arrive for another hour, so I joined my badged-up colleagues standing around another rickety table, this one holding coffee. I didn't need more caffeine, but then, need had never been a factor in my decision-making processes.

I picked up a sheet with the running order for the day. I sometimes wondered if Bruce had been a spy in a previous existence, because he fiercely guarded all information, no matter how innocuous, circulating memos on a purely need-to-know basis. Maybe he worried that if we knew who was going to present which craft book at what time, we'd rush out and sell the information to the Russians. My eye snagged on an entry for *The Great Fire of London Colouring Book*. The craze for adult colouring books was paying my salary that year, but really, what next? Maybe we could do battlefields? *World War I: Colour in Trench Foot, Mud, Rats, and Lice*, or *Crimea: The Valley of Death*, with the massacred five hundred carefully outlined and ready for the creative colourist.

It was probably fortunate that Bruce began to herd everyone inside to the dance floor, where the presentations were being made, before my imagination took me further. The first group of presenters stood at the back of the stage—the stage where Madonna had performed, Bruce reminded us for the ninety-seventh time—while the sales reps, the booksellers, and the chain-buyers all sat uncomfortably close together at small club tables. The setup probably worked better when lubricated by alcohol, not coffee, and accompanied by Madonna, not muffins.

First up was Ben, whose list ran to literary fiction. Ben and I had spent most of our time as colleagues barely tolerating each other. Recently, however, we'd come to a relative détente in order to present a united front against an infestation of management consultants. (What was the collective of management consultants? A scourge of management consultants? A slurry?) Then Miranda, in her first foray into editing, had discovered that a book Ben had acquired under the impression it was a memoir of a gang member was, in fact, entirely fabricated. She and I had managed to work with Ben, in somewhat grumpy harmony, to get the author first, to confess, then to rewrite the book as the fiction it had been all along. Ben was now onstage to present this newly created novel as though no one—neither author nor editor—had ever imagined the material was anything else. I watched admiringly: he was really good at it, and the buyers were industriously making notes. Then it was my four minutes, and, if I do say so myself, I sold the hell out of my fashion-gossip book. It wasn't difficult: a handful of anecdotes from the manuscript conveyed its sheer outrageous pleasure, helped along by a brilliant jacket from the design department projected on the screen behind me. Again, the buyers wrote busily, and I jumped down from the stage, confident it would get good book-trade support.

Ben returned with his next book, and I tiptoed out to the foyer to wait for Carol. She and I had spoken several times about her presentation. I'd prepped her on the people she'd be talking to and the kind of information they needed, but I was leaving the content, and style, to her: if I was going to spoon-feed her a text, I might as well have saved myself the weeks of argument and presented the book myself.

She was already there waiting, and we did the London publishing double-cheek kiss (without the accompanying "mwah" sound—that was for the fashion world). I fetched her some coffee, and only just managed to refrain from asking whether she needed to go to the loo before we went back inside: there are large areas of overlap in the duties of an editor and those of a primary-school teacher, and the lines sometimes blurred in my mind.

I suspected Carol knew it, too: there weren't many flies on her. She had been an oncology nurse before her books had begun to earn enough that she could write full-time, and she carried with her an aura of competence, a sense that whatever the situation, she would manage it, and you. I stood at the back as she confidently took the stage as Ben finished. They were an interesting contrast. Ben, young, dark, and handsome, thought people listened to him because he was interesting, whereas in fact they listened because he was young, dark, and handsome, and also because he gave them little opportunity to do anything else, talking over and interrupting people without ever being aware that that was what he was doing. Carol was middle-aged, with a warm, friendly face, and she wore what I privately thought of as Mum clothes: sensible cardigans and dark trousers, and slightly flirty shoes that were her breakout gesture to personalizing her wardrobe. And yet, after only a minute, she had the buyers' interest. They were listening to her not because her demeanour said she was interesting and clever, but because she had persuaded them that *they* were interesting and clever.

I tuned back in as Carol wound up. "*The Alien Corn* is not only about Ruth and her family. It's about all of us. It's about getting older, and being overlooked, not because we're any less interesting than we were a decade earlier, but simply because we're ten years older. In the Bible Ruth tells Naomi, *whither thou goest, I will go; and where thou lodgest, I will lodge: thy people shall be my people.* Today we assume that we choose our friends, while we are given our family. Yet we choose our families too: there are those who we see once a year at weddings, and those with whom we share our most intimate thoughts. Ruth makes choices, and those consequences affect not just her, but her family, both chosen and given."

She raised her hand to make her final point just as one of Bruce's damned interns flashed the lights to signal her four minutes were up. Instead of merely gesturing, therefore, she looked like a Jack Nicholson double in *The Shining*, her shadow flickering ominously across the dance floor. She didn't stumble, though, gracefully finishing her sentence, and presentation. I checked out the buyers from behind. I did that at every sales conference, as though I could guess the orders they'd place from the way they were scratching their elbows, or easing a shoe off a blistered heel. Most had made notes during Carol's talk, but there was no way of telling whether they read: *Fascinating. Must order thousands of copies*, or, *Yawn, avoid*, or even just, *Remember to pick up dry-cleaning!*

Ben's "promotable" author followed her onto the podium, and as I moved to intercept Carol at the door I kept an eye on the buyers. Were they more persuaded by this young woman's good looks than by Carol's good book? By her shiny pretty hair? I liked to think that they had seemed more engaged by Carol, but I was probably deluding myself. It's one of my better-developed talents.

"That was great, thank you," I said quietly as Carol joined me.

"I wasn't sure about ending with that Bible quote. Did it make it sound too worthy?"

I kept my eyes on Miss Literary Novelist and shook

my head. "No, it was good. Although it did make me realize I don't know who Ruth was, what she did, I mean, apart
from her goest-ing wither Naomi goest. Where were they
goest-ing? And for that matter, who was Naomi?"

"Naomi was her mother-in-law, but it doesn't matter:
the phrase is shorthand for loyalty and—Good god"—she
clutched my arm, horrified—"is that what would have
happened to me if I hadn't stopped?"

The lights had flashed for Miss Literary Novelist, and
then, when she continued without pause, flashed and
flashed again in a continuous visual siren warning. She finally came to a stop, mid-word, her mouth open. Either
Ben had failed to tell her that four minutes really meant
four minutes, or she hadn't believed him. It would be unkind of me to think that when she was no longer young and
beautiful her expectation of being heard would get a short,
sharp shock. It would be unkind to think that, so I didn't.
Of course not.

And then I stopped, just the way she had, frozen.
Carol was saying something, and I roused myself for long
enough to thank her again for coming, arrange to be in
touch the following week if we'd received any feedback on
the book or the jacket, and see her out. I looked at my
watch. The presentations would go on for another hour,
and then there was a sandwich lunch meet-and-greet with
the buyers, which I couldn't skip out on.

I stood with my colleagues at the back for the presentations. I went through to the foyer for lunch. I ate sandwiches; I met; I gret. Many of the buyers did genuinely

seem excited by *The Alien Corn*; even more, as I had expected, loved the fashion world exposé. It was, overall, a positive session, but I couldn't give it my full attention.

And then it was over. Miranda was away from her desk when I got back to the office. I left her a note: *Doing spreadsheets. Hold the fort and take messages.* It wasn't a lie, as such. I was doing spreadsheets, just none that related to my job. If people wanted to assume I was doing budgets, they were entirely at liberty to do so. And one day I would definitely do them.

I opened up a blank form and made a timeline of events, from the first night of *The Spanish Tragedy* onwards. Then I opened a second form, filling in the details of Sander, and Maurer, and what we knew about the two of them, and their work. I could see why crime shows made fabulous television: the glamour of typing data into spreadsheets was hard to beat.

I plodded on. I admit it, I'm a neat freak. I don't like it when the forks get put into what I have decided is the spoon section of the cutlery drawer, and I didn't like it when murder got mixed into the friendship section of my life.

But finally I was forced to stop avoiding the issue. I opened a third sheet, and typed at the top, "What if." Because, standing at the back of Spritz!, with Carol filling me in on family loyalty, with Ruth refusing to leave her mother-in-law in the alien corn, I began to wonder if the story we should have been following was not that of Liz Henderson's mother and brother, but of her father. He had made no appearance in the lawsuit, and if I had thought about it, which I hadn't, I would have presumed he was either dead or long-divorced. But realizing I knew the names Ruth and Naomi without ever knowing they were related, and listening to Carol talking about choosing—and not choosing—your family, made me type, "What if Campbell Davison was Liz Henderson's father?"

I stared at that for a good long while. What if? I'd gone through Helena's notes on her for Spreadsheet One, and Davison was old enough, certainly. He had been in Germany at the right time. But if he was her father, how did that change the way we were reading her story? And why was she keeping it a secret? Or, for that matter, *was* it a secret? What happened to the way we were reading this if she knew, but he didn't? Or vice versa?

After a few minutes, almost reluctantly, as though I were doing something that others would disapprove of if the word got out, I went online and found the government's Births, Marriages and Deaths website. I was only briefly sidetracked by the idea of changing my name by deed poll, and then sidetracked again when I discovered the government thought it needed to tell the general populace that they wouldn't need to apply for a new passport if they decided to dye their hair, or grow a moustache. I shook my head at the general imbecility of the world, and then again at my lack of focus, and returned to the birth certificate page.

After a registration process so laborious you'd think I was signing up to rent the Crown Jewels for an evening on the town, I discovered that I wouldn't be able to access the birth certificates online, just order copies. So I did. Then, since the registration had taken nearly a quarter of an hour, and I felt that shouldn't go to waste, I ordered a certified copy of my own birth certificate—you never knew when one might come in handy. And then I did the same for Sylvie Sander. We knew nothing about her background, and if it was a waste of £9.25, it was money that I would otherwise only fritter away on grey cardigans, my office-wardrobe staple. Thinking about the cardigans made me feel the need to rebel, so I ordered Davison's, too.

I probably would have gone on to order Jake's, and Helena's, and the entire editorial department's, if Miranda hadn't tapped softly and put her head around the door.

"Sorry to interrupt," she whispered, as if lowering her voice made it less of an intrusion. "I've got your neighbour Bim's school on the line, and I thought it might be urgent."

I couldn't imagine any emergency that involved both Bim's school and me, but at least I was no longer spending money. I'd probably forgotten to sign something when I picked up Bim. I picked up the phone.

"Mr. Clair, please," came a high-pitched voice.

"This is Sam."

"No," said the voice firmly. "I'm trying to reach Mr. Clair."

I was used to this confusion. "If you want to speak to Sam Clair, you're talking to her. I'm Sam. Samantha."

There was a pause, and a miffed "Oh. Well. I didn't know."

I crossed my eyes at the phone. "Now you do." I was taking out my unease at the questions I had been raising on this person, which was unreasonable. I softened my tone. "How can I help you?"

That cleared the logjam. "Ms. Clair, I'm ringing all the parents. I was hoping you might still be near the school."

Near the school? "I'm at my office," I said. "Why?"

"What a pity. We forgot to give the children permissions letters for their school trip, and as it's on Friday, I'm ringing round instead of emailing. Since you've only just collected Bim, I hoped you might be near enough to turn back and pick his up."

"Collected Bim?"

The voice faltered. "Yes, you signed him out—" A page rustled before the voice continued more firmly, "You signed him out twenty minutes ago."

"I'm afraid I don't know what you're talking about. Who are you, anyway?"

"I'm the school administrator. I told you, the children weren't given permissions le—"

"Yes, I understand about the letters. What I don't understand is why you think I signed Bim out. I'm at work, and I have been all day."

"No," she said, absolutely secure in her piece of paper. "You collected him at four ten. I wasn't at the collection point today, but I have your signature here."

"I—" I began to argue, then saw the futility. "May I have your name, please?" I asked, trying not to sound accusatory.

I must have failed. "We don't give our names out on the phone to just anyone," she said, pulling the old something's-gone-wrong-and-I'm-going-to-make-damn-sure-it's-not-me-who-gets-the-blame card.

My words were pure acid. "I'm not 'just anyone.' I'm Sam Clair, authorized to collect Bim Lewis, and you know this because *you* rang *me*. Whereas you," I added, "apparently *you* are the person who handed Bim over to a total stranger."

She had no answer to that.

I told Administrator Woman, who finally confessed to being named Ida, that she was going to have to ring Kay, but she wasn't listening. She was in a full-blown panic, which took the form of telling me repeatedly how carefully they had devised their systems to ensure that only authorized people collected the children. It took me five minutes before I realized there was an easier way to get her off the line than by trying to interrupt her. So I hung up.

Miranda had heard my raised voice through the wall, and was standing by, in full emergency mode, pen and pad out: "What shall I do? Who do you need me to ring?"

I wasn't sure Ida was in any state to phone Kay, even though that should have been her first move. So I dialled her number. Her phone was switched off. I scrolled to Anthony's number. Voicemail. Kay had said he was away filming, but I didn't know if "away" meant Luton, or Edinburgh: half an hour away, or half a day. My message tried to convey urgency without hysteria: "Please ring me the minute you get this. It's important."

Then I asked Miranda, "Will you find me a number for the Duchess Theatre? There must be a listing for the offices, or the stage door, or something." Thursday was matinee day. The play ran about three and a half hours. I looked at my watch. Kay would be there for at least another hour.

I tried to think. When Kay and Anthony were both working, Bim was collected by a child-minder. I'd seen her coming and going at the house, but all I knew was that her first name was Lisa. If anyone had ever mentioned her last name, it hadn't registered. And anyway, Kay had said she was away: it was the reason I'd been dragooned into that first rehearsal. Who else was there? Anthony had introduced us to Kay's parents on opening night, but they didn't live in London. And their last name was Cummings. I had no idea how to locate a couple named Cummings who might live anywhere in England. Or possibly Scotland. Or Wales.

I tried to slow myself down. Maybe I was overreacting. I rang Mr. Rudiger. At least I didn't have to worry about him being out. I didn't say hello, just, "Do you know if Bim is home from school?"

There was a pause. "No," he said slowly. "I'm the only person in the house right now."

If he said no one was there, no one was there. Mr. Rudiger always pretended he didn't keep track of all of us, but he did, and I was grateful for it.

I explained what had happened. "There may be some simple explanation . . ." I trailed away, hoping he would fill in with what that simple explanation might be.

He didn't.

"Will you ring me if Bim—if anyone—comes home?"

I disconnected as Miranda reappeared with a slip of paper. "The stage door number."

I tried to look as if I wasn't as frantic as Ida as I snatched it out of her hand. The phone was picked up on the first ring.

"I need to speak to Kay Lewis, and she isn't answering her phone. There's an emergency at home."

The voice at the other end was firm. "She's onstage."

I thought about the play I'd now seen twice. Until she was messily killed, Kay spent most of the second half on-stage sitting behind Frankie, as her lady-in-waiting, or maid, or whatever she was called, essentially being wallpaper. Maybe they could signal to her from the wings and she could slide off. "May I speak to Jenny—" I blanked her last name too. When I wasn't having a nervous breakdown, I'd find time to berate myself for how little attention I paid to other people. But not now. "Jenny," I repeated more firmly. "The stage manager."

No dice. "The show comes down at five forty-seven. No interruptions during a performance."

"It really is an emergency."

"Give me a message. I'll pass it on."

I took a deep breath. "Will you tell Kay to ring Sam as soon as possible? We're not sure—" I had no idea how to say this gently. "Her child has gone missing. He's only six."

That got me somewhere. "I'll pass the message to Jenny right away, and she'll see that Kay is notified."

I gave him all my contact information, in case it was Jenny who responded, not Kay. I called Anthony again. Still nothing.

I tried Jake, but got a recording saying his phone was switched off. His phone was never switched off, so he had to be out of cell reception. I texted: *CALL ME! Bim's school rang, he was signed out under my name, but I was at work. Don't know where he is, can't reach K or A.*

I opened a new box and texted Ida: *News?*

She replied seconds later: *No.*

There was no choice. *You need to report this to the police.*

I got back: *I have.*

Then I rang Helena. Not because I thought she'd have Bim stashed in a filing cabinet under "B," but because she would know what to do. But I wasn't even going to have the comfort of knowing she was on the case. Adenike, her assistant, picked up her phone: Helena was in court. Helena is a solicitor, not a barrister, but she does sometimes make court appearances. My luck, today was the day.

"When she's back—" I began.

Adenike was chipper. "She's not coming back," she said, before going on chattily: "She was planning to have a drink with Connie, and then they'll go to Gray's Inn together."

The sodding party. I'd forgotten all about it. I took a deep breath. "I'll text her, but in case she misses it or you speak to her first, will you ask her to ring me as soon as she can?"

I explained about Bim, and Adenike, only a few months back from maternity leave herself, promised to use her court contacts to try and get a message through before the court rose. Adenike had worked with Helena for years, and despite being still in her twenties, was almost as formidable. If she said she'd do something, I had no doubt it would get done.

But I couldn't sit there and wait. I grabbed my bag. "I'm gone for the day," I called to Miranda as I ran down the corridor: moving fast gave me the illusion that I was doing something useful. "Call me if there's news."

I might not be responsible for losing Bim, but I could be at the theatre when Kay found out.

Chapter 16

My office, tucked away in a street behind the British Museum, was only ten minutes' walk from the theatre—less if I ran, dodging tourists walking blind as they held guidebooks up in front of their faces, office workers also walking blind, but with their heads down, checking their phones, and deliverymen *also* walking blind behind huge boxes of goods carried in and out of shops. As I ducked and wove, I dedicated a tiny smidgen of energy to wonder if anyone looked at other people, or their surroundings, anymore.

It was only because I was looking for side streets to turn off, where there might be fewer pedestrians, that I realized I was passing the side street where Davison's production company had its office and rehearsal space, the place where I'd been with Kay and Bim.

I hesitated, stopping dead on the pavement, and, uncaring, became the kind of obstruction I'd just been curs-

ing. The theatre was only a few minutes away. But then
I'd have to talk myself past the stage doorman, and this
time I had no Jake, and no warrant card. Maybe there
would be someone at Davison's office who could help. It
would only take five minutes.

I rang the buzzer, and then, impatient, again. Nothing. I might not be able to remember people's names, but
Bim's singsong rendition of the code was stuck in my head.
I keyed it in. The rehearsal room took up the entire top
floor, so the offices were probably somewhere below. There
was no directory on the wall; I took the stairs.

The first floor said RED ARROW ADVERTISING on the
door, but the entire floor was dark, and the space was
empty: no furniture, nothing. Red Arrow was apparently
not in business. The next level had a sign for a television
production company. Here too it was dark, and they were
even more obviously not in business: there were no walls,
and the light from the windows revealed—nothing. No
furniture, no office equipment. Whatever company had
rented the space, they were long gone, or possibly yet to
arrive. I went up another flight.

The third floor was more promising. There was no
name on the door, which might be right for Davison's temporary stay. The door made a ghostly squeaking noise as
it opened, and another as it swung closed behind me. No
one called out, and there were no lights, but at least this
time there were walls, and furniture. I set off down the
corridor. Several of the rooms were set up to be used as

offices. All but one had a docking station on the desk, but none had computers—whoever worked here brought their laptops with them, which also suggested a temporary office. I was a floor below the rehearsal studio, so I might be on the right track.

I continued down the hall. More of the same. The first room had what looked like some sort of technical drawings hanging on the walls, and a drawing board with printouts of ground plans. There was nothing else in the room, apart from a stool and an Anglepoise lamp. The next room was empty. The third room had a desk and chairs, and also filing cabinets, all labelled. I drew nearer. "Contracts," "Personnel" and "Duchess Theatre." Bingo. I was in Davison's offices, all right. But I was no closer to finding someone to talk me through the theatre's doors. A quick check of the files might give me Jenny's mobile number, though. I tugged at a handle. Locked.

I moved on. The final room was different. It had an oriental rug on the floor, and prints and posters on the wall. It also had no computer dock. Instead, the desk held an old-fashioned blotter, a marble ashtray, and a leather desk diary open beside it. It looked like an office in a 1950s movie.

From the far side, I pulled over a file sitting open on the blotter. "Dear Campbell . . ." I was in Davison's office. I rounded the desk to see if he kept his drawers locked too.

And tripped. I looked down.

Bim. Half in, half out of the kneehole under the desk.
And not moving.

I dropped to my knees beside him. "Bim," I called. "Bim,
sweetie, open your eyes."

No response. From this close, I could hear he was
breathing heavily, as though he had asthma. I tapped at
his cheek. "Bim. Sweetie. Wake up." Nothing. The rhythm
of his breathing didn't even change.

He was wearing a coat, and a pair of rain boots, with
a scarf around his neck: he was dressed exactly as he must
have been when he left school. I ran my hands over him to
ensure he wasn't injured. The only injury was mine, when
I caught my hand on the top of the junior screwdriver in
his tool belt, still perma-fixed to his waist. With no physi-
cal injury visible, he had to have been drugged.

If I were Sam Spade, or, for that matter, Carol Dennison, I'd be able to tell from his pulse if he was all right,
but I wasn't sure I knew how to find a pulse, much less
know what it was supposed to feel like. And I'd check his
pupils too, but that would leave me in the same cloud of
unknowing. I made a mental note to sign up for a first-aid
course.

In the meantime, I reached for my phone: 999 first, for
an ambulance, then the theatre, and then Ida, in that order. Since I didn't know the building's address, I hit "call,"
and then moved back to Bim. He didn't stir when I lifted
him: no noise, no movement, no change to the heavy gasp-
ing breaths. Nor did he do what children normally do

when they're carried, even asleep: wrap his legs or arms around his mode of transportation. I grappled him onto my hip and his head lolled back. I gave him a little bounce to push him against my shoulder, and nearly dropped the phone. At six, he was big for his age, and I'd stopped picking him up a couple of years before.

He was far too heavy for me to carry him down three flights of stairs, even if it meant other people in the building might see me. I was connected to 999, which gave me a sense of confidence. By the time I'd manoeuvred him into the lift, out of the lift, propped him up against the wall by one knee while I wrestled with the locked front door, I'd explained the situation, and the dispatcher had promised an ambulance was on its way to the nearest cross street. And it was. I could hear it even as I came out of the building, and almost immediately Bim was lifted out of my arms, and someone was checking his pulse and his pupils (See? I knew that was what I should be doing) and an oxygen mask was put over his mouth and nose and he was moved to the stretcher.

"Mum," said the driver, as I stood there, suddenly at a loss, not sure what I should be doing.

He assumed I didn't respond because I was terrified for my baby, not because I wasn't Bim's mother. He shook my arm gently. "Come on, Mum, get in, stay with your little boy."

Now wasn't the time to explain my relationship, and possibly get left behind. I got in.

"Where are we going?" I asked. "Which hospital?"

I was dialling even before the doors were closed. Kay's phone was answered by a man's voice, but I could hear her in the background. And, as the ambulance driver had assumed for me, she was terrified for her baby, crying as if the end of the world had come, and she was the only person left behind.

I didn't bother to ask whom I was speaking to. "Tell her it's OK," I said urgently. "Tell her I've got him. He's going to be—" I raised an eyebrow at the paramedic beside the stretcher, who was looking relaxed, and sitting by, just watching. He nodded, so I continued: "He's going to be fine. Tell her," I repeated.

He turned away from the phone, and there was only a sentence before Kay was on the other end, crying and shouting and entirely incomprehensible. So I just kept repeating: "It's OK, Kay. I've got him. He's going to be fine."

She finally took a breath, and I went on. "It's me, Sam. I've got him. He was in the rehearsal studio offices. He's unconscious, but he's with the paramedics and they don't seem worried." The paramedic nodded affirmation again. "Really, he's OK. We're in an ambulance, and they haven't even got the siren on." I looked out the back window. "We'll be at the hospital any moment. They're taking us to St. Thomas's. Get in a cab, and I'll text you when I know where they take Bim."

I hung up and texted Jake. *Have Bim. He was unconscious in theatre offices. On the way to St. Thomas's.* And then I texted the gist to Ida too. As I did, Bim moved, his hand coming up to the oxygen mask. "Mama?" he asked drowsily.

"Not Mama," I said, stroking his hair away from his face. "It's Sam. Mama's coming."

He nodded and curled into a tight ball, my hand in his.

By six o'clock, I was sitting in a very crowded hospital room, entirely surrounded by police. Bim had woken more fully as he was being admitted, and he would be kept overnight for observation, despite being clearheaded enough half an hour later to announce with absolute firmness that he had never eaten applesauce, he never would eat applesauce, and he certainly had no plans to eat the applesauce that—he pushed fretfully at the tray—was being presented to him now. But when the police asked him who had collected him from school, he'd pressed himself back against the headboard, his hands out as if to ward off an attack. And then he started to scream. And scream.

Everyone froze except a wild-eyed Kay. She leapt up, a whirling dervish of motherhood, ready to beat back the world.

"That's it," she said definitively. "Everybody out." When one of the police began to speak she dared him with a single look. "If you aren't happy with that, you can go and get a court order. And," she wound up, "if there is a court in the country that will authorize you to question my child"—she repeated "my child," banging her breast— "if there is a court in the country that will give that authorization, before he is ready, then you'll have to go through me, because you *damned well aren't going around me.*"

Kay did her drama school proud. She was a power-house standing there, still in her stage makeup that she'd half cried off, her hair covered in one of those flesh-coloured bands that wigs get attached to, and dressed in her normal street clothes, which that day meant a lavender dirndl embroidered with pink sunflowers, and a pink glitter belt.

Anthony, who had arrived only minutes after her, stood behind her, dark and glowering. The police, very sensibly, made pacifying noises and said they'd talk to her again in the morning.

Which left them free to focus on me. They shepherded me out into the corridor. Jake had arrived with Kay, and I ignored the police and turned to him. "How did you get here so fast?"

He sighed and kissed the top of my head. "I was interviewing a witness when you phoned to say Bim had gone missing. By the time I finished, you weren't answering your phone. I didn't know where he went to school, and Kay's phone was off, so—"

I pulled out my phone. Yes, six missed calls. Jake went on: "Unlike you, though, I could pull rank on the theatre people. I headed over there and I was liaising with the Child Protection Officer the police had sent to the school, when your text came in."

The adrenaline I'd been running on since Miranda knocked on my office door had now drained away, and what I really wanted to do was curl up on the extremely uncomfortable waiting-room chair and have a nap. But that wasn't going to fly. Instead, "What do you need from me?" I asked.

"Just go through what happened."

So I did, from Ida's phone call, through deciding to go to the theatre, seeing the turn-off to the offices and then finding Bim. I finished with my own questions. "Do they know who took Bim? A description?"

The uniformed officer began to sing the we-have-no-information-at-this-point-in-time song, but Jake must have decided he didn't care what his colleagues thought. He spoke over them. "No one at the collection point remembered who picked Bim up. 'She must have been ordinary,' they said, 'or we would have noticed.'"

"Or him." I'd thought of that earlier, after I'd spoken to Ida.

Jake looked interested. "What makes you think it was a man?"

"Nothing. I mean, I don't, necessarily. All I'm saying is, if you're going to sign your name as 'Sam Clair' you can be either. You might be looking for a man."

"Another reason we need to speak to Bim."

Since that wasn't going to happen until tomorrow at the earliest, I asked, "Were there CCTV cameras anywhere near the school?"

Jake nodded. "The film for the surrounding streets is being gathered now."

I tried to work the timeline out in my head. "Could it have been Liz Henderson?"

Jake ignored the increasingly restive movements of his colleagues, who clearly weren't used to information being shared. He looked even more interested. "Why Liz Henderson?"

I wasn't going to share my wild idea about her father in front of the others. Particularly since Bim's abduction made it seem ever-less likely to have any foundation in reality. Instead, "Why anyone? Why Davison, why Sylvie? Why a six-year-old? None of it makes any sense."

Jake rubbed his eyes. "Welcome to the wonderful world of the CID."

Jake's colleagues, and the uniformed officers, left. The Child Protection Officer told me he'd be in touch, although why I couldn't fathom. I was too tired to ask, though, and just nodded as though I regularly spent my days and most of my nights speaking to Child Protection Services. Whatever.

Bim and I had arrived at the hospital through the ambulance bay, which was basically every woman's worst nightmare of an empty car park at night, with fluorescent lights casting creepy shadows, making every passer-by look like a suspicious character loitering. The main entrance, however, where Jake and I now stood, was even more disorienting. Apart from an information desk, it looked like a small-town shopping centre. I could see the reason for the two chain-store cafés, and the newsstand; even the flower and gift shop made sense. But in what universe did a hospital have need of—I counted—three

clothing stores? And why a chemist? Surely patients' pre-
scriptions were filled by a pharmacy department, and it
was hard to see why after admission for cardiac arrest
you'd feel the sudden urge for sunblock, or travel-size nail
polish.

And yet, that was where Jake was nudging me now.
He picked up a basket and began dropping items in: small
shampoos, deodorant, shower gel. I stared, puzzled. I
mean, I'm all for miniature anything. In hotels, I pretend
I'm Gulliver in Lilliput when I unwrap the fiddly little
soaps. Or, if I'm feeling less literary, the giant from Jack
and the Beanstalk.

Jake broke me out of my reverie. "I'll do this. You go
do clothes."

"Clothes." I wasn't going to admit I had no idea what
he was talking about.

He knew. "For Kay and Anthony. They'll be sleeping
here tonight with Bim. We can either trek all the way
home and pick up their own things, or—" He waggled the
basket at me.

"Good thinking, Batman," I mumbled, and headed off
to buy his 'n' hers underwear, ridiculously annoyed at Jake
for being so thoughtful. Still, I consoled myself, I bet he'd
never thought of waving the mini bottles around in a hotel
shower, singing, "Fi-fi-fo-fum, I smell the shampoo of an
Englishman."

Chapter 17

We said good night to Kay and Anthony and I sagged against the wall of the lift.

Jake put his hand on the back of my neck. "Can you face Gray's Inn Gardens? I could go alone, but it won't seem as uncontrived."

I stared at him like an owl on tranquillizers. Why was the man burbling on about gardens? Then, Gray's Inn. Helena's "casual" meeting with Liz Henderson. I banged my head against the lift door. That didn't help, so I did it again.

"I take it that's a 'No, I don't want to go' in Sam-speak."

It was nice to be with someone who spoke fluent Sam, but I took a deep breath. The day had lasted about four months so far, so what did a couple of hours matter? I blew out all the air in my lungs and pasted on a fake smile.

"Oooh, I *lurve* parties," I said in a breathy Betty-Boop voice. "Wouldn't miss this one for the world."

Jake snorted. Luckily, I spoke fluent Jake, too, and understood it to mean both *Sure, I believe you,* and *No, I can't think of anything I'd like to do less either.* But he just said, "Do you need to go home and change first?"

I checked my clothes in the reflection of the lift door. I'd worn my posh suit that morning, in honour of the sales conference. It didn't, perhaps, scream "festive dress," but then even if I went home to change, a festive-dress section in my wardrobe wouldn't magically manifest itself.

"I'm not really dressed for a party. This was for work," I said in a tired non-answer.

He looked me over. "You should be fine. You're clean."

That cut through my exhaustion. "I'm always clean."

He held up a palm against my outrage. "Sorry, I had a man moment. What I meant was, you look fine." He tried again. "You look like you always look." A ringing endorsement, but he stuck with it. "There's no point in getting pissed off. You don't care about clothes. I don't care about clothes. I like the way you look, and you look the way you always look. Which I like." He paused to suck in some air. "Is this getting me out of that big hole I dug?"

It wasn't bad, and he was right, I didn't really care. I let it go and moved on. "Let's go straight to the party. If I go home, I'll sink into the sofa and you'll need a three-sixty-degree earth-excavator to lift me up again."

He gestured me toward the door. "What do you know about excavators?"

"Absolutely nothing apart from their name. It was in a book I did once." The editor's answer to everything.

Gray's Inn Gardens is one of those places that Londoners keep secret. It's barely off the tourist trail, only a few minutes' walk from the British Museum, but it might as well be in another country. One side is blocked by an unattractive stone wall; on the other, you have to know which alley to dodge down. Then, behind the wall, down the alley, suddenly you're not in the centre of a city at all, but in a huge garden with tree-lined paths and walkways, surrounded by Georgian—or, at worst, Georgian-style—buildings. It's private, belonging to the lawyers, and officially it is only open to the public a couple of hours a day, but if you walk through with enough confidence in the daytime, it's not often you get stopped.

On the way there, Jake had taken a call. He didn't say anything about it, just reminded me, "We're listening tonight, not asking questions. Understood?"

Fine with me. We walked past the now firmly locked gardens and passed through a foyer, where we left our coats and umbrellas, and then moved with the other guests up the stairs, through three (I counted) anterooms before we reached what was, undoubtedly, called the Great Hall. I didn't know how old it was—if the history of the area was anything to go by, it was probably fairly new, since the World War II bombing had been heavy around here. But it was designed to look like it had been there since the Middle Ages, all panelled wood and candle sconces in the walls, although these were now wired for electricity.

I didn't bother to search for Helena. She's tiny, and would inevitably be surrounded by a group of men, all of whom would be finding her enchanting. Once she'd finished enchanting them, she'd extricate herself and locate me.

Instead, we stopped by a long table that had been set up by the door, laid with a smooth white tablecloth, and with large silver tureens at each end, which, from the smell, and the steam, were filled with mulled wine, or punch. The November evening was just one level up from drizzling, and the damp had been bone chilling. I would have liked something hot, but punch to me tastes like someone has spent the day boiling down a locker-room's-worth of socks. I picked up two glasses of wine, waving one in Jake's direction questioningly. Normally it wasn't a question, but even if he was "just listening," that was work. Apparently not enough for it to matter: he took the glass without hesitation, and we turned and faced the crowd.

"Do you know anyone here apart from Helena?" he asked.

I was about to say no, and then revised. "There's Connie," I said, indicating her general direction with my chin. "Do you remember her from Helena's party? She's the one who helped Sam." Sam, whom I usually called boy-Sam, to ensure no one thought I talked about myself in the third person, was a young neighbour who had been what was euphemistically referred to as "in trouble" with the police, mostly because he was young, had had difficulty finding work, and hung around with a lot of other young, not regularly in work kids of his age. Helena had sicced Connie onto his case, and, as with everything Helena touched, the story had ended happily. I'd only met her briefly, but in this crowd of lawyerly strangers, that felt like we had spent our teen years selling Girl Scout cookies together.

We joined her, and did the air-kissing thing. (Not Jake: no air-kissing in the CID. It was in their employment handbook.) I updated her on Sam: he had a job, a girlfriend, dee-dah, dee-dah. Then she was carried away in a tide of networking, and Jake and I were left in a corner by ourselves once more.

Which was fine with me. I was happily silent, not thinking about the endless day, or any of its events, when Jake nudged me gently. He spoke softly, like those voiceovers in nature documentaries, when the patient zoologist finally uncovers the nest of the rare thingummy bird. "Look," he said.

I followed his gaze. Everyone was becoming more animated as the wine circulated—by waiters, and in their veins. They laughed and chatted and figuratively and literally patted one another on the back. All except two. One couple was standing at the end of the room, in a small alcove shielded by screens. They were hidden from the room unless, like Jake and me, you were looking at the mirror that hung over the central fireplace. It was Liz Henderson and Cyril Bosworth.

Their actions unrolled like a silent film. Gone was the flirting, pouting socialite, the unctuous and supercilious grandee. These two knew each other well, and they weren't happy with each other, said their body language. She was saying something vehement, her hand gripping his forearm and shaking it in time to shaking her head was doing as she told him no. He responded, also with a slashing negative: whatever she had thought, or said, he wanted none of it.

I kept my eyes on the mirror as I said, "She's in charge, isn't she?"

He considered the pair. "I think so. He doesn't like it that she is, and he doesn't like what she's saying, but however forcefully he's saying no, she knows, and he knows, that she's going to get her way."

I watched for a couple of minutes. "It's about something, though, isn't it? I mean, it's not about them." I stopped. "That makes no sense. Even I don't know what I mean."

"I do. You mean it looks like they're arguing about something concrete, not *Why were you looking at that woman when you're with me*, or, *You keep saying you're going to tell your husband about us, but you never do.*

He was right: that was what I meant. I was glad one of us knew what I was talking about. "It doesn't look like there's an 'us.' It's not a relationship fight."

Jake was quiet for a moment, then said, reluctantly, "That call earlier, in the car, was from Chris." One of his colleagues. "They sent a couple of uniforms to interview everyone after Bim was found. All the theatre people—the actors, the crew—were doing their jobs, in sight of everybody else. Liz Henderson was at home, but the porter in her building said she had just arrived when they got there."

I waited while he very obviously decided how much he was going to tell me. Since he hadn't told me in the cab on the way over, it was more than he'd planned already.

"She said she had been shopping, but she had no receipts. She said she'd tried things on at Selfridges, but hadn't seen anything she liked enough to buy."

"It's a big enough place that no one would remember if she was there or not, even if they'd been helping her."

He nodded, still with his eyes on the couple in the corner. "The uniforms thought that maybe she'd had an assignation."

"Assignation?" I repeated it, deepening my voice to parody levels. "*Assignation? The police really use that word?*"

Jake pushed at my shoulder with his. "No. They said they thought she'd met someone for a quick shag. I'm protecting your delicate sensibilities."

How kind. But if that's where she'd been, it would take some serious weight behind it to get her to admit to it. More than the police could bring, based on the flimsy bits of coincidence that were all that they had now. I was about to point that out, when in the mirror we saw her lift up both her hands, palms out: enough, they said. She turned and strode away, pasting a fixed smile on her face as she emerged from the corner. Squirrel watched her with a savage frown on his face.

"Give me your glass," said Jake.

I looked down, confused. "It's full," I said, tilting it toward him. "It's been a long day. I'm not really drinking."

He lifted it out of my hand nonetheless. "I know." He kissed me absently on the nose and sauntered off, on a direct line that would intersect with Liz Henderson. Oh.

I turned and contemplated Squirrel. I had no chance of getting anything out of him. I had nothing he wanted from a woman. I wasn't young and pretty and flirtatious enough on the one hand, nor powerful enough on the other. This was a job for Superwoman. I looked for Helena.

Who was still not visible. And Squirrel, I saw now, was moving to the exit. Maybe I could use the fact that he thought I was unimportant. He might not watch what he said.

"Thank you for a wonderful evening," I said as my path ever so accidentally on purpose crossed his. "Helena always says you have the best parties," I added, hoping to god they had enough parties for that to make sense.

They did, because a look of complacency replaced his scowl. He paused long enough to expand on the splendours of his chambers, and their client base. Nodding and smiling admiringly were all that was required, which gave me time to consider what I was actually hoping to achieve. Asking, *Why were you quarrelling with Liz Henderson, and what did she want you to do that you didn't want to?* was not viable. I racked my brains, but Squirrel was winding down. "Is Hugh here?" I asked wildly, grateful for my afternoon of timeline-ing, so that I remembered Liz Henderson's husband's name. "I saw him and Liz the other night, but didn't have a chance to catch up."

He hesitated, trying to work out what our connection was. I didn't want to give him time to realize that there wasn't one. "It must be so reassuring for Liz to have you as her advisor." I patted him on the arm admiringly. I had no idea what the hell that meant.

Neither did Squirrel, but he took it as intended. He patted me back, and smiled benevolently. "Would that more women thought like you," he said, a priest bestowing a blessing, before he left me flat-footed, staring after him as he headed for the exit.

Shouting, "Yeah, right, buster," after him seemed undignified, so I didn't.

It was a good twenty minutes before Jake returned. I'd hidden in the loo for a while, then gone and got myself a glass of water, before pretending I wasn't a wallflower, keeping myself entertained by trying to spot a woman who didn't dye her hair, or a man who did. I failed on both fronts.

"Having fun?" I asked snidely when he finally reappeared.

"There's a reason men don't put 'toy boy' down as their career of choice," he said, wiping his hand across his face as though to clean it of toy-boy-ness.

I tried to look understanding, but snorting water the wrong way never makes it sound as though you sympathize. Anyone less toy boy–like than Jake it was hard to imagine. Maybe a pro wrestler might be higher up the list. I mentally shaved Jake's head and added some tattoos and a pair of shiny satin wrestler's shorts. Then I attempted to find enough brain-bleach to remove the image again.

"So?" I prodded.

"One's hair is ruined—*ruined*—by this weather. And *everyone* wears fur in Italy, so the fact that one can't wear fur—just a charming little fur jacket—in London, because a handful of bleeding-heart liberals will assault you— *physically assault you*—makes winter in town sheer purgatory," he recited.

I tucked my imaginary violin under my chin and played him a sad tune. "You're a detective, for goodness sake. There can't be an IQ requirement for suspects."

He laughed at the idea, good humour restored. "If you could arrange for that to be made law, the entire CID would nominate you for a knighthood."

"I'll get onto it tomorrow. In the meantime, did she say anything useful? Did she know who you were?"

He shook his head. "I said I'd been sitting behind her at the theatre, and let her assume I was an investor too. If her conversation is anything to go by, she knows almost nothing about investing, or theatre." He paused. "Either she's a very stupid woman, or she's very clever, and plays at being stupid. But I don't know which."

"Did she react when you mentioned Sylvie Sander?"

"How do you know I did?"

"Because I'm quite sure you don't want Liz Henderson's views on sixteenth-century revenge tragedy, Thomas Kyd, or his influence on *Hamlet*."

"What influence on *Hamlet*?"

I waved it away. "You don't want my views on that either."

"You're right. She did react when I mentioned Sander, but it was just *Oh poor Sylvie, she must have been so unhappy*. I asked if she had known her well, and according to her, they were the closest of friends—" He twisted his index and middle fingers together to show me how tightly the women were bonded. "Neither she, nor 'poor, dear Campbell' ever made a move without consulting their close chum Liz on matters of taste, art, fine dining, fashion, and probably what type of loo paper to buy. But how much of that had some basis in fact, and how much was look-at-the-important-people-I-know, I can't say."

"Does that mean we're done here?" I asked hopefully. We hadn't seen Helena, but I could tell her in the morning we'd spoken to the people we'd needed to speak to. And I'd already felt like I'd had a long day after the sales conference, never mind the rest of the day. I was now officially about a thousand light-years of overtime on the long-day front. Apart from anything else, I'd caught sight of myself in the mirror after Cyril left. I may have been clean, as Jake had so kindly mentioned, but I also had red-rimmed eyes and a dead white face. I looked like Dracula, if Dracula's office had had a dress-down Friday policy.

We began to move to the door, Jake pushing ahead to

manoeuvre us through the crowd. "What did you get from Cyril Bosworth?" he asked once we were clear.

"I'm not sure. Nothing, I think. I suggested that Liz Henderson relied on him for advice, and he agreed in a way that said they had some sort of ongoing relationship. Not necessarily intimate, but more than that he had once been the barrister who represented her in a court case a few years ago. Apart from that, his main contribution was that if only more women like me listened to men like him, the world would be a better place."

Jake didn't just laugh at that. He laughed so hard that he had to stop walking and bend over, hands on knees. When he finally caught his breath: "You're more likely to take off your shoes and stage a sock-puppet performance of the complete works of Shakespeare than you are to listen to men like him."

He knew me well.

Chapter 18

I would like to state, like the heroine of a Victorian novel, that I didn't sleep a wink, either kept awake by the trauma, or beset by unending nightmares. In reality, I started to strip as the front door closed, dropping my clothes behind me as I headed straight to bed. I fell in dressed only in my underwear, and that was all I remembered until my bedside light went on.

I squinted up. Jake was up and dressed and my clock said it was a quarter to seven.

"Here."

He held out a cup of coffee and I sat up to clutch at it like a lover. But I wasn't born yesterday. "What are you hoping to sweet-talk me into?"

He sat down beside me. "It's not sweet talk. I had a text last night. They want to interview you at the office. I suggested eight o'clock, and then it'll be over."

The "office" was Scotland Yard. The one time I'd been there, they'd been in what they now called the old building. I hadn't been impressed. It took the worst parts of 1960s design and strapped it onto an airport-style security system. It was an ordeal to get cleared to go in, and once you were in, the orange-and-blue tartan carpet made your eyeballs scream to get out again. I didn't imagine the new place would be any more aesthetically enjoyable. But I kept that to myself. "Mmm," seemed like a good thing to say, so I said it.

Yesterday I hadn't had time, or the energy, to discuss anything that had happened before Bim's disappearance. Now seemed a good time.

"I had this idea," I began.

Jake frowned. "Your ideas make me nervous."

Join the club, bud. "I had this idea," I repeated firmly. "Yesterday. Before Bim. It's probably nothing, but—" I rushed it out now. "But what if Liz Henderson was Campbell Davison's daughter?"

Jake opened his mouth to respond. Then he closed it again. He looked away. He scratched his neck. Finally he said, mildly, "Why would you think that?"

"I don't think that. I think 'what if?' She's the right age, her mother was in the right place. She lied about being backstage with Jenny when she wasn't, at around the time Davison was died. She has some connection with Davison—" I held up a hand when Jake began to speak. "Some connection, both in investment, and historically through her brother, who worked closely with Davison before his death. Basically, she's all over this story, but with no reason for her to be."

Jake rubbed his eyes. "You've got to stop reading so many books. We don't really worry about *why*. *How* tells us the answers. We need to find out how Davison was killed, and"—he hesitated, no doubt sanitizing the phrase for me—"and displayed. And how Bim was taken. That will tell us why."

That was complete and utter drivel. We knew *how* both things had happened. It was *why* that was going to tell us who had done it. But Jake and I had an unspoken division of labour. I didn't tell him how to detect crime, he didn't tell me how to edit books. So I finished my coffee in silence.

The interview went more easily, and more quickly, than I'd expected. Although someone from Child Protection was present, the case had been taken over by the CID team working on the deaths of Davison and Sander, which meant Chris was in charge. I told him once more what I'd told his uniformed colleagues, and Jake, the night before. Then they asked me questions, the answers to which were almost all "I don't know," or "As I said . . ."

After half an hour, I decided it was my turn. "Did Bim tell Kay or Anthony anything useful?"

I understood then why they had been focusing on me. Chris rubbed his eyes. "He doesn't know."

"He doesn't know who took him?" He was six, but he was a smart six. "He went off with a stranger?"

Chris nodded. "A woman. She said that Kay had sent her, that they needed him at the rehearsal studio. So he went. She knew his mother's name, what she was doing, and where she was doing it. A sixteen-year-old might not have queried it."

Or a sixty-year-old.

"We've got a sketch artist who will work with him when his parents say he's ready, to see if we can get some idea of what she looked like. At the moment, all he can say is that she was tall, and old, and had brown hair. But then"—he looked tired—"when we asked his mother to get him to describe you, he said you were old and tall and had brown hair. If you look at the world from three and a half feet high, everyone over four feet is tall."

"After yesterday, I feel old, too."

He ignored that. "We've got CCTV images from cameras near the school, and Bim is easy to identify. The woman is bending down, though, talking to him, or hidden under an umbrella. We'd like you to look at it."

He turned a laptop to face me and ran some footage. Lots of adults and children milling about, then pairing off and walking down the street. There was maybe five seconds for each before they passed out of camera range. I spotted Bim right away, his tool belt on over his jacket, and his satchel and pirate treasure box held carefully in front of him. The woman who spoke to him was facing away from the camera. There was a fraction of a second where part of her face was visible, but I doubted if her own child would have been able to identify her from that.

I reached out and hit "replay." The entire clip lasted little more than ten seconds, and nothing stood out. Contrary to Bim's description, she wasn't tall, and she didn't move like an older person. She could be anyone: not tall, not short, probably neither young nor old, in a raincoat with its collar turned up and carrying an umbrella that shaded her face. That was it.

I shook my head. No one looked surprised.

"Are there any CCTV cameras near the theatre offices?"

The Child Protection Officer spoke for the first time. He was barely out of childhood himself, probably in his mid-twenties, yet he looked tired and worn, as if he'd seen far too many bad things happen to good people. "We're still checking the films. So far, there's one where it might be them, just turning the corner, but her umbrella was up, and we're not even sure it was Timothy. We can't see the woman's face at all."

I stared blankly. I'd never heard anyone use Bim's real name. He'd been Bim since he'd first mispronounced Tim, and it felt odd, like we were talking about an imposter.

I shot a quick glance at my watch under the table. Not quick enough. At the far end of the table, where he'd been listening but not participating, Jake smiled slightly, a tiny uptick at one corner of his mouth. I looked around, but no one said anything, just stared at me as if I had all the answers. Hell, I didn't even know what the questions were. It pushed me, however, to ask the one thing that had been buzzing around in my head.

"She signed my name," I said.

They all waited.

"How did I get connected to this? It's obviously linked to Davison's death, because Bim was taken to the theatre offices. How did the person come up with my name? Who would know I had anything to do with Bim?"

They all looked at one another. I thought I'd brought up a good point, until I realized they were embarrassed. Jake spoke gently, as to a child of limited abilities. "You were at the rehearsal studio looking after the boys. You collected him after the second opening night. Your name is probably all over the paperwork."

Oh. I moved on seamlessly. "Where is his satchel?" They all looked blank. I pointed to the laptop. "He had his satchel and his pirate treasure chest with him."

One of the men whose name I hadn't forgotten because I hadn't listened to it in the first place now spoke. I could tell he was working very hard at being polite. "Why? Do you think there's something in a six-year-old's bag that is going to help?"

Two could play fake polite. I smiled, showing all my teeth. "No, of course not. But *where* it was located might tell us something, mightn't it?"

The deafening silence that met this made clear that they were all screaming *No* in their heads.

Moving on. "Is there anything else?"

That stirred Chris into gathering his papers, and he passed me a card with his number. "We might need to talk to you again, but in the meantime, ring me if you think of anything, will you?"

Jake walked me out, and we stood on the pavement. "Chris sent a couple of the team round to interview Liz Henderson again this morning," he said. "She wasn't there. She was at her solicitor's, according to her husband. He said he didn't have the details, and we would have to ask her."

I looked at my watch. It was only just past nine now.

"She was at her solicitor's, before nine o'clock? I didn't know solicitors got to their offices that early."

"Tell that to Helena."

Good point. I summarized. "Liz Henderson was asked where she was yesterday afternoon, and by this morning, she's already at her solicitor's." I had no idea what that indicated, but it sounded as though it indicated something. "Maybe being questioned by the police frightened her." That seemed perfectly reasonable to me.

Jake did that head nod-shake thing that meant "maybe." Or maybe not.

I spent the rest of the day on all those boring, mindless tasks that I normally postpone in the hope that, if I leave them long enough, they will no longer be relevant and I can bin them without doing them at all. I filed; I went through minutes for meetings I had never attended and didn't care about; I read memos on revised procedures for approving cover copy, and how to work the new scanner;

and a hundred other fun, action-packed accompaniments to office life. I didn't dare do any real work, since I couldn't concentrate, and I knew I would only have to do over again later.

By five o'clock, I admitted defeat. I threw a couple of manuscripts into my bookbag and headed home. Carrying the manuscripts home and then taking them back to the office the next day would have to do as a substitute for reading them. I knew the futility of the gesture even as I made it, but it didn't prevent me from making it all the same.

As I put my key in the front door, it opened in front of me. Two startled squeaks sounded, one on each side. We sounded like hamster sisters.

Then, "*Darling,*" a voice breathed, as if the mere sight of me was the culmination of decades of hopeless yearning. Frankie.

At some point during our massive drinking bout, which I was still firmly calling "dinner," we had silently agreed that her over-the-top-ness was much funnier if countered by my withdrawn, undemonstrative personality. So, "Hey," I said, stepping inside, as if I met West End stars in my front hall every day of the week, with an extra side order of film star on Sundays.

"I've just been to see Bim," she said.

Chris had told me that they were saying nothing about the day before. The people who were in the theatre when Kay heard Bim was missing had been told that it had been a misunderstanding, that Bim had gone to a friend's house and his babysitter had panicked when she couldn't find him. So, "Bim?" I repeated dimly as I searched desperately for a way to say *Why?*

Frankie held her hand at waist level. "About yea high? Snub nose? Lives in the flat above you?"

"Oh, Bim." I gave up. "Why are you visiting Bim?"

"Didn't you *hear*?" she breathed. "He has a cold, poor little pet. I don't live far"—she swept her arm dramatically across the hall, to indicate the not-far-ness of her house—"so I popped in."

"I hadn't heard he was sick. How is he?"

She made a face. "Asleep. I sat and chatted to Kay and Anthony for ten minutes, but they said he'd been sleeping on and off for the whole day, so I didn't stay as long as I'd planned."

She looked at me expectantly, and I felt obliged: "Why don't you come in?"

She mimed hesitation, but it wasn't meant to be taken seriously by either of us. "Only for a few minutes. I need to be at the theatre a good hour before curtain to get into that pig of a headdress. And nothing to drink, obviously, before a show. Tea would be lovely. Camomile if you have it." We moved into the kitchen and I put the kettle on. "The sooner this run is over, the better." She slumped down at the table.

"Don't you have another play coming up with the same company?"

She made the noise a beer bottle makes when you open it, *Pfft*, while her hands made a simultaneous explosion gesture.

Apparently that explained everything, because she didn't say anything further. After a moment I repeated the noise, and the gesture, but with a question mark at the end: "*Pfft?*"

"Completely *pfft*. *Pfft* to the nth degree." She took the cup I handed to her. "We can't work together again. We can barely do it now. After Campbell was, well—" She waved it away. "But since Sylvie, it's—it's like one of those nightmares when you wake up and think, *That was a nightmare*, and then you go back to sleep and it begins all over again. Even if Sylvie did kill herself and it's nothing to do with Campbell, we're all on edge. Jenny has gone into uber-dictator mode, barking at all of us, even more than usual. Which is still better than Tom, who isn't speaking to the lighting designer, the lighting designer, who isn't speaking to the techs, or half the cast, who isn't speaking to the other half." She stretched in her chair. "I, of course, am speaking to everyone, and everyone is speaking to me, because I'm so lovely."

I laughed. "Yes, you are."

She nodded: it was her due. Frankie was the strangest combination, humorously self-aware while also being starrily pleased with herself. And I never knew which side was going to be uppermost at any moment.

My phone rang, and I checked the screen. Sandra. It could wait. I let it go to voicemail, but Frankie took the opportunity to stand and get her coat. "I'm off. I told Kay to let me know if there's anything she needs, but if she doesn't, will you keep me posted?"

"Of course. But since you're here, why aren't you going to the theatre together now?"

"She's taking a couple of nights off because of Bim. She doesn't have a cover, so I'll be without a maid. It's no big deal: Campbell wanted the stage to look very lush, very dressed, but she only has a few lines, and they can be redistributed, and her murder can happen offstage." She rolled her eyes. "Jenny is cross, of course, muttering about how children onstage always cause problems, but Jenny is permanently cross. So I should say, she's crosser than usual, though I would have thought that that was physically impossible." She finished wrapping herself in her scarf and then her coat and hat. She looked like a very chic woolly mammoth. "Ta-ra, love. See you on the other side."

I put the flat door on the latch and followed her into the hall, going up instead of out. Since Kay wasn't going to the theatre, I'd check on Bim before I started dinner.

I found Bim and Anthony laying out the components of a model railway that looked as if it would take over the entire flat before they were done. Kay was standing in the doorway by the kitchen, watching them. Bim was back to his usual ebullient self, while Kay looked like she was the one who had been abducted and drugged.

Her clothes reflected what the dark shadows under

her eyes were saying. Instead of one of her usual outfits that looked as if it had been rejected by a Disney Princess as too pink and sparkly, she was wearing a pair of jeans and a T-shirt. I hadn't ever seen her in jeans before, and while her T-shirt announced that she was Glinda the Good, normally she wouldn't have had to announce it: she'd be dressed as Glinda the Good's frillier, if definitely cooler, more hip, sister.

But she smiled when I came in, and waved a wooden spoon in greeting. "Will you stay for supper?"

Bim looked up from his trains. "You have to stay. You haven't had supper with us forever!"

That wasn't strictly true, but when you're six, a few months is forever.

And Bim had been abducted, and drugged, and I'd held his hand in an ambulance. I had hardly ever brought myself to refuse him before. Now I had this to justify what I knew I would have done anyway. "Of course I'm staying for supper. I wouldn't miss it." I shot off a text to Jake to come up when he got home, and sat down beside him. "What are we playing?"

Bim showed me how to join up the track, and gave me instructions on the siding that needed to be built to extend the loop around the coffee table, but "Leave the bridges. They're the hard part." He patted his tool belt, as if to say *Man's work*.

By the time Jake joined us, and spaghetti was eaten, and wiped off Bim and the floor around him, it wasn't until we were clearing the dishes that I had a chance to speak to Kay out of Bim's hearing. "Are you OK? Is he?"

She smiled faintly—everything she'd been doing had been faint that evening, as though she were seeing the world through a piece of gauze, dimly. "He's fine. Much better than me. He thinks he got sick, and the woman who collected him called you, which is why you were at the hospital with him."

"But he screamed when he was asked about her yesterday."

She shrugged. "After he slept, that seems to be what he remembers. He calls her 'the bad lady,' but he doesn't say why, and the hospital therapist thought it was better just to let him tell the story however he wanted. I half think that the bad lady is only bad because she lost his satchel and his pirate box somewhere between school and the office."

"If his spelling homework was in the satchel, she'd be 'the good lady.'" I remembered the struggle I'd had to get him to concentrate on that.

Kay smiled faintly again. "True." She hadn't taken her eyes off Bim as we'd washed the dishes, and, much to his disgust, Anthony had kept him just as close as they'd played trains. He was used to being a more free-range child, with his own private games. "I don't know what I'm going to do," Kay continued. "I've got three days off, but I can't imagine letting him out of my sight, even to go to school."

"Understandable. When is your regular sitter back?"

"Not for another ten days. I'll take him to school and collect him on Monday. I need to have a little discussion with them anyway."

I wondered if Ida had considered emigrating to avoid that "little discussion." Antarctica might be far enough.

Chapter 19

On Monday night I was looking back fondly to the day when I'd eagerly been anticipating attending a performance of *The Spanish Tragedy*. Because now I was standing in the wings, waiting for Bim to exit, and if I never saw the sodding play again, it would be about a hundred years too soon.

Kay had remained jumpy over the weekend, and she and Anthony had both walked Bim to school that morning. They had considered withdrawing Bim from the production—they didn't trust Gordon to keep an eye on him, Kay couldn't do it from the stage, and Anthony had had to leave that afternoon for a job in Sheffield. But the hospital's therapist had advised against changing his routine without explanation, and they had reluctantly agreed.

"If you can get me approved, I'm not doing anything on Monday evening. At least for the first night you're both back, I can watch him while you're onstage." The offer was out before I had even thought about it.

So there I was, once more watching death and devastation, this time from backstage while I ate a stale sandwich and drank the oily, burnt coffee that one of the crew had brought over to me. And I was bored out of my mind. I didn't know how actors could find something fresh every performance: I thought I was going to expire from the tedium, and it was only the third time I'd seen the play.

I leaned back against one of the flats, making sure to keep behind the tape on the floor that marked the area past which I'd be visible to some of the audience. Instead of the stage, I watched the crew. Onstage it was theatre, but behind the scenes it was ballet. The black-clad, head-setted techs moved around with barely a sound, in an elaborate dance as they prepared props, shifted scenery, moved ropes and counterweights into place. At their centre, the focal point from which all action eddied, was Jenny, always on the move, shifting in and out of focus, here one moment, gone the next, only to reappear where you least expected her.

In the rehearsal studios I'd admired the efficiency with which she'd kept the day on track. But here it was more than efficiency. Here, she was queen. Tablet in hand, she moved from place to place, never raising her voice above a murmur. She stood behind one of her crew who was poised, waiting; the cue came, he let launch his rope. She nodded, ticked off an item on her tablet, dropped her spectacles to her chest, and moved to the next point, the lighting board. She stood behind once more, waited again; the next cue, the next action, the next nod, tick, spectacle drop. Even when she was still, taking a break—even when she repeated her grande dame gesture from the rehearsal, handing a lowly peon her water bottle to open, she was formidable. If Marcel Marceau had ever had the chance to see her work, he would have created an entire evening in homage to her dance of efficiency.

Bim appeared beside me, flushed and happy. "Did you see?"

"Every second. Come on, let's get you cleaned up and ready to go." We moved along the dark corridors cunningly booby-trapped with bits of furniture and strange, draped unidentifiable items, and then through the safety door, and into the light.

Bim galloped up the stairs. "Avast, my hearties." He waved an imaginary sword as he boarded the enemy vessel, which looked remarkably like any other concrete landing in any other turn-of-the-century building.

"Where's Black Bart?" I asked. "Has he walked the plank already?"

He stopped mid-gallop and stared at me severely. "Sam. You know we hangded Black Bart. You saw Robbie and me do it during the rehearsal you was at. With the special pirate noose in black and red. The pirate colours." He tone was disappointed.

"Of course I did. I remember. It was very exciting. I meant Black Bart's cousin," I improvised. "Rowdy Rufus."

Bim looked interested in this new arrival to his cast

of characters, but Gordon was waiting at the dressing-room door. "Here's Black Jack, returned from sea safe and sound," he called. "There's a towel and cold cream ready for him."

What every pirate needs on shore leave. I sipped at the coffee I was still clutching. It was disgusting enough that I'd only barely touched it, but it was still caffeine, and since it would be more disgusting once it was cold, I persevered. I manoeuvred around the pirate-cleanup as Gordon sat in the room's only chair, Bim firmly pinned between his knees. Previously, I would have pictured dressing rooms to be colourful and warm, stuffed with costumes spilling off racks, and with lots of makeup laid out in front of one of those mirrors with the lightbulbs in rows on the sides that you see in films. In reality, I had discovered, they were tiny little bare cubes, usually with too many people crammed into them, and for some reason always both overheated and draughty, a combination that previously I would have said was impossible to achieve. Although the mirror and dressing-table part was right, there were no costumes spilling anywhere—there wasn't space for a clothes rack, much less an abundance of clothes. Bim and Robbie's costumes were covered in plastic and ti-dily hung on pegs. Apart from some crayoned drawings they had done that were taped to the whitewashed brick walls, there was nothing else in the room.

I hitched a hip up and leaned against the dressing table while Gordon began the de-blooding process. While his reputation as a slacker may have been true before,

Bim's disappearance had put the fear of god into him, or perhaps it was fear of Kay. He had barely been a metre away from Bim when he wasn't onstage. Understandably: I would certainly be afraid to cross Kay in her current mother-lion-defending-her-cub mood. I was relieved. The past few days had suddenly caught up with me, and I could barely keep my eyes open. He could take over for the moment. I didn't even try to cover the huge yawn that overtook me.

"Bim!" said Gordon. "Stop wriggling. Arms up."

Two small hands poked in the air, the black velvet page's tunic pooling around his wrists, making his little paws, which he clenched and released in pirate death throes, seem disembodied, as if they were floating in the air.

And a series of images crossed my mind, falling like dominoes, one hitting the next. Campbell Davison's clawed hands as he hung suspended. Carol Dennison, arm flung out, the shadow of her hand elongated by Bruce's light show. And Jenny Rogers, passing her water bottles for her assistants to open. I'd taken it as part of her assumption of grandeur, her Queen of All She Surveyed routine.

But really, who did that? It had to be covering up some deep insecurity. Or—just covering up?

Gordon broke into my thoughts. "He needs to shower." I nodded, searching the dressing table for my phone, which I'd had to leave there while I was backstage. What I needed would be on it. And it was. One quick Google and I was reading when the door clicked shut behind me.

"That was fas—" But it wasn't fast, because it wasn't Gordon and Bim.

It was Jenny.

I kept my face as bland as possible, my voice level. "Aren't they going to miss you?"

She spoke quietly into her headset, and then to me: "I have nine and a half minutes. As long as I continue to talk to them, possibly another two after that."

Nine and a half minutes. I could surely keep her talking that long. "Why are you doing this? And how did you know I'd worked it out?"

"I heard Bim on the stairs just now. I didn't know you had worked it out, but it was possible that you would, and I don't like loose ends. And you're more than a loose end, aren't you?" She gestured to my phone.

I tried frantically to remember what Bim had said on the stairs. Apart from more pirate factoids, there was nothing. I certainly wasn't going to tell her that whatever she thought I knew, I didn't, so I stared at her silently. She returned the look. I was hoping we might keep it up until Gordon and Bim returned, or her crew realized she'd gone rogue, but then she added, in a conversational tone, "Delay won't help. The shower room door gets stuck, and it takes ages to find someone to release it. And about ten minutes ago you texted that police boyfriend of yours to say you had news, and you'd meet him at Scotland Yard. He'll be waiting there for you now."

I flicked over to my texts, and I had, apparently, done just that. She must even have scrolled back through my earlier messages, because it was signed the way I always signed them to him: "xxxS." She snatched the phone out of my hand before I had time to think.

I considered my situation. Jenny had nine minutes. She didn't appear to have a weapon, and if experience was anything to go by, she liked to keep blood down to a minimum. She also, according to the god of Google, was unlikely to be strong.

I gestured to my phone. "I'd only just worked it out. It was your hands first of all." Jenny held her hands out, looking down at them as if she'd never seen them before, turning them over and looking at both sides. "Davison, when he was onstage," I said, still having trouble finding a decent substitute for *when you hung him up on a meat hook for people to laugh at.* "Davison's hands were extraordinary. At first I thought the designer had given the dummy claw hands intentionally. Later, I was told it was cadaveric spasm. But I'd seen hands that looked like his, I just didn't know where. You handed people your water bottles to open. I thought it was to show you were in charge and they were there to serve you." She smirked. "It was only a couple of minutes ago I realized your hands looked exactly like his."

She sneered. "That was enough? Campbell Davison"—she said his name the way most people would say "festering maggot-ridden pond-scum"—"Campbell Davison and I both have arthritis, and you decide I killed him?"

I put on my most patronizing tone. "Jenny, you cornered me alone in a dressing room. You made sure Gordon and Bim were held up. You texted my boyfriend to delay him. You wouldn't be here if you thought I worried that you got a bit rheumatickey on rainy days." I took a noisy slurp of my coffee to make a punctuation point.

Her eyes flickered, but she remained steady, once more whispering into her headset. I spoke more loudly, hoping it might carry. "It's amazing what you can find online with a reverse search," I said. "Just a couple of minutes looking for 'inherited genetic condition' and 'claw hands,' and you get Ehlers-Danlos syndrome. Imagine what the CID will find when they look."

She had to have known that this was coming, but even so, she flinched, as if I'd marched across the room and slapped her.

"Five more minutes on the government website gets me a birth certificate." She didn't have to know that I'd had it all wrong, and it was Liz Henderson's I'd ordered—and even that hadn't arrived. I'd let her assume you could see them online. "You're Campbell Davison's daughter," I said, with far more certainty than my knowledge warranted, "and he had a genetic condition he passed on to you."

She snarled. "His daughter? He was nobody's father."

"That's not what your birth certificate says." Maybe.

"He was my father just long enough to pass this on—" She lifted her hands. "He wasn't a father in any other way. He had no idea I even existed. My mother was a twenty-year-old would-be actress. By the time she knew she was pregnant, he was back in Germany, and had turned into The Great Director. She never told him. The end."

Only for him. "He didn't know who you were when you were hired?"

Until that moment, I'd been worried, but not frightened. The smile she gave now terrified me. Somehow, in my tired mind, it swelled and grew. "He didn't know until his last moment. Then his child, the one he did *this* to"—she made the same gesture with her hands—"*that* child was the last thing he ever saw."

She was crazy, but unfortunately in full control, dropping her head once more to speak into her headset. I needed to keep her talking to me. "I don't understand. He didn't intentionally pass on his condition. It's not as if he gave it to you to spite you. He had the same problem."

"The same problem?" She was fury personified, a seething pool of rage. "He had the *same problem*? You think a few joint aches and pains, a bit of *Oh poor Campbell, his knees give him trouble* was anything like what he gave to me?"

"What did he give to you?"

She had just told me she'd killed her father, and then hung his body on a meat hook for public mockery, but the raw pain on her face now was almost unbearable.

She never raised her voice, but she might as well have shrieked it aloud. "He killed my babies. That's what my father's genes gave me. The *only* thing he, and they, ever gave me was seven dead babies."

I cry easily. I cry all the time. At sad films. Advertisements. Even seeing a Labrador puppy walk by might do it. I can cry at them all. But standing locked in a dressing room with a self-confessed murderer threatening me, I could not have stopped the tears had I been Joseph Stalin's tougher, harder-hearted brother.

"Seven miscarriages," she went on, unheeding. "Oh, and two destroyed marriages caused by the seven miscarriages. 'Cervical insufficiency,' it's called. Not that that's a symptom of Ehlers-Danlos that would trouble The Great Director. Only those he abandoned." She thumped the table beside her, and I jumped. "That's my inheritance. So." She gathered herself. "So, you see why I had to kill him. For them. It wasn't right that my babies died, and he got to live."

That brought me back to the brute facts. "And—what you did after? What you did to him? Why that?"

She had never lost track of the time, and she spoke once more into her headset, enjoying making me wait. I leaned against the wall, everything combining to make me feel weak, as she turned back to me, vicious and smug. "Why not? He needed to learn what being an object of ridicule was like. Having people prod and poke at you, laugh at you, because you weren't good enough."

If I had any brains I would've pushed past her and yelled and banged at the door. But I had questions.

"But Bim. Why would you hurt Bim?"

She was horrified. "I didn't hurt him. I'd *never* hurt a child."

"You drugged him. You were going to kill him." And then I saw it again in my head. Jenny backstage—action,

nod, tick, spectacle drop—versus Jenny in the rehearsal
studio, when she'd pushed her specs up on her forehead
and they kept falling down. And then Bim's pirate talk on
the stairs that Jenny had overheard, the red-and-black pirate noose. "Your spectacles. He had the cord from your
spectacles in his pirate box." I reworked it in my head, and
then almost simultaneously aloud. "He didn't get too light
a dose by accident. You wanted to make it seem that way,
so no one would question the disappearance of his pirate
treasure."

She nodded as though that explained everything. She
spoke into her headset, eyes on her watch. "Time's up.
Yours too."

She moved toward me, but I stood firm. "Where do
you think this is going? You're not bigger than me, you're
not stronger. How do you plan to stop me?"

She didn't even trouble to glance my way, just turned
to the door. "The same way I stopped Sylvie."

And that's all I remember.

Chapter 20

People were speaking, low-voiced and serious, but I didn't pay any attention to them, because my head was a helium balloon. I let go of the string and watched as it drifted away, above the clouds. It sailed off, taking my thoughts with it. Helium heads were a wonderful invention, I decided dreamily. We should all have helium heads, and just let go of the strings. Although, what was I thinking with if my head had floated away? I frowned. It must mean my brains weren't in my head, which went against all conventional wisdom. If I still had a head, I'd worry about that. Since I wasn't worrying . . . I got a bit lost in the middle of that sentence, and gave up.

A voice, which I shouldn't have been able to hear, because my helium ears had floated off with my head, said, "She's waking up."

I opened the eyes that, by rights, ought now to be somewhere overhead. They weren't, because I saw a dressing room. I could tell from the dressing table with its lightbulbs, but it was more elaborate than the one I'd been in, bigger, and with an extremely lumpy sofa, which I could vouch for from firsthand evidence, because I was lying on it. The painted brickwork was the same, however. What was it with painting bricks, I wondered. Who decided that naked bricks were embarrassing, and needed a G-string and pasties of paintwork to cover them up?

I decided I'd worry about that later, and turned my eyes to the group of people standing by the dressing table. Somehow, Jake and Chris had appeared, together with a man I didn't know. Sitting near them, at the table, was Frankie.

This must be her room. It was nice of her to let me have a nap there. She was a good person. Unlike Bim, she was sitting in all her blood, just staring at her hands. So much blood. That—I sat up. "Jenny! She's—"

My head was, apparently, still attached to my body. So was my throat, because it felt like I'd swallowed razor blades. My stomach was too, because it lurched alarmingly. The man I didn't know stepped forward quickly, already holding a basin. A Boy Scout, I decided as I retched into it.

Then Jake was sitting beside me, and as I swilled out my mouth, the basin-holder was introduced. He wasn't a Boy Scout, he was a doctor.

"What happened?"

Jake looked grim. "You got a nice dose of Valium. This is Dr. Stearns, who was in the audience. He pumped your stomach, and has given you activated charcoal, but I want to get you to the hospital."

I ignored the last part, although it was good to know I hadn't actually swallowed razor blades. "When? How?" Then I made a mental note. The next time a cup of coffee tastes like it's been sitting on a burner for a week, it might be an idea to stop drinking it. "Never mind. Back up. How did you find me? What happened? And where's Jenny?" I looked around wildly, as if she might emerge from behind a door.

Chris pulled a chair around and sat. "We'll get to that, but we need to know what happened to you first, and why. We saw the open screen on your phone, but it's not very clear." He took out his notebook and nodded to the door. I looked over and saw another two men standing just outside the room. One came in, his notebook out too. "Can you tell us?"

I nodded agreement, but repeated, "Where is she?"

"In a dressing room across the hall, with a PC. We wanted to hear you first."

I paused for a moment. "She told me quite straightforwardly that she'd killed Davison. And that she'd 'stopped' Sander. I don't know if that means she drugged and suffocated her, or drove her to suicide. If she threatened to reveal that Sander's career was based on someone else's work . . ." I stopped. "No, wait, there's no reason for her to have known that, is there?" I chewed on that for a moment before I gave up. "I don't know. She said she'd stop me the way she stopped Sylvie. I guess if she drugged me, it means she drugged Sylvie too, but why, I don't know."

No one jumped in, so I started again from what seemed to be the most important point. "Campbell Davison was her father." I felt a charge run around the room. Even having read what was on my phone, they clearly hadn't got that far. "I had only guessed that part. I told her I'd seen a copy of her birth certificate, which wasn't true, but of course even if he was her father, and it was true, her mother might not have put his name on it." I realized I was rambling. "I'm trying to get this in the right order."

"Take your time." Chris was professionally soothing.

I began again. "Davison had a brief affair with a young actress, who didn't contact him after she found she was pregnant. Jenny was the child. So far, so ordinary. The bit that made it different was that Davison had a genetic condition, something called Ehlers-Danlos syndrome. I only had a chance to skim read." I waved my hand to the phone. "Basically, in mild cases it causes a few problems in men—clawlike, or other deformation of the hands, joint problems; in women, those symptoms too, and it can also create a thinning of the cervix, meaning that women with the syndrome can become pregnant, but have little chance of carrying a child to term. Jenny had had seven miscarriages." I saw Frankie wringing her hands out of the corner of my eye. It should have looked absurdly melodramatic. "She blamed Davison for that, for her two marriages that couldn't take the strain. She wanted him not just to die, but to be considered"—I cast around for the right word—"be considered lesser, a joke. She thought that's the way the world saw her because of her infertility." I thought back. "I saw it, but I didn't know what I was seeing. The day at the rehearsal studio, I saw her staring in Bim's direction. She looked sick with longing."

The uniformed policeman by the door moved restlessly.

It wasn't my imagination. "It was lots of little things. Jenny ran the theatre like a machine. She was everywhere, and knew everything, but no one knew anything about her. Nobody knew she'd had a series of miscarriages, or that she was desperate for children, or what was wrong with her hands—no one even knew there *was* anything wrong with her hands. No one paid her much attention at all. She made their lives easy, and they ignored her otherwise."

Frankie flinched. I hadn't meant her. Chris intervened. "I'd like to go through this step by step. You say she told you that she'd killed Davison, and said she'd 'stopped' Sylvie?"

I nodded in agreement, then said "Yes" when the constable making notes looked up to confirm.

"She could have introduced peanuts to Davison in almost any way, at any time." Chris was speaking to his colleagues now, not to me. "Anyone could have, and anyone could have sent a text from his phone afterward. She had access too, to the stage machinery, if he didn't die in precisely the right location. Not all the others did."

He returned to me. "She had the same access to

Sander that many others did, but no motive for her death. If she knew about Maurer, she might have used Sander's death to lead us away from her, but that assumes that Jenny knew about Maurer, and there's no reason to think she did. The only way Sander and Davison could have kept up the fraud for this long was if they were entirely tight-lipped about it."

I agreed, but "They could only keep the fraud going because the drawings are only ever seen in Sander's workspace. No one notices Jenny. She's there, but no one pays her any attention until they need her. She wouldn't have needed to have overheard more than a couple of fragments to set her on the right path, and she'd have the drawings right in front of her. We figured it out based only on the drawings and a bit of theatre knowledge. If Jenny had done the most basic reading about her father's career, together with those images, she would have the story."

"All right," said Chris. "It's possible. Let's set that aside for the moment. What about Bim?"

"Bim was a serious danger to her. Bim was telling everyone how Davison had been given the peanuts, and he also saw Davison after he died."

"No. We interviewed him. He never said any of that." Chris, always so slow spoken, was sharper than I'd ever heard.

"He doesn't know he knows. We all heard it, and didn't know. But Jenny knew. Bim does an imitation of Davison. He does it all the time—I've seen it at least half a dozen times. He pretends to be Davison reading a script, and he makes a finicky little gesture, licking his finger before he turns each page. My guess is that Jenny put nut dust on Davison's script, and waited for him to read it, licking his finger as he turned the page. She—"

Jake interrupted. "That's risky. Davison could have done that at any time, in front of—"

I interrupted right back. "In front of anyone, or everyone, which wouldn't have mattered in the slightest. Jenny wouldn't have been able to stage her coup de théâtre, which she probably really wanted to do, she wouldn't have been able to reveal herself to him as he lay suffocating, which I'd bet good money she did, but he'd still be dead, and no one would look twice at her."

Chris was dotting his I's and crossing his T's. "Bim saw this?"

"I don't think so, but his constant imitation of Davison reading must have been nerve-wracking, especially once she realized he'd seen Davison dead backstage."

All three men spoke at once, the gist of which was, again, that Bim had been interviewed and had said no such thing.

"He didn't know Davison was dead. He was telling me about having stage blood painted all over him. 'Sticky' was the word he used, and then he said, 'Campy was sticky and smelly.' There was no reason for Davison ever to have had stage blood on him, to be 'sticky.' As to smelly"—I turned to Jake—"when people die, they—their bodies, that is—"

Jake helped me out. "His bowels or bladder might well have released, yes."

I moved on hastily. "He told me that once, at home, but he told you too," I turned to Jake. "He said it backstage that night we collected him. Kay was cross because he was shouting and doing his imitation where everyone could see. I don't know if Jenny heard, but she was there right after."

I could see Jake was searching his memory, trying to visualize who had been in the corridor that night, but I went on without waiting. "He also told me that 'Campy was stuck.' We were talking about spearing toffee apples with forks, so he didn't mean Davison was stuck *in* something, he meant the spearing kind of stuck. We've been told repeatedly that the chaperone often didn't watch the boys because he was flirting with one of the techs, and Kay said Bim was 'free range' at the theatre, which annoyed Jenny. I think that on one of his backstage jaunts, Bim came across Davison's body with the hook already fixed onto the back of his costume."

The men all looked at one another, but didn't speak. I continued. "And somewhere near the body, he found the cord that Jenny kept her reading glasses on when she wasn't using them."

Now even the detective who was making notes looked up. "I didn't know what it was until this evening. Bim had a box of what he called pirate treasure. There were bits of pamphlets that he called maps, and stones that were jewels. He also had what he said was a noose that one of the pirates' enemies had been hanged with. It was a thin red and black woven cord. The box got knocked over at rehearsal, and everything spilled out." I pictured the scene when Bim had bitten Bill Rose. "Jenny bent down to help tidy the treasures, and then stopped suddenly. I thought it was because she thought she was too important to be cleaning up after a child, but she must have seen the cord, and realized where Bim had found it. I only worked it out this evening. Bim was shouting about it on the stairs, describing the cord. Earlier I had been watching Jenny, and she had kept putting her glasses on to read, then letting them fall onto her chest from a cord. At the rehearsal, her glasses weren't on a cord: she kept pushing them up on her forehead. My guess is that the cord snapped, either when Davison was dying, perhaps he made a grab at it, or when she moved him to get him onto the hook. She didn't notice, and Bim picked it up and later added it to his pirate box. She didn't want to kill him, just get the cord back. It was pretty well the only thing that said she had been near Davison's dead body."

There was a silence, so I felt obliged to press it, as though Jenny killing only two people, not three, was an extenuating factor. "She didn't. He was almost awake by the time I found him. And everyone focused on his abduction, not on the box, thinking it had just got lost in the shuffle."

Chris said, "It wasn't Jenny who collected Bim at school. There was a matinee on, and her absence would have been noticed."

Of course that hadn't been Jenny. Bim knew Jenny. He didn't know the woman who collected him.

"We'll find her, now we've got a starting point." Chris sounded sure.

"Who would do that?" I wondered. "Who could she find who would do that? I don't know anyone well enough to ask them to drug a child for me, much less well enough to trust they'd never say a word after."

"She didn't have to trust them. She could do it just like she drugged you, and, presumably, Sander: in a drink or a sandwich. She says to her friend, please collect this child for me and drop him off at our offices. Oh, and here's a sandwich and some juice for him. The woman leaves, Bim falls asleep, and that's it."

I thought of Jenny's face when she said she'd never hurt a child, how shocked she had been, even as she spoke calmly to her crew. "What is the range of the headsets they all wear?"

There was a silence. Then Chris said, "You think she left the theatre and went to the office *during* the show, and no one noticed?"

I rubbed at my face. Now that the adrenaline was wearing off, my throat hurt, my head hurt, and my stomach was still turning over. "I don't know. I know that today she had her glasses on a cord around her neck that is the same size and colour as the one I saw in Bim's box, ten days ago, when, coincidentally, her glasses were not on a cord at all. How or when she got at his box, I can't say, but he had it, and most likely the cord, before he was abducted; a day later, the box had vanished, and her specs appeared on a cord around her neck."

I paused. "There is one other thing. The money. Davison probably earned very nicely, but it's worth remembering that he recently won a million-dollar prize. If he didn't know he had a child, she wouldn't be in his will, but might she have been able to sue his estate after his death for a share? That might have something to do with the timing."

Jake added, "And Sylvie Sander's death. She was a legatee."

Chris made a note. "Jenny Rogers told you she'd killed Davison. She said she'd stopped Sander. We'll find the person she sent to the school. We'll check her medical history. It will all unravel." He nodded to the other two men, and they both stood. "I'm going to start processing Jenny." He paused. "Thank you for your help. And I'm sorry this happened to you."

There was a silence after he left. The doctor had faded out at some point during the story. Jake didn't say anything, just sat beside me, a solid, comforting presence. Finally I roused myself to ask, "How did you get here? One moment I was alone with Jenny, the next moment I was in here, among a cast of thousands."

"I got your text—or, as it turns out, Jenny's text from your phone. It felt wrong, but I didn't know why. I texted you back, but got no reply. Then, a few minutes later, Frankie rang me."

Frankie had been so silent, I'd forgotten she was in the room, and when she spoke I jumped as though I'd been poked with an electric cattle prod. "I saw her watching you all night when you were waiting for Bim. Whatever Jenny was doing, wherever she was, she kept staring at you. I'd never seen such naked hatred. When I was killed, she always stood on the prompt side, waiting for the gunshot effects. They were tricky, and she never missed them. But tonight she wasn't there. Then I saw Bim in the corridor, without you, and you hadn't been more than a metre from him all night. So . . ."

Jake picked up the thread. "So, very sensibly, she rang me."

I stared between them. "You rang Jake? At the office? To say I wasn't watching Bim?"

"Put like that, it does seem an overreaction, I admit," Frankie replied, not even slightly abashed. "But with Campbell and Sylvie both dead, and something horrible having happened to Bim—" She waved away my protest. "I know, it's all a deathly secret, but it was obvious that something horrible *had* happened to Bim. Kay would never have missed a performance for a *cold*." She held the word out in invisible tongs, as though no one in the history of mankind had ever stayed home with a cold. "Anyway, darling," she concluded, returning to her breathy drama-queen style, "I never thought I'd have the chance to ring 999 and demand to be put through to Scotland Yard when I wasn't in costume. *Such* a thrill."

"So pleased to be able to broaden your horizons," I murmured.

Jake kept his focus. "Frankie began by saying she was sorry to trouble me at Scotland Yard. When she said the words, I realized that that's what was off in your text. We all say 'the office,' not 'Scotland Yard.' You do too. Given the text that had probably been sent from Davison's phone after his death, I called the local nick to get someone into the theatre to look for you."

I stared at Frankie. "You're not onstage."

"That liquid cosh didn't do any damage, did it?" She tapped her head smartly. "Nothing gets past you."

"I mean—what time is it? Is the performance over?" I looked around wildly, as if I would be able to tell the time from the four walls of the room.

She smiled, but it wasn't real. "We brought the curtain in ten minutes from the end. We had to stop to see if there was a doctor in the house once you were found, and no one could continue after that. There'll be an official announcement tomorrow, and the company will quietly fold. It's people's jobs, and salaries, but we can't work together anymore."

"What will you do?"

She shrugged. "I'll be all right. I have a few offers." She pursed her lips disapprovingly. "And there will be more offers tomorrow, when the news hits. Nothing like a bit of free publicity."

"No more 'The show must go on'?"

None of her drama was left now, just sadness. "There's the show must go on, and then there's madness. Our director and designer were both murdered. One of the cast—the smallest, and most vulnerable cast member—was abducted and drugged. And our stage manager, it turns out, did it because she was crazed with grief over her unborn children, and none of us knew anything about it." She added quietly, as if to herself, "However I shield them, they must die. And, seeing that they must, it is I who shall kill them."

She didn't say anything else.

"Was that in the play?" I asked.

She shook her head, but didn't reply. And then I remembered what Kay had said about Frankie's drunken appearance the previous week, when she'd shouted about killing her invisible babies. "The whole thing," I said. "It wasn't about revenge. It wasn't *The Spanish Tragedy* at all, was it? It was *Medea*. It was about a woman killing her own children: Jenny's body turned on her, and killed her babies. It was Greek tragedy all along."

Chapter 21

The police had finally left. Jake had closed the dressing-room door, so I didn't see when they took Jenny away to charge her. Frankie went to clean up not long after, and Jake and I went home with Bim.

Jake took Bim upstairs. I'd fought off going to the hospital by promising to tell him if I got any worse, and agreeing to go for a check-up in the morning. But I felt a lot worse than I was letting on, and was heading straight for a shower and bed. As I walked in, my landline was ringing. The police had taken away my mobile, but I was happy to remain unreachable for a while. I ignored it.

The silence lasted no more than three minutes before there was a knock on the door. My flat door, not the front door of the house. I braced myself before I heard, "Sam?"

Mr. Rudiger.

When I opened the door, he was standing with his hand outstretched, phone in it. "Helena," he said.

"Really?" I said into the receiver. "You couldn't just leave a voicemail message like a normal person? Or, I don't know, call back later?"

"Don't be silly, darling." Helena was unruffled. She rang my neighbour because I didn't answer my phone, and *I* was silly? She went on without waiting for a response, which was fortunate, as Miss Manners would disapprove of all the ones that came to mind. "Jake filled me in on the stage manager. As long as you're all right, we don't need to discuss that now. I want to know why you didn't tell me about the Theatre Museum."

I blinked. "The Theatre Museum. Why didn't I tell you what?"

She didn't sigh, but I could tell it was a close-fought battle. "Why you didn't tell me you went, and that you had found an unidentified person who had been looking into the same files."

Mr. Rudiger was leaning against the wall, arms folded, visibly amused by my side of the conversation. I widened my eyes at him and put the phone on speaker. "I didn't tell you what I ate for breakfast this morning, either. Why should I?"

"A banana. It's what you always eat for breakfast." She was tart. "And as to the museum, if you had, I could have told you who it was, and you could have tied up that loose end much more quickly."

"Who what was? The person from the Barbican?"

Her voice had that edge of patience that always drove

me crazy. "The person from the Barbican who was not a person from the Barbican. Who was an employee of Liz Henderson's investment company."

I closed my eyes. "Smithfield," I said. "You even told us the name of her company. When I saw it at the Theatre Museum, I thought it was an address."

Helena never wasted time gloating. "Exactly."

"All right." I was working it out in my head. "So Liz Henderson had someone look at the files in the Theatre Museum because . . ."

Helena picked up for me. "Because she wanted to track down the details of her brother's estate. As an investor in Davison's company, she had been backstage, and possibly even at his offices. She'd seen her brother's drawings up on the walls. And then, possibly after speaking to Sylvie Sander herself, she sent someone to the Theatre Museum to check their archive."

I broke in: "And, because she wasn't the sharpest knife in the drawer, she made Sylvie suspicious, and Sylvie went and checked out the archive too, worried that there might have been some drawings there." I paused. "That's the wrong order. The catalogue said there was design material. When it wasn't there, I thought Sylvie Sander had taken it."

"Instead, it was Liz Henderson's employee. I've had lunch with Cyril—a very long, *very* dull lunch," Helena added waspishly. "Liz Henderson had some drawings which she said were her brother's, and she had photographs of others, which had Sander's signature on them. The first must have come from the Theatre Museum, the latter from the production offices. It was these that caused the argument with Cyril. She wanted to bring a suit against Sylvie Sander's estate: theft, and misappropriation of intellectual copyright. He was trying to explain that since she had come by both the drawings and the photographs illegally, she might have just contaminated what would otherwise have been a very straightforward case."

Helena continued down her own path. "She invested largely in the company to get closer to Davison. That gave her access not only to the designs, but to the personnel. According to Cyril, she had taken Jenny Rogers out to lunch to pump her for information months ago, no doubt giving away far more information on Maurer, and Davison, and Sander, than she collected."

I remembered her alibi on the night of Davison's death. "When she said she had been with Jenny, and Jenny said she hadn't, everyone thought it was Liz Henderson who was lying."

"Whereas Jenny Rogers was simply misdirecting—a little suspicion here or there to weight the scales if necessary."

"Everybody was out for their own interests," I said sadly.

Helena was serene. "Is that necessarily wrong?" she asked, and hung up without waiting for an answer.

I stared at Mr. Rudiger. "Isn't it?" Then I reconsidered. "I need to make a call," I said, and dialled. Voicemail, but it didn't matter. "Kit, will you give me a ring when you get this? I think a book on a four-decade-long design fraud might sell nicely, don't you?"